PENGUIN METRO READS

EX

Novoneel Chakraborty is the author of fifteen bestsellers, two novellas and one short-story collection. His works have been translated into multiple Indian languages. His Forever series made it to the *Times of India*'s Most Stunning Books of 2017. His latest, *Roses Are Blood Red*, is still on the list of top ten books across India even nine months after its release. His twists, dark plots and strong female protagonists have earned him the moniker 'Sidney Sheldon of India'.

The first book in the Stranger trilogy, which became a phenomenal hit among young adults, has been adapted into a web series, *Hello Mini*, on MX Player, produced by Applause Entertainment and Rose Movies. The show already has more than 100 million views. His erotic thriller novel *Black Suits You* has been adapted into a hit web series, titled *Bekaaboo*, by Alt Balaji. His novella *Red Suits You* is all set to be adapted as well.

Apart from novels, Novoneel has written and developed several hit TV and web shows for premier channels like Sony, Star Plus and Zee. He lives and works in Mumbai.

BY THE SAME AUTHOR

Half Torn Hearts
The Best Couple Ever
Cheaters

FOREVER SERIES
Forever Is a Lie
Forever Is True

THE STRANGER TRILOGY
Marry Me, Stranger
All Yours, Stranger
Forget Me Not, Stranger

How about a Sin Tonight?
Black Suits You
Roses Are Blood Red

EX

...a tw!sted love story

NOVONEEL
CHAKRABORTY

Penguin
metro reads

An imprint of Penguin Random House

PENGUIN METRO READS

USA | Canada | UK | Ireland | Australia
New Zealand | India | South Africa | China | Singapore

Penguin Metro Reads is part of the Penguin Random House group of companies whose addresses can be found at global.penguinrandomhouse.com

Published by Penguin Random House India Pvt. Ltd
4th Floor, Capital Tower 1, MG Road,
Gurugram 122 002, Haryana, India

Penguin Random House India

First published by Random House India 2013
Published in Penguin Metro Reads by Penguin Random House India 2020

14 13 12

ISBN 9788184004328

Typeset in Palatino by Eleven Arts

Printed at Repro India Limited

www.penguin.co.in

FSC www.fsc.org MIX Paper from responsible sources FSC® C047271

This is a legitimate digitally printed version of the book and therefore might not have certain extra finishing on the cover.

For
my Iron Lady.
I love you didi

'If you are accustomed to see only black and white, then you'll never see me.'

Later in the story

SHARADA HEIGHTS
NEAR TANK NO. 4
SALT LAKE, KOLKATA

'Now tell me, what were you saying?' asked the boy rapidly climbing the stairs with nervous energy. His attention towards the girl, who was ardently trying to catch up with him from behind, was undisturbed though. They were climbing the stairs of Sharada Heights; a five storey apartment. By the time they reached the third floor, both of them were soaking wet.

'Just like a river has different names as it traverses different territories,' the girl said climbing the stairs. The boy was ahead of her but she was breathing harder than him. 'Our love too shall have different names as our life traverses different births. But the essence, the nature, the taste of love shall remain the same,' she continued.

They continued to climb the stairs.

It was around midnight. No moon, no stars. Only black clouds. There was heavy rain, though, with an interlude of lightening and thunder. There was no one on the streets. Everyone everywhere seemed to be fast asleep. And just when everything seemed like a prelude to an impending doom, the old door of the terrace of Sharada Heights opened with a creaking sound. The sound lingered in the air for some time.

The girl, dressed in a blue top and cropped trousers, and the boy, wearing a white T-shirt tucked beneath a pair of black jeans, peeped out from the half-open door. The sound of heavy rain hit their ears. They slowly stepped out on the wet terrace.

The moment they stepped out in the open, the rhythmic beating of the raindrops on the floor muted all other sounds. The sky seemed to relentlessly kiss the earth—just the way lovers kiss when they meet each other after a long time or for the last time. *Does the sky and earth,* the girl wondered, *gossip about spring, summer, and winter through raindrops*?

The girl and the boy, grasping each other's hands more firmly as the rains drenched them, stood still. For the world, perhaps, it would have been just another abrupt shower that year, but for them it was the first rain of confession in eras that was drenching them. There are certain relationships which don't necessarily start when two people meet. Even their first meeting has the vibe of an unexplained continuation. The girl and the boy were in one such relationship even from the time they were not in a relationship.

Standing under the rain, together, they finally understood how much they loved each other. It wasn't that they didn't realize it before, but the journey from a 'gut feeling' to a 'concrete knowing' happened at that instant. They kept looking into each other's eyes. The rain by then had polished off their appearance, transforming them from stones into glistening diamonds that emanated an alluring desire for the other. Desire gives love its wings—they understood.

The boy took her to the edge of the terrace. He stood up on the cemented barricade that fenced the terrace, and then pulled up the girl beside him. She was visibly scared. The boy feigned his fear better. They were standing on the edge facing each other. The girl didn't let go of his hand even for a second. They stood so close to each other that they could feel their breaths on each other's skin. Their breaths, by caressing their skin, soon gave birth to a feeling in them whose wail drew their heart's attention. The latter asked the feeling what it was seeking. A kiss; the feeling told the heart. The latter was instantly alert because a kiss was the heart's only way to share its deepest secret with the soul. Should the kiss happen, the heart will have to bare open all its secrets, in all its nudity.

The boy brought his hand to the girl's inquisitive face and tucked a strand of her wet hair behind her ear. He then cupped her face gently with both his hands. For her, it was like a giant dream within the tiny capsule of reality. For him, it was a certain reality inside an uncertain drop of a dream.

A few raindrops trickled down her forehead. The boy interrupted one raindrop with the tip of his tongue. When a promise and a prayer come together, a commitment is created. She was the promise, he was the prayer, and the unprecedented feeling their kiss triggered within them was the commitment.

Why this commitment? her mind asked her heart. *This commitment is an assurance,* her heart answered the mind.

'That I'll choose him in whatever form, and whenever, he presents himself in front of me. It's not because our choice will claim we are the best for each other. But just like a student passing out from a school knows the basic of everything, we would be the basic of each other.'

The boy sucked hard on her lips. The girl felt nothing for some time after which she opened her eyes to realize her deepest core had evolved. An irreversible ritual had taken place in her heart. With this new self, now, she sucked his lips. *Did his heart undergo a similar ritual too?* she wondered. Soon the two tongues prattled amidst the torrential rainfall.

The fear the girl had felt after climbing up the cemented barricade had now been conquered. Trust, after all, rinses a heart of almost every fear, eventually. Hope takes care of whatever residual.

Their lips parted. Nothing will be able to wash his imprints off her now, she knew. As their eyes met again, she wondered whether she really existed or had she been a mere fragment of his imagination all these years? Could it be that she was leading a life of death till now? And when he happened to her, life happened?

The boy, in an indescribable trance, sat down by the cemented barricade. He pulled the girl's hand as an invitation to come and sit close to him—and she did. The outside was chaotic, the inside calm. In that calmness she could hear her heartbeats loud and clear. The beats seemed to have graduated from mere sounds to a language through which she was translating what the boy had penned on her heart with the ink of love.

A minute passed by. They kept exchanging furtive glances gravid with romance. As the hypnotizing moment was busy making a space within their hearts which both would visit every time a separation beckoned, the boy leaned sideways and kissed her on the cheek. She gave him a half-nervous, half-shy smile. She leaned a little more towards him and they kissed again. Only this time the kiss made them slowly swing between life and death, love and despair, destiny and coincidence, choice and consequence, decadence and redemption, forgiveness and revenge, light and darkness, sexuality and spirituality, blame and guilt, consciousness and subconsciousness, instinct and experience, fame and oblivion, future and...

The kiss broke. They sat by the edge of the terrace for some more time; hand in hand. Finally, they both stood up.

'I had to tell you this...' said the boy as they stood facing the other. 'I love you because that's my best bet to mean something to you. My love for you is only a means to an end. And the end is I want to *mean* something to you.'

The girl couldn't hold back her tears. Crying is the heart's way of embracing pain. And love.

'I don't know how long this separation of death will be, but until life gives us a chance to meet again, my soul shall be burning,' she said with tears rolling down her cheeks. In the rain, however, the tears lost their distinction.

The boy's body was shaking from an inner catharsis.

'Just promise me one thing,' the girl said, locking her fingers with the boy's.

'What?' The boy held her hand tight.

'Even if death touches us, you shall always remember me as yours?'

The boy nodded.

It was time to carry out their plan.

Chapter 1

Six months back

A middle-aged man is pacing about restlessly in a sophisticated lobby. He is semi-bald, lean, almost to the level of being skinny, wearing black cotton trousers, a plain white half-sleeved shirt, and shining brown Khadim's sandals. He casts an occasional glance at his wrist watch. 7.45 pm. He has been waiting in the foyer for the last half an hour, along with a few others perched at the edge of their seats, nervously waiting for the receptionist to announce their names.

The man adjusts his square-shaped spectacles a little and stands up. He soon locates what he is looking for; a water cooler at the end of the hallway. He ambles towards it, takes out a paper glass from a stack beside the cooler, and pours himself some cold water. He quaffs the water in one go and then pours himself another glass. The moment he gulps it, his eyes fall on a woman right ahead in the foyer where he was sitting. The man particularly notices her because she has raised her hand a little to draw his attention. Also, she is his wife.

She has come dressed in a gorgeous chiffon sari with a matching blouse and sandals. Unlike the other ladies present around her, she has applied oodles of makeup on her face. At her age, her overall dressing looks loud and bizarre. Even though the air-conditioner in the room is on full blast, the woman keeps pretending to wipe non-existent sweat drops from her forehead and cheeks with her handkerchief. Her hair is jet black, almost like she is wearing a wig.

As the man by the water cooler fills a glass of water for his wife, an intercom buzzes loudly, breaking the otherwise brittle silence to pieces. The receptionist, a young female sitting behind a semi-circular table at one end of the entrance, picks up the receiver on the second ring.

'Yes ma'am,' she says. After a few seconds, she calls out to the man by the water cooler, 'Mr Chatterjee, please go in. You're next.'

Atul Chatterjee quickly empties his glass in the cooler's sink and joins his wife, Sonakshi. The urgency in their demeanour alarms the onlookers.

In his head, Atul had formed a picture of the woman they are about to meet—middle aged, well past her menopause, and a strict feminist. There was no particular reason why Atul had that image of the woman. But the person waiting for them shatters his perception completely. This is a girl, and not a woman to begin with. She is wearing a crisp business suit, her hair is neatly done up with a couple of loose strands falling on either side of her face. She is sitting straight with her hands clasped together on the large woooden table behind which she is sitting—a very corporate pose. Her black carbon square specs suit her oval face well.

'Good evening ma'am. May we please come in?' Atul says hoping he has subdued his male ego enough in his voice. Rarely before has Atul ever needed anyone's permission for anything. But this, of course, is different.

'Yes please Mr...' The girl glances at her iPad once, kept beside her, and says, 'Atul Chatterjee.'

The couple come in with a pseudo-smartness about them and take seats opposite the girl. Sonakshi gives the girl a plastic smile and says, 'Mr Dasgupta recommended you to us.'

'Dasgupta?' There is a slight twitch in the girl's eyebrow as if she is trying to recollect.

'Bibhash Dasgupta...'

'Oh yes, I remember.'

Atul and Sonakshi share an assuring glance presuming that if the girl has finally recollected who Bibhash is, their own importance in her eyes would have escalated.

'It's about my son,' says Sonakshi uneasily.

'Where is he?' The girl—realizing her mobile phone is vibrating—turns it upside down. The vibration ceases. Sonakshi makes a mental note of the fact that the girl didn't take the call. She herself wouldn't have appreciated any disturbance at this point of time.

'If you want to talk about your son, you'll have to bring him here,' the girl says.

'That's the problem. We can't bring him here,' Atul says.

'Then I'm afraid I won't be able to help you.'

Atul and Sonakshi exchange a nervous look.

'I'm ready to give you as much money as you want.' Atul's helplessness is quite transparent by now.

'It's not about the money,' the girl says with an unflinching look towards Atul. Only her jaw moves as she speaks, like she is a programmed robot.

'Please do something,' pleads Sonakshi. The helplessness has possessed Sonakshi equally. 'We have come here with a lot of hope.'

The girl keeps staring at the woman as if she is trying to judge whether the mother's concern behind the painted face is real or not.

'What's your son's name?' she asks.

'Neel,' Atul blurts out.

A slight frown appears on the girl's face. Her jaws lock themselves and in the next instance releases. Her eyes swiftly studies Atul and Sonakshi sitting in front of her. Something about their appearance tells her that she isn't seeing them for the first time. She unfolds her hands, slowly takes off her specs, and says, 'Do you have any photograph of your son?'

Atul quickly brings out his mobile phone and hands it over to the girl. His phone has the photograph of his son on the home screen.

The girl stares at the photograph. A touch longer than necessary. She gives the phone back to Atul.

'Excuse me,' she says and goes to the washroom, her heart pounding hard.

Inside the washroom, she stands by the washbasin for some time pondering over something. She looks up at her reflection. It looks surprisingly happier than what she is feeling from within.

The girl slowly comes out of her business suit. She unbuttons her white formal shirt and takes it out too. Next she unhooks her bra. She turns around and tries to see her back in the mirror atop the washbasin. In the reflection she can see several burn marks. She caresses the few marks near her shoulder and breaks into a sadistic laughter.

'You had your chance, Neel Chatterjee. And you fucked me *good*. Now it's my turn. I'll fuck you *bad*.' The girl tells her reflection.

Chapter 2

ROOM NO. 332
HOTEL SAVOY RAJ
MG ROAD, JAIPUR

Neel Chatterjee is climbing up the stairs to the third floor of the hotel. He does so a little too quickly than his usual speed, hence he ends up gasping for breath. Blame his speed on the message he received a minute back on his mobile phone from the girl who, he knows, is waiting inside room 332 for him. The message read: *I'm wet*. And before that he had seen her slip off her bra from her shoulder, standing by the roadside-view window in her room, when he was entering the hotel gate.

Now, standing in front of room 332's half ajar door, Neel waits to bring his breathing back to normal first; two deep breaths and he feels better. Next he presses his erect penis between his legs. He doesn't want to make things too obvious for the girl inside the room. He takes one final breath and pushes the door open.

As the door slowly opens up, light peeps in the room from the tubelight in the corridor outside in the otherwise dark room. And somewhere from the darkness he hears her say, 'What's the most important thing in your life Neel?'

As he takes some time to speak, Neel locks the door behind him. The room is completely dark now.

The girl throws a packet of condoms at Neel.

'We'll need this in sometime, not immediately.'

Neel wishes he knew what 'this' was that the girl threw at him.

'It's a pack of condoms.' The girl's voice clarifies from the darkness as if she is reading his mind.

'Answer me now,' she adds. Her voice is strict yet soft.

'I don't know,' Neel says staring at the darkness ahead, 'Probably to soon become a published author?'

The girl switches on the bedside light. The room is now filled with a soft erotic yellowish tinge. She smiles at him. The room has one television, one single bed, two lamps, a centre table, a telephone, a wardrobe, and a mirror. As Neel looks at the girl, he notices that her firm erect breasts are rising and falling, in a sensual rhythm, with her slow but deep breaths. He can tell both her smile and her breasts are blatantly attention-seeking. In fact everything about the girl seems like black magic. He feels an insane pull towards her, just like an unscrupulous man would feel for a woman apt for his most primitive need.

The girl has a mysterious aura about her. When she looks at him with a certain quietude, Neel feels like he is standing alone in front of a vast ocean which can throw up gigantic waves any moment to swallow him. And when she talks to him, it's a sandstorm; he doesn't know what to focus on—her moving lips, her blinking eyes, or her animatedly moving hands. For the time being, Neel decides to focus only on her smile.

'Strip. And be quick,' the girl says and switches off the light.

Neel's mind is already bouncing off thoughts about his girlfriend Titiksha. How would she react if she saw him like this? He had taken a decision twenty days ago and that punched a hole in his five-year-old 'steady' relationship with Titiksha. Before tonight, he never knew he had the guts to cheat on her.

All Titiksha knows is that he is attending the Jaipur Literary Festival. He even told her the mobile network is weak where he is putting up and thus he won't be able to take her calls. In reality he has removed his mobile phone's battery while coming up to the room so that his number is unreachable. The girl had remarked that she hated interruptions. It has only been two days and three nights since he met her and he is already more loyal to her than his half-a-decade old girlfriend.

Men!

Right now, he only wants to live in the moment. The guilt, the moral bugs, and the canines of relationship ethics—they can all wait.

Neel has taken off his black jacket, pullover, tee, trousers, shoes, and socks. He is about to tug his underwear down when the girl switches on the light and says, 'Keep that on.'

And he does.

'Come to me,' she says. He follows.

A couple of steps and Neel shrieks out with pain.

'There are glass pieces all over,' he complains pulling out a sharp piece of glass from under his feet with a distorted expression.

'Pleasure is more exciting when you get to it by confronting pain,' the girl hisses.

A confused Neel somehow manages to stand straight as he notices the girl sitting on the bed. She is only wearing a pair of shorts.

'Some Tequila?' she asks holding up a bottle.

'Fine with me.' Neel keeps the other bottle of alcohol he had brought with himself on a nearby shelf.

He observes how swiftly she readies a shot of Tequila for him. Her preparation surprises him because it means she knew he would give in. Men are pretty straight that way. Women, on the other hand, are always a work of translation. If you want to get to a woman's essence, you have to read her in the language she has originally been written in, and not the one she has been translated into. *What's her original language?* Neel wonders and watches her spread a pinch of salt on her bare shoulder line.

'Take your shot Tiger,' he hears her say with intent.

Neel goes to her, licks up the salt from her shoulder line, gulps the shot, and sucks the lime which she has kept in her mouth with the juicy side outward. The sucking seems like a small mouth-duel.

For the next shot, the girl lies down on the bed and spreads the salt on her navel and puts another lime wedge on her mouth with the juicy side out. Neel licks the salt, making sure he has every grain of it in his mouth—even the ones which have gone inside her belly button. He gulps the Tequila and sucks the lime harder this time. While licking the salt, he feels her squirming sexily. It arouses him.

For the third shot, the girl rubs the salt on her lower lip. She is holding the lime in one hand and the Tequila shot in another. First the salt, then the shot, and as Neel is about to suck the lime, she moves her hand upwards. Neel tries to reach it, she moves it downwards. Neel suddenly grabs her hand, sucks the lime, and compulsively kisses her on the lips till she pushes him away.

He distances himself presuming she has taken offense.

'I'm sorry,' Neel apologizes wiping his mouth.

She reacts by getting up from the other side of the bed and going around it to reach him. Somehow the more time she takes to get to the final act, the more fire Neel can feel in his loins.

'Look out!' Neel warns her but by then she has already stepped on a tiny glass piece.

'Pain has become such an intrinsic part of me that it has

stopped disturbing me anymore,' she says. Neel is amazed to see that she doesn't even flinch even once though a glass piece has pierced her feet. She plucks out the glass like it's nothing.

She is standing right in front of Neel now. He looks down at her breasts. Her chocolate brown nipples seem tight. It calls for a high degree of will-power to avert his eyes from the nipples and look up at her.

'You told me what's important in your life. Won't you like to know the most important thing in *my* life?' she says caressing his chest softly with her fingertips. All Neel can manage is a subtle nod.

'Okay. I'll do something to you now. It's the code for the most important thing in my life. You have to decode it if you want me tonight right there on the bed with you,' she says with an air of mystery.

The intensity of the statement makes Neel glance at the bed. He can visualize their bare bodies on the bed in a carnal wrestle.

'Okay,' he manages to blurt with a semi-dry throat.

The girl raises her heels slightly to stand on her toes and reach his ears. From his left ear she licks him downwards, with the tip of her tongue and stops at his shoulder blade.

'Clue number one,' she says looking straight at his eyes. She then kneels down next and slowly encircles his belly button with her tongue. She does so with a fervour Neel always wanted to see in Titiksha but never did. He wonders if they are in a dream and if he will wake up soon? But how should he confirm if it's a dream or not? Probably if he never wakes up it's reality else it's a dream. But what if this reality is the biggest dream of all?

'Two,' she whispers next. He looks down at her but this time instead of returning his look, she goes further down and moves her tongue over his underwear, on his crotch: first a slanting lick downwards from left and then a slanting lick upwards towards right.

'Three,' she murmurs and stands right up on her toes, reaching his right ear. She licks him there as if making two 'C's; one below the other.

'And four.' She smiles at him. 'Now tell me.'

Neel has no idea what the clues stand for. Judging from his face, the girl tells him she can do that only once more for him. This time Neel is able to make sense of it. The lick from his left ear, down to the side of the neck, and then towards her right following his shoulder blade seems like an 'L'? The encircling of the belly button is an 'O'. The slanting lick downwards and then upwards is a 'V', and the final licks on the ear—a 'C' below a 'C'—could be...

'I got it.' Neel sounds relieved more than anything else.

'The word is L. O. V. E.,' he says.

The girl sucks in both her cheeks a little and pouts her lips looking at him with an intent which smells of raw lust.

'Congrats. You've just won yourself a ticket to a lot of places inside you.' A pause later she adds, 'Take me to bed Neel.'

As he picks her up, she looks deep into his eyes and says, 'There are two kinds of love: one that exists because it has never been tested, and one that lives on because it has passed all its tests. What kind of love do you have for Titiksha?'

Neel doesn't care to answer. Instead he places her on the bed. He is about to kiss her when he notices she has tears in her eyes.

'What happened?' Of all things, Neel hadn't expected her to cry.

'I told you I'm wet.'

Before Neel can understand what she means, she forcibly bites his left ear.

Chapter 3

WHO EXACTLY IS NEEL CHATTERJEE?

Couples fight. The ones that don't, smile unnecessarily all the time. That way they remain at peace with each other. Sooner or later, one of the two gets bored with the peace in their relationship, and then start talking honestly about it. Next, they fight.

Titiksha and I have been a couple for four years, ten months, and twenty-one days. I have never understood why we fight. But we do. Not all the time. In fact, it wasn't like this always. The time when we knew less of each other, things were better. A relationship is always allergic to possessiveness, giving it rashes of insecurity. Titiksha is extremely possessive about me. Worse, I am insecure about her.

Two things pissed her off today. One, when I told her I want to be an author. And second, while she was shouting at me, I told her that I had an erection. I couldn't help it. Her anger is one of the sexiest things about her. And if you are a guy, or a girl who has a guy in her life, you will know how involuntary an erection is. It can happen anytime, anywhere, and for any reason. Or at times for no reason at all. I was trying to fight Titiksha's anger, but seeing her in the taut black shorts and white spaghetti top which gave me a glimpse of her bouncing boobs every time she shouted at me rendered me off track. I didn't tell her about the bouncing-boobs part else she would have scratched me bad. Why? Wait, you don't know Titiksha yet. I do. She simply needs an excuse to scratch me with her long nails.

But she had noticed the erection, after all. She told me to stop being an animal at odd hours. Going by her logic, her horniness is 'her love for me' and my horniness is an animalistic trait. I agree we haven't had sex for a long time now, but I wouldn't have caused such a thing for distraction. I even apologized stating it wasn't my fault that she looked incorrigibly edible so early in the morning. It was the truth. Her hair was all muffled. The kajal she had applied the previous evening was smudged. She smelt of dry sweat. She doesn't know it but I like her this way; stale. I couldn't convey this to her because she can't even take praise when she is angry. And if this was not enough, I could also see her nipple poking out from her top. That's serious distraction, ask any guy. How could I argue with a girl with her nipples eyeing me?

Coming to the primary thing that pissed her off this morning was my decision to quit my three-year-old managerial job at a private bank. It was the first thing I told her when I opened my eyes. She asked me why I didn't consult her or my family about this, and whether I knew how insecure is the life of an author, or how she had planned our future. Did I mention Titiksha is a financial analyst?

According to her, we would get married by twenty-eight, have a child by thirty, adopt another by thirty-two (she says every financially stable couple should conceive one baby and adopt another), and then together we would retire by forty-five in some hill station and watch our kids grow. All my life I have lived by others' expectations of me. I'm twenty-seven now. I haven't yet done anything that I thought I should do.

Twenty years from now I'll be forty-six and I want to use these twenty years in-between to do things my heart stands for, so that after forty-six I don't waste time having life-consuming-monologues all the time concerning my self-chosen cowardice. I really loved to write but nobody ever encouraged me. And now when I see someone's novel in the market or read about the Indian Publishing boom in newspapers and magazines, only I know how much I want to be a part of it.

Of all people, I thought Titiksha would understand the latent pain associated with the non-realization of my long-nested dream. She said I should have consulted her first. I don't understand this. Is being in a relationship customary to lose one's individuality? I didn't feel like discussing it with her. Period. Does that mean I don't love her? Five years into the relationship, and only this morning I realized how much we chew on each other's choices.

In angst Titiksha left me with an erection. What kind of girlfriend does that? In the five years that we've been together, she should have known I can't tolerate a wasted hard-on. I CAN'T! But she left. I doubt she must have done a crash course on how-to-be-rude-to-your-horny-boyfriend, if that sort of a thing is possible.

Alone, I sit down on the floor. There is nothing in this rented flat of ours except a mattress, a few old saris of Titiksha's mother which we have turned into curtains, two laundry bags (hers is bigger than mine), and a small almirah. We earn considerably well but we never buy anything for the flat. She never lets me. 'I'm saving', is her excuse. Titiksha is like that—weird about certain things.

I wipe my face and chest with a towel. It's very humid in Kolkata today. I'm only in my knickers. I rest my back on the wall and look up at the ceiling. To be precise, I stare at the ceiling fan which is rotating furiously. There's something about its movement which makes me ponder…

As far as I remember—and I don't remember very much—I have always been a loner. Ma was there. Dad was there. But nobody was there by my side—you know what I mean? I never felt the need for anything except the basics. My basic needs were always met, and hence I concluded my family did well.

From the time I was a kid, I was kept away from people. Ma once told me I was allergic to some dust ailment which, if I was exposed to, could be fatal. Her statement was never tested so I don't know if it's the truth. But then truth is what one thinks it is, isn't it?

Now I have somewhat recovered in the last few years of the dust ailment. Or so I'm told. I'm free to roam about freely, though I don't go to many places as such. I live-in with Titiksha here in this rented flat in the Lake Town area of north Kolkata. My parents let us live-in together because they think we'll get married eventually, even though Titiksha and I have never even discussed marriage yet. Marriage is only a social license to procreate. Titiksha and my relationship is more serious than that. We are seeking companionship and that doesn't need any social licensing.

Let me tell you something funny. I have a couple of photo albums of me in hill stations, beaches, or riding a camel in a desert—but I don't remember these moments well. Perhaps I was too young. Is the ability of making one memory after another so that secretly we can be with it at our leisure, one of the signs of maturity? In that case I matured pretty late. That's what my parents tell me. Hence I never attended school. Not like others. Private tutors used to teach me at home while I went to school whenever there was a class test or a term exam. The other students never talked to me. I was an alien to them. I could tell from the way they looked at me. I was physically different from them as well—bigger in size. The school uniform undoubtedly looked funny on me while I had a definite thick moustache compared to the others who only had a soft thin line. And only I know how disgusting my stubble looked in comparison to others' supple cheeks.

The girls looked at me with a sense of pity. One or two smiled. It made me nervous. A girl smiling at me is something that petrifies me the most. No, second most. The foremost is a girl giving me a flying kiss. It has happened a few times in the past. Even now whenever Titiksha and I make love, which is rare, she initiates it. I have a problem initiating anything. Except an erection.

In a way I was happy to be at home. Within the four walls of my room, I had my best friend—my imagination. Self-talks. Headaches. Masturbation. Medicines. Tears. Smiles, too. And some music. I never read newspapers. Never sat in front of a computer until I joined college. Even the window panes of my room were done with black glasses through which I could see outside but nobody could see me. Just imagine eighteen-shit years, like this! You may ask if I didn't get bored or how I hadn't turned plain crazy by the end. I didn't. Why? How? I was made to believe that everyone, by and large, lived exactly the same life as me—again and again and again. I always believed what I was told. Like I have been told that God is everywhere around us, and humanity within us, and nobody controls anything. Everyone is controlled by destiny. That respecting one's own religion and taking part in rituals is important to keep the Gods happy and seek their blessings. That blessing is stronger than karma, and so on. Funny thing is, I believed it all without asking for proof.

The good thing about being alone all the time was that I never had to share anything with anyone, or I wasn't ever back-stabbed, never wasted time advising anybody what he or she should do, never killed time by thinking about someone. The same thing happened after school. I told my parents I wanted to study computers. Thanks to Pritam, a friend whom I lost all contact with after school, I made the decision. What happened was I saw him cheating during a school term exam. He saw me notice it but I didn't complain to the teacher. He thought I could have complained when the reality was the concept of cheating was new to me then. I understood he was cheating much later. Anyway, so when I went to school for the next semester class test he gave me a disc, out of gratitude, saying it was his favourite computer game. I took the disc alright but had no clue what to do with it. I had computers as a subject then, but all I learned were some silly languages. A computer game was alien to me back then. I went home and read whatever was written on the cover. That curiosity led me to take up computer science during my graduation but I knew that only few colleges would have agreed to have me as a student. I always had low grades in school. I studied alright. Teachers said my grasping power was pretty low. Surprisingly, I passed AIEEE with better marks than most students, and got into a good college on the outskirts of Kolkata to study computers.

The college was good. The seniors, professors, freshers—everybody kept to themselves. Nobody talked to me. Nobody ragged me. I was dropped at the college gate in my father's car and picked up right after college. My academics improved during college. I once heard someone say real friendship begins in college hostels. But I could never experience it. My parents would have never agreed to it. They always have been protective about me. I rarely have any interaction with them except about what I should or shouldn't do. And of course the medicines. I have frequent headaches. I get them since childhood, they say. And for that I have to regularly go for check-ups, have medicines, and answer some irritating questions thrown at me by doctors. I try hard to avoid going to the clinic but headaches get the better of me always. To cut a long and boring story short, I have lived a very shitty life than most of the people out there. But tell you what, there are certain fragrances, if followed well, take you to that very point in life where everything seems perfect. Love is one such fragrance. And it happened when Titiksha joined my college in the second year.

There's a power cut. The fan rotation slows down and I come back to the present. I hear the main door open and shut. Titiksha has come. I tell her I knew she would be back. Hearing this she rebukes me for not reminding her that she wasn't wearing a bra while going out. But how could I? I was enjoying the bra's absence. I don't tell her this. I only tell her that I shall stick to what I have decided to do with my life henceforth: that I would be an author and for inspiration, I shall visit Jaipur in the coming week for the Jaipur Literary Festival. Titiksha is staring at me now. She shows me both her middle fingers and asks me to go to hell. She leaves again, and I shout at her from behind in a mocking manner.

'I'm going to Jaipur, not hell!'

Chapter 4

HOW DID NEEL MEET THE GIRL?

It's 7.02 am. The Indigo Airlines flight touches the aerodrome of Jaipur. This is the first time Neel has come out of Kolkata to a new city—Jaipur. All his life, his parents have made him tread on one single track: first school to home-home to school, and then college to home, home to college. It's only when Titiksha came into his life that he started going out a bit—malls, cafes, restaurants, even though not very regularly since Titiksha is a workaholic. While others would look forward to a Friday night, Titiksha would look forward to get back to work soon.

As Neel confessed earlier, the work-obsessed streak in Titiksha is only because she wants to secure their future together. She has never told Neel much about her family except that her parents hate her independent streak as much as she hates their regressive mindset. And that she has been on her own financially from a long time now though she is only twenty-five. Is it because she never had a cohesive family to begin with that she wants to desperately make one with Neel? As a child whatever you think you deserve but miss in life, you go after it like a hunter dog the moment you become an adult. What Titiksha doesn't know is Neel's parents have told him that they are friends with her family and have no problem with them living together. Neel has kept this family-friendship part a secret from Titiksha fearing her reaction. She reacts weirdly at times, and violently too, to insignificant things.

Twenty minutes after the flight has parked itself, Neel comes out from the airport exit. It's a small airport and everything is in order. There is a sizeable crowd maybe because of the popular annual literary festival, Neel guesses, which draws literature lovers to Jaipur from across the globe.

As Neel moves out, a few taxi drivers clog him. Neel feels nervous with this sudden attention but he doesn't make it obvious. For a moment, he thinks he should have carried on working in the private bank in Kolkata. To be where one always is, seems comfortable all the time. But now he has taken a decision, and his being in Jaipur is a consequence of it. Life is anyway a tennis-match of sorts between one's choice and its consequence. As Neel ponders which cab to choose, studying the eager looking faces of the drivers, a short and stout man with a bushy hairdo and long sideburns reminiscence of the 70s, comes to him pushing the other cab drivers aside.

'Dur hato madarchodo. Yeh mera hai,' Neel hears him say as the man snatches his American Tourister bag from him. The other drivers move away to other passengers.

'Is taraf sir sahib,' the man says while walking away from him and towards the other side of the road where most of the cars are parked. Neel follows him urgently lest the man steal his Tourister.

'Myself Lappan sir sahib. Your flight is early or I is late?' His English makes Neel avoid answering immediately.

'My flight landed early,' Neel eventually says after a long pause.

'Thank Godji. I'm pick you up and drop you on Diggi Palace. You have booking?'

'I have a booking?'

'Yes sir sahib. You are Neel Chatterjee, right sir sahib?'

'That's right. But who booked a hotel for me? And how do you know me?'

'I.' Lappan focusses on the traffic as he takes a left from a signal.

'You?'

'I not knowing you, sir sahib. Same people who booked I for you.'

'Who is that?'

'Titiksha ma'am. She emailed me your foetoo. So I know you.'

'Foetoo?'

'Yes. Foetoo-garph.' Lappan takes off his hands from the steering wheel and turns to gesture Neel what exactly he means.

'Photograph.' Neel makes a correct guess.

Initially Neel was feeling uncomfortable because the car had transparent windows. In Kolkata he always moved in his father's car which had black tinted windows. He is feeling okay with every passing second.

So typical of Titiksha, Neel thinks to himself, beating his fingers rhythmically on the seat reacting to the song playing on the car's radio. Whenever they fight, Titiksha stops talking, but makes sure all is fine with him. This is one reason why Neel thinks he will always love Titiksha. She may fight like a bitch but always cares for him like a mother. He wants to call her and give her a long kiss but he knows she won't pick up. A faint smile appears on his face. He knows Titiksha will continue to avoid him till he goes back to Kolkata and pleads mercy by promising her that he has given up his dream of becoming an author. But, will he be able to back track on this decision? His smile dries up. No, he won't go back to the mundane life he has been living as a bank employee. That's death and he won't be able to live death anymore. Neel has understood life is too rare an occurrence to waste it doing something other than what you want to.

'Jaipur you come first time, sir sahib?' Lappan speaks.

'First time.'

Lappan slows down the car, rolls down his window pane, looks to his right, and folds his hands in a namaste, touching his forehead. A curious Neel follows his sight and realizes they have just passed by a small Shiva temple below an archaic looking tree.

As Lappan's foot presses on the accelerator again, he glances at the mirror atop and smiles at Neel.

'You believes Godji, sir sahib?'

Belief is a tricky word Neel has never come to terms with. What to believe and what not to? Is belief a product of a personal experience or a subliminal acceptance of an already prevailing protocol?

'Yes,' Neel lies. The truth is he hasn't been able to understand the concept of God ever. Or religion for that matter. All he has inferred is men love to make shelters for themselves; from psychological to emotional to spiritual. God is one such shelter. Love is another. Probably.

They arrive at yet another traffic signal. Traffic is heavier here. Lappan turns off the car's engine, takes out a cigarette from his jacket's pocket, and lights it. As he exhales in peace, the smoke slowly floats in the air to reach Neel. He feels a knot in his stomach while inhaling it. In that chilly winter morning, a sweat drop trickles down his sideburn. Another travels down his forehead. His breaths suddenly become shorter and faster than normal. He is looking at the cigarette obliquely, almost petrified. He thinks he may choke to death. Neel tries to unlock the car's door and move out but he isn't able to. He screams out for help clenching his throat which seems to be narrowing down. By the time Lappan turns to realize what's happening, Neel manages to unlock the door and stumbles out. People around don't care. The traffic signal turns green. A biker applies brake else he would have almost hit Neel. He hurls abuses at Neel and drives off. People have stopped in their tracks to see what the commotion is about. Neel has managed to get what he abhors—everyone's attention. He is all the more nervous. Lappan gets out of the car and tries to help Neel get up.

'What happened, sir sahib? How you get out?'

'That thing...' Neel tries to point out but there's no cigarette with Lappan now.

'What thing, sir sahib?' Lappan looks genuinely concerned.

'The smoke...' Neel is feeling a tad better now but he has brought half the traffic to an unnecessary halt.

'Oh! I not knowing cigarette air is bad for you, sir sahib,' Lappan says finally getting the point.

'Sorry sir sahib. But please get inside the car now else the police kicking my hard pumpkin behind harder,' Lappan says guiding Neel into the car.

Cigarette...its smell brought back something. Something vague and warped.

Neel is satisfied with the room Titiksha has booked for him. After a quick hot shower, he comes out to see his breakfast laid out on the table. But he leaves it untouched since the day's events at the literary festival venue have commenced. He knows this because his hotel—the Diggi Palace—is also the venue of the festival, and at that very moment, he can hear a lady sing an Indian classical song. The festival schedule said the song shall start the proceedings for the day. But what he is troubled about is why Titiksha took care of his hotel bookings when she doesn't want him to become an author in the first place. Does it show she is actually coming to terms with his decision to become an author? She has to; reconsideration is out of the question for him. Neel picks out a well ironed beige coloured kurta, a Nehru jacket, and a pair of jeans to wear.

He is now at the Front Lawns where one of the talk sessions is in progress. Multiple such sessions have started simultaneously at a few more places within the Diggi Palace. But Neel decides to be in the Front Lawns for he has heard a lot about the author who is speaking now.

Neel looks for an empty seat. But there's none left. He looks around. He finds a bit of space for standing on the other side beside a cameraman. From there it may be difficult to see the author but he will be able to see him clearly on the giant screen which is at an angular direction from the cameraman.

Neel goes there and stands with folded hands admiring the international author on the screen. He is yet to read any of his books but he stands with an expression as if he has read, analysed, and re-read all his works more than the author himself. He glances at the crowd and realizes most of them have a clone of his expression on their faces. Are they all being pretentious like him?

He is an international author known for his unconventional, almost pushing onto profanity for many, take on relationships. This author's latest book, which is also available in the festival's bookstore, talks about a memory pill which, when popped, helps people select their memories, and how a small town decides to hold an annual sex day every year where anyone can sleep with anyone with the choice of the memory being with oneself. What the author claims and wants to relay through his work is the possible memory of something and its uncontrollable ramifications that makes people often shy away from their innate wants and desires. If human beings, the author says, were not capable of making memories, then as a race our dark desires wouldn't have had any filters.

Some people applaud the author's thought, certain women wonder how rough the author would be in bed, few detest his thoughts, and the rest behave they understood whatever the author is saying by nodding their heads constantly.

For the next forty minutes, the author talks about what all hardships he faced prior to getting published, his style of writing, and why people should write. He believed that writing is the most effective and constructive stressbuster. The audience is allowed to ask questions. Neel has a question ready in his mind. He raises his hand too like others, and his turn comes after three questions have been asked. The people present are looking at him with anticipation, making him more nervous. He sees himself on the screen and doesn't like it. He puts across his question to the author uncomfortably.

'What should a debutant author do when he wants to tell a story but he has none?'

'Well, in that case, sir,' the author says in his native accent, 'You have to simply wait for the story to come to you.'

People applaud as the convener of the session announces the author will be available for a book signing event opposite the Mughal Tent. The crowd disperses. Neel stands there. He is in a dilemma: whether to go for a quick breakfast since his stomach is churning or to get the author's autograph. For that he will have to buy his book first from the book store in the campus. Breakfast! He decides and follows the crowd to the other side of the venue where there's a coffee-sandwich-tea corner. But the queue is too long. Precisely then the man across the counter shouts at him, 'Sir, your chicken grilled sandwich.'

Neel is taken aback. He is not even in the line, and he has been offered a sandwich. And it's the exact one he had eyed after seeing the menu pinned on the nearby wall.

'Mine? Are you sure?' Neel inquires.

'Yes. That's what the girl said. She has even paid for it. Please take it.'

'Girl? Which girl?' Neel says in surprise. For a second he wonders if Titiksha has followed him to Jaipur. The very thought gives him the creeps.

The man gives Neel a your-shit-is-not-my-shit glance and gets busy catering to another customer. He clearly doesn't have time for this. Neel turns to see if there's anyone looking at him. Girl, the man had said. People around are in small groups, busy, either chit-chatting or having their breakfast. The ones who are standing alone are busy talking on their phones. Then he notices a girl walking away rather urgently and yet not quickly enough for him to not notice her. Gaping at her butt with his mouth half open, Neel's first thought is—*a perfect butt—one that could arouse even a hermit*. She is wearing such taut cotton trousers that they define her butt's shape in a left-nothing-to-imagination manner. And as she walks her left butt cheek wiggles in a funny manner. Isn't she aware so many would be checking out her butt right now? Neel looks around to realize nobody except him checking her out. He feels ashamed but the temptation ahead of him wins. Sometimes it doesn't matter how sure one is about one's moral lock, someone does turn up and twists open that lock. The girl has just done that to Neel.

The girl turns ever so lightly, just enough for her to see Neel. He notices her noticing him. Is she the one who bought him the chicken grilled sandwich? The girl slips her hand in her back pocket and brings out her mobile phone. Neel now knows it was the phone's vibration that made her left butt-cheek wiggle funnily. She smiles at Neel. It is difficult for him to see her face since she is wearing big shades covering most of her face. Neel gives a compulsive smile. She takes a turn towards the Front Lawn where he was minutes ago. *She has to be the one!* Neel infers from the smile she gave him. Certain smiles are subtle clues to profound secrets of the heart. He goes running towards her but she is nowhere in sight. *She should be somewhere in the crowd,* Neel tells himself. He will find her and pay for the sandwich.

He keeps thinking how did she know he likes chicken grilled sandwich, and more importantly why did she buy it for him.

Right then the author's words ring in his ears: *You'll have to wait for the story to come to you.*

Neel is shaving inside the bathroom by the mirror atop the washbasin and shaving. He only has a towel wrapped around his waist. He keeps pulling it up every time it slips down, exposing his butt cleavage. As he shaves he keeps thinking about Titiksha and himself. From the time their relationship began, both kept dabbing emotional makeup, one day at a time, to remain appealing to each other, for each other. But now they have put on so much makeup that the real emotion seems to have lost forever. Why is he thinking like this? He has called Titiksha many times since last night but she has not picked up his call even once. He left her two messages as well:

Message one at 9.33 pm: *Thanks for the hotel booking*

Message two at 11.38 pm: *I am missing you a lot*

In the morning he got a reply but isn't sure which message did she respond to.

Titiksha's reply at 7.02 am: *Okay*

The minimalistic reply had the perfume of arrogance sprayed all over it. Should he act like a snob too? Or should he try hard to pacify her? Should he abuse her and make her his emotional slave or should he simply beg for mercy? What should he really do? With this question in mind, Neel takes a shower, dries himself, and rummages through his Tourister to find his best outfit. Why is he doing that? He can wear anything. Nobody is coming to see him. *Nobody?* Really?

One simple action—a turn of head and a smile—and how someone can hook a person. That's what the girl with big shades and a perfect butt did. Along with the girl's piercing look, Neel also remembers the chicken grilled sandwich she bought for him just like that. But why him of all people?

It is funny how you meet an absolute stranger who pulls you in a mystic way, drowning you into a sea of questions. You fight hard to swim in the beginning. But with each passing day, as each question gets answered, you learn to swim in the sea. The stranger becomes an acquaintance and the attraction turns into once-upon-a-time kind of a fairy tale. Neel hasn't been able to forget the girl from Diggi Palace because of the sea of questions she has immersed him in: Who is she? Why did she buy him the sandwich? Was she planted by Titiksha to spy on him? Will she be there in the festival today as well? It's in response to the last question that he wants to be at his best attire: a black kurta this time with the same black

Nehru jacket he had worn on the first day of the festival. He empties half the perfume bottle on himself. He didn't do so yesterday. The girl with the big shades and perfect butt has, in an incredible manner, managed to alter his preferences. The thought makes him shrug at his reflection in the mirror. He changes his hair parting from right side to a bit in the middle. He thinks he looks smarter this way contrary to what Titiksha thinks. But today she isn't around him. He can be himself. If that's really the case then what is he in front of her? Who is he in front of her?

Neel reaches the Darbar Hall at 9.05 am. The session on 'How to write a bestseller' is going on with full gusto. This time Neel gets a seat next to a girl. He looks at her from the corner of his eyes not sure if it's the same girl he saw yesterday. She is reading the festival schedule. Neel looks up and sees the author on the stage animatedly declaring to the audience that 'a bestseller cannot be planned' and that 'one needs to connect to the readers in order to feature in the bestseller's list'. What he doesn't say is that every month he has a dedicated PR team who makes sure they buy 70 percent of the overall sales of his book for the month, keeping his book in the coveted bestselling list for most part of the year.

Neel notices the girl sitting next to him toying with a cigarette between her fingers. Neel swallows a lump in his throat and gets up. There's a sudden escalation in his breathing. But nothing worrisome happens because he shifts his place quickly.

Neel sits with an expression which is similar to the one with which he attended all the sessions yesterday—as if he has read, analyzed, and re-read all the works of the author. Time and again he keeps looking at the crowd to see if someone—preferably a girl with oversized shades and a perfect butt—is looking at him. Behind the author, on the stage is a big mirror in which Neel can see the reflection of most of the people attending the session. He suddenly spots the girl in one of the seats behind him. He turns his head to confirm if it's her. It indeed is. Neel can't make out whether she is looking at him or not because of her shades. Why is she wearing those shades inside the hall? He looks at her a few times but nothing encouraging happens. Neel is waiting for the session to get over so that he can go to her and pay her for the sandwich.

The session gets over on time and as the crowd disperses, Neel quickly makes his way towards the seats at the back. The girl isn't there anymore.

Standing outside the Darbar Hall and trying to hunt the girl with the big shades amidst the crowd, Neel feels a tap on his shoulder from behind.

'Neel Chatterjee?' the girl says. Before Neel can answer, he notices she is wearing Ray-Ban Wayfarers, black breast-defining high-neck sweater, a royal blue hipster jeans, brown leather belt, and black high-heel boots that make her taller than him by an inch. She has a brown purse hanging from her right shoulder and a furry coat folded on the forearm of her left hand. There's a Nikon D90 dangling from her left shoulder. Her hair is silky, with a red strand in front, and fall loosely on her shoulders. Her thick, slightly pouty lips are accentuated by the lip gloss. And on her fair and supple right cheek there is one tiny red dot of a pimple.

'Yes,' Neel blurts out. He is not sure what his expression should be like. But he is sure he is looking like a fool nevertheless.

'Remember me?' she says removing her Wayfarers.

'Yes.' It's a lie. He doesn't know why he says so. Maybe he didn't want to sound too rude to her. Her eyes have as much lust in them as they have a longing. The lust is to conquer.

The longing is there so that the one being conquered enjoys the process.

'Really? Who am I Neel?' she says with a tight smile.

He gives her his most unsure smile and thinks hard. He isn't sure if he ever knew her. Who the hell is she?

'Actually...' he begins but is cut short.

'Oh it is okay, I won't mind. I know you don't remember me.'

Relief!

'I'm sorry,' Neel says apologetically as if he should have known her. If she didn't have a knockout figure and a forbidden-desire inspiring eyes, would he have stood there apologizing for not knowing her? Neel knows the answer. He remembers an adage Titiksha always tells him: men will be men.

'I realized you didn't recognize me yesterday.'

'You bought me a chicken grilled sandwich. How did you know I wanted to have it?'

'I know a lot many things about you. I'm your ex.' Her face has a shine of amusement.

Neel doesn't know if she is joking or serious.

'I'm kidding. We were in the same school. You used to come there for exams. I was pleasantly surprised to see you here yesterday.' Her right cheek flexes just a bit into a smile and the next moment the tip of her tongue comes out of her mouth. He loves the way her tongue wets her dry lips. ' Chicken grilled sandwich is your childhood favourite, isn't it?' she asks.

Is it? Neel isn't sure. But if the beautiful girl says it is, then he doesn't mind accepting it as the truth.

'Right,' he says and wonders how piercing her eyes are. As if they can fish into his subconscious and pull an alien desire out.

'What brings you here? I didn't know you had a penchant for literature,' she says.

Neel wants to say something smart that will floor the girl. But he can't find the right words. He notices the girl looking at her mobile phone.

'Come let's go to Baithak Hall. I want to attend the next session there.'

As she walks ahead, Neel follows her feeling amused about the fact she didn't even care to ask him if he is interested in attending the session that she wants to go for. And it's even funnier that he didn't even mind her not asking.

Before they take the narrow route to the Baithak Hall, Neel glances at the topic of the session on the giant programme schedule put up as a billboard. The topic is 'Sex in contemporary English novels'.

As they sit in separate bamboo chairs, she asks him, 'How is life?'

'Good.'

'You didn't tell me what you are doing here though.'

Neel hopes the answer he has conjured in his mind blows her over.

'I want to be an author.'

'An author? Wow, That's great! Authors are the only liars women love to sleep with. One second...'

He observes how swiftly she opens her bag, brings out a pen, and gives it to him.

'Autograph please! What if you forget me again tomorrow?' *Again?* How many times has he forgotten her already? Isn't he meeting her for the first time?

She pulls up her sleeves. He is supposed to sign on her forearm. The suddenness of it makes Neel uncomfortable. He doesn't know if she is kidding or is serious. Should he really give her an autograph? *An autograph*! She is definitely kidding.

'I insist,' she smiles with such warmth that it convinces Neel that it's not a joke. He takes the pen and scribbles his name in a complicated manner. He doesn't even know if it will be his autograph once he becomes an author.

'Thanks,' she says kissing him on his cheek. It's a normal, friendly, asexual kiss but Neel feels funny between his legs as she takes the pen back and keeps it inside her bag. He has always been like this. The slightest touch and he feels funny between his legs. In order to distract his mind, he asks the girl, 'What do you do?'

The girl leans closer to his ears and says, 'Later.'

Neel likes the way her breath tickles his ears. The funny feeling between his legs becomes funnier. He likes the way she... *By the way what's her name?* he wonders. She may remember his name but the truth is Neel remembers nothing about her. Should he ask her directly? He takes out his mobile phone and asks her, 'What's your number?' The girl looks at him as if he has interrupted her attention. She takes his phone, types her number herself, and gives it back to him. He chooses the 'save as contacts' option and inquires, 'How do you spell your name. I mean I remember the name but the spelling...'

For few seconds, she keeps looking at Neel. He doesn't know what to infer from the look.

'Tell me Neel,' she says softly, 'What if we didn't have any of our senses? What if we couldn't see, feel, taste, smell, or hear anything? Would we still fall in love with the person we are in love with otherwise? Don't you think Neel, love is only a trick of the senses?'

What was that? Neel seems baffled. It is too heavy for him to comprehend. He only asked the spelling of her name, damn it!

She leans towards him again and speaks softly into his ears, pronouncing each alphabet of her name distinctly as he types it in his mobile phone. The way her breath caresses his ears makes him hear a thunder within him each time.

Neel is taking a shower in his hotel room's bathroom. He has kept the geyser on for a long time by mistake, as a result of which the vapours have invaded the entire bathroom, blurring every glass. Neel writes her name on one of them with his fingertips.

Nivrita

He keeps staring at the name all through his shower. The other day he had followed Nivrita to all the events she wanted to attend. There is a primitive magnetism in her which he finds undeniably attractive. Passion is a devil. It's there in all of us. It is hungry, has canines, and is ferocious to the core. Most importantly it is blind too. It doesn't have limitations, doesn't associate itself with any stigma. More often than not it remains chained in all of us until you come across someone who unchains it for you, within you, and you suddenly realize you are exactly all that you always loathed in others. Nivrita has been able to unchain that passion in Neel in one single meeting.

They didn't talk much after the small talk in Baithak Hall the previous day. Sometimes she seemed all open and chirpy but the moment he wanted to ask anything personal, she turned reticent. Right before they bid each other goodbye, she asked him, 'How about roaming around Jaipur tomorrow?'

Neel looks at two outfits alternately—one is a light green kurta which Titiksha likes a lot and the other one is a T-shirt. He remembers a casual remark from Titiksha: 'I think you look better in kurta'. He decides to go for the T-shirt.

He has been wearing Titiksha's choice for a long time now so he thinks of giving Nivrita's suggestion a chance. Nivrita had gifted him a cologne—Bogart Pour Homme—as a parting gift for the day saying: *this smell turns me on*. And it indeed had a better smell than the perfume he used.

Was Nivrita taking him away from Titiksha? Neel shuns the stupid thought since he knows Titiksha from half a decade now and Nivrita, only a few hours. And yet when he looks into the mirror, his reflection seems more like a personification of Nivrita's desire than Titiksha's wish. Does he mind it? Neel doesn't know yet. He is now ready to roam the city of Jaipur with his 'supposed' ex, about whom he remembers nothing. He doesn't remember anyone from his school anyway.

Last night was an extraordinary night for him. He had done something for the first time. He had messaged Titiksha that he was missing her when the reality is he is at peace in her absence. The realization surprised him. He loves Titiksha and yet is happy about the momentary freedom. Why was he finding it hard to tell Titiksha about this alleged school friend of his? Maybe if he did, Titiksha would be in Jaipur first thing in the morning, curbing his freedom. But what is this freedom about? Why is it making him feel elated? It's not that Titiksha's presence stifles him, so why does her absence feel like a relief? Is he being unfaithful to her? Should he not go out with Nivrita and instead do what he is here for: attend the literary festival, feel inspired, and return home to start writing his debut novel?

His mobile phone buzzes. It's a message from Nivrita: *I'm here. When are you coming downstairs?*

In the momentary silence that follows, Neel locks his decision.

He types: *In a minute*, and presses on the send option.

As they come out of the hotel premises, Neel sees Lappan waiting with his Indica by the road. He waves at him. Neel wants to take Lappan since there would be sufficient space between Nivrita and him in a car. In certain ways, he is scared of her. No, he corrects himself, he is scared of his reaction towards Nivrita which may be favourable for her but not for him or his relationship with Titiksha.

'But from a car, it's difficult to click photographs. I want to click the city as it prepares to take on the day,' Nivrita says almost pulling Neel away from Lappan. She is wearing the same boots she was wearing a day back along with black denims and a red poncho over a white shirt.

'I'll call you if need be,' Neel tells Lappan.

'Okay sir sahib.'

Lappan drives away with an I-know-you-want-to-be-alone-with-this-chick smirk. Neel only hopes he doesn't mention it to Titiksha on the phone if he talks to her anytime. His fear makes him call out to Lappan.

The car reverses till it reaches him.

'Keep this,' Neel says stuffing a hundred rupee note in his shirt pocket.

Lappan gives him a now-I-exactly-know-*why*-you-want-to-be-alone-with-this-chick smirk and drives off.

Neel and Nivrita take a cycle-rickshaw. It's almost crawling on the busy MG Road. Nivrita is continuously clicking pictures with her DSLR while Neel is trying hard not to notice that they are sitting so close that their legs are touching. To divert his mind, he keeps asking her questions which she replies to while moving around her eyes furiously and clicking anything that interests her.

'Are you married?' he asks.

'Nope!' She doesn't look at him while answering.

'Committed?'

'Nope!'

'Why is that?'

'Why is what?' She glances at him.

'How come you are single?'

'Why, does that make me an outlaw?'

'No, I mean a girl like you…'

Neel cuts short his sentence as Nivrita turns to look at him. It makes him feel as if he shouldn't have said what he did. She clicks a close-up of his.

'What do you mean?' she says examining the pictures in her camera.

Now he will have to tell her what he thinks of her: that she has an amazing figure, that he would have doted on her had he not been committed, and that he had mentally stripped her the first instant he saw her, but a silent sigh later, he answers, 'You are beautiful.'

'Thanks,' she beams. 'I believe I can only be loyal to one thing: either my life or a relationship—not both. I have chosen to be loyal to my life.'

'What's that supposed to mean?'

'Love and life are two parallel tracks, Neel. I believe I can put myself only on one track at a time. I made the mistake once of expecting my life to be better because I was in love. Not anymore.'

In the silence that follows, Nivrita continues to click

pictures. It amazes Neel how she can be aloof and involved both at one go. Being in a committed relationship with Titiksha, is he allowed to be amazed by someone to this extent? In this manner?

The cycle-rickshaw climbs a steep speed breaker. Both Nivrita and Neel suffer a sudden jolt. She grasps his hand while he grabs her thighs for support. By the time the cycle-rickshaw climbs down the speed breaker, she is still holding onto his hand while he removes his hand from her thighs almost instantly. He looks at her expecting a reaction but there's none.

Few silent minutes pass by. Neel is getting bored. If not for Nivrita, he would not have visited any place in Jaipur. New places bore him. Rather, they make him feel uncomfortable. They somehow make him want to go back home, to his comfort zone, where he lives with Titiksha. Since the time they shifted together, Titiksha has become a symbol of the domesticity he finds himself chained to at all times and whose non-negotiable pull he feels every time he moves out of that comfort zone. Only Neel knows how he has dared to fly from Kolkata to Jaipur. And every dare has a prize, Neel wonders, looking at Nivrita as she climbs down the cycle-rickshaw. They are in Hawa Mahal now.

As Nivrita moves about inside the Hawa Mahal to capture a nice frame, she asks him, 'Do you know, Hawa Mahal was made so that the women could see what was going on in the city? But the windows, or Jharokhas as they were called, were made so small that nobody from outside could see them. Don't you think that made them voyeurs?'

Neel doesn't know what to answer and more importantly doesn't know how it matters what he thinks.

'Yes, I think so.' When in doubt, Neel always agrees.

'Are *you* a voyeur, Neel?'

A tricky question for sure. He has no clue what to say now. Should he agree he is a voyeur? Is he one? How will it harm him anyway if he lies?

'No, I'm not.'

He notices her pause. She gives him an appreciating smile which could also be read as a don't-kid-me smile, and then gets back to clicking pictures.

'Have you ever wondered that the moments we are living now with each other may well be the moments we desperately wished to live in some other life but somehow couldn't?'

Neel feels it's an interesting thought. *Is it true? Can be. Who knows what's on the other side of life.*

'Not really,' he says.

Next, they go to Amer Fort. With each passing moment words become lesser and lesser between them, as if Nivrita is slowly forgetting about his presence. After roaming around Amer Fort, Neel calls Lappan to come and fetch them.

In the car, every time Nivrita comes and sits dangerously close to him. He compulsively glances in the mirror atop the driver only to realize Lappan has his you-owe-me-another-hundred-rupees-now smirk on his face. It has appeared three times now. Neel mentally calculates that he owes Lappan three hundred rupees.

Finally he conjures up something to ask her.

'Weird, I haven't yet asked you, but what you do?'

'I make my life interesting.' Neel hears her say, 'Every now and then I ask myself what my goal is and what's the most interesting of roads that will *not* take me to it. That's what I do. I set goals and choose roads not to reach it.' She smiles, examining the pictures she has been clicking in her camera. At first Neel thinks it's her sense of humour at work and he is even on the verge of laughing at something he didn't quite get, but then good sense prevails, and he chooses not to prod.

'Stop here please,' she tells Lappan who by now has realized the lady is calling the shots.

'Let's ride a camel.'

This has to be a joke now, Neel tells himself.

The camel ride turns out to be the worst experience of Neel's life. He doesn't want to even think about it. They sit by a bench overseeing the Jal Mahal and have some vanilla ice cream. To distract himself from the horrible camel ride, Neel keeps noticing how her tongue comes out to lick the melting ice cream and reverts back to the mouth with each lick.

'What I meant in the car was what do you do for a living?' Neel says.

'I'm the senior commissioning editor at Word Tree Publishing, India,' she says in a matter-of-fact manner.

Word Tree Publishing? Did he hear her right? He wants her to repeat because for some inscrutable reason he knows it is good news for him. Instead he hears her say something better.

'What's the premise of the story you have in mind for your debut novel?'

None! That is the truth and that's what he says, 'Nothing.'

She looks at him inquisitively and says, 'Great!'

Great? An aspiring author with no story idea. What's so great about it? Neel is confused.

'I have a story. But I'll share it with you if you promise me to make it your debut novel.'

Where was this kind of good luck before? Neel can feel happiness imploding in him.

'Don't worry. If you say no, I won't mind nor shall our friendship be affected in any way. But if you do accept my proposal, then it's my promise that I shall personally look into the matter that your debut novel gets published soon and marketed as the best novel ever from Word Tree, India. What do you say?'

Neel opens his mouth and tries to say something, but words fail him.

It's 10 pm. The temperature in Jaipur has suddenly dipped by five degrees. The chill has ascended. Neel is standing alone below the budget hotel which is at a ten-minute walk from Diggi Palace. It is where Nivrita is staying.

After reaching Diggi Palace post their Jaipur darshan, she requested him, in a subtle way, to shift from Diggi Palace to Hotel Savoy Raj.

'I think a piece of this cold night, a bit of alcohol, and a lot of you and me getting to know each other would make the trip memorable. What say?'

While going out with Nivrita early in the day, Neel had confirmed with the receptionist that the Hotel Diggi Palace booking was indeed done by Titiksha. Hence, Neel didn't shift his luggage lest Titiksha calls the hotel, and realizes that he has changed his hotel. That would mean a lot of explanations required of him.

Standing below Hotel Savoy Raj by a quiet road he is waiting for the vendor, opposite to the hotel, who is supposed to bring the alcohol he ordered a minute back. In two days, Nivrita seems to have caught hold of something within him, which being with Titiksha all these years had turned into wood. And now suddenly with Nivrita's touch, that wooden something seems to be producing music of an unheard and strange quality. That something is his heart.

Neel has been handed over the desired alcohol in a paper packet. He pays the money and turns to walk towards the hotel entrance. It is then that he happens to look up at Nivrita's hotel room which has a window with a road-side view. Neel pauses. He doesn't believe what he has seen. Though Nivrita's room is dark right now but a second ago there was light and he saw her by the window doffing her tee. It must be an illusion. He prepares to walk on but pauses again. The light in the room has been switched on. Nivrita is standing by the window now in a bra. He has a feeling that she is looking directly at him. He looks around swallowing a big lump down his throat. There's nobody else noticing them. The distance doesn't allow him to see her clearly in the nude, and that adds to his emotional arousal and carnal intentions. Nivrita slowly slips off one of her bra straps from her shoulder. The light is again switched off. Neel is standing like a fool and hoping for the light to come on once again. The next instant he gets a message on his mobile phone: *I'm wet.*

Neel can feel his breathing escalate reading the message. He rushes inside the hotel.

It's 4.50 am now. Neel is used to the darkness of the room. He is lying straight on his back, naked, eyeing the ceiling, while Nivrita is lying beside him on her stomach with the blanket giving shape to her curvaceous body. Neel can see the reflection of her nude back on the clear ceiling fan. He notices some marks on Nivrita's back but he is too consumed in the post coital bliss to even care to ask her about it. But the thoughts recur. Who could have done this to her? Did she have an abusive father or husband or boyfriend or what? Whoever did that to her should rot in hell. Should he ask her about it when she wakes up? Neel decides against it because scars are always a private matter. Neel covers her back with the blanket.

Minutes back they were involved in an emotionally and physically intense and desire-draining sex session. Neel in particular liked the way Nivrita made him lick up the salt from her body. How she made him realize what the most important thing in her life is, and how casually she offered her body to him. A body he has been waiting and wanting to devour in every manner possible from the time he saw her. The only thing he couldn't guess was why did she cry? But there is another equally troubling thought trying to gain Neel's attention.

Neel knows he has cheated on Titiksha for the first time. And he is busy choosing the best excuse for it to calm down his busy mind. The mind is such a nice salesman; it keeps selling the best of excuses to the heart. But the heart is both a curious and cautious buyer. It doesn't buy what the mind has to offer every time.

Neel is trying to keep it simple. He believes—or better still, has compelled himself into believing—that he has done what he has in the last few hours because he wants to get his debut novel published by the big publishing house Nivrita works in. After attending some of the author sessions at the festival, he has come to understand how difficult it is to get one's debut work published. Rejection can quickly become a way of life. And here he has been almost accepted before he has penned the first word, even before he knows the story himself. He tries not to think about it for some time. Then he wonders: if love is a huge sea, then Titiksha is a boat which has eventually led him to a giant ship, Nivrita. Should he leave the boat behind and climb up the ship for his book's sake? He can always clarify it to Titiksha later. Or, what if he doesn't tell anything to Titiksha ever? Hiding the truth is not lying. Hiding the truth is hiding the truth.

'Neel?'

He hears Nivrita speak. Her voice is groggy. She turns her head to look at him.

'What if I tell you that love itself is afterlife? From the time one loves someone, he or she transcends normal life as we all know. And death is a means to bring someone back to that very life so that one can fall in love and transcend it yet again; a cycle of sorts?'

Again one of those queries which if he responds to, he knows, will make him sound stupid since he doesn't know what she is actually talking about. First she said love and life are like parallel tracks and now she says love is afterlife.

'I'll believe you.' A safe answer indeed. 'But why do you say so?'

'I heard it from someone.'

'Who?'

'The one on whom my story is based.'

'May I know your story Nivrita?'

'For that we will have to go back to Kolkata first,' she says and turns her head in a concluding manner as if she wants to use the subsequent silence as a lullaby.

•

Chapter 5

WHAT IS THE STORY NIVRITA HAS FOR NEEL?

'Lit by day, clit by night.'

Neel smiles to himself remembering what Nivrita had whispered to him during their carnal encounter the night before. It was vulgar for his standard but it definitely gave him a kick. Both are sitting side by side in an aeroplane flying them back to Kolkata. Their being in the same morning flight, as Neel has learnt, is a coincidence.

'Thanks for the pleasure pilgrimage, Neel.'

Pleasure pilgrimage, the words amuse him.

'Pleasure because the skin was involved. Pilgrimage because we were pursuing the soul through the skin,' Nivrita clarifies. Neel loves her way of expressing how well he has fucked her.

Thirty minutes in air and breakfast is served. When Nivrita sees a tiny piece of bread on his chin, she leans sideways to lick the bread piece off Neel's mouth, and swallows it herself. Neel doesn't react. By now he is used to her impulsive kisses, sudden touches, and abrupt licks. Nivrita reads Mario Llosa's *The Bad Girl* for some time, and later takes a short nap while Neel sits still trying not to think of the sex session that had occurred last night, and what he will tell Titiksha if and when she asks, 'How was Jaipur?'

The flight lands in Kolkata on time. As they stand by the pre-paid taxi queue, Nivrita asks him, 'Where do you stay?'

'Ultadanga. And you?' asked Neel.

'Salt Lake. Tell you what, let's take a single taxi. I can get down at the Ultadanga crossing and take another taxi from there.' Nivrita says with a smile and in that smile Neel reads an emotional fetish for taking decisions for others. Or is it she likes to control only his choices? Before he can answer, he reminds himself that whatever Nivrita asks him, he is not going to say no. Not till he writes her story and gets it published on his name. Once success comes his way then—only then—he shall call the shots. He smiles at her hoping she doesn't read his intention. By now he knows she is a sharp girl. At that time the premise of the story which Nivrita told him a few minutes before the plane landed echoes in his mind:

My story is about two innocent lovers and the not so innocent world around them. The story shows how their inability to cope up with the world they don't belong to, but have to live with, costs them their love. In the first half, the protagonists are teenagers.

'What about the second half?' Neel had enquired.

Nivrita had dismissed his question by plugging her iPod in her ears and closing her eyes to surrender to the music. Neel didn't dare ask her again.

After standing for fifteen minutes in the queue, one minute to book a taxi, and another five minutes to get the taxi number from a counter outside the airport, they finally get a taxi. Nivrita doesn't seem to mind sitting with Neel but he is somehow acutely aware of the distance between them. Maybe for her it's an unnoticeable distance, but for him it's a disturbing proximity.

Not a word is exchanged between them throughout the journey. The taxi slows down behind a bus whose driver is verbally abusing a rickshaw-wallah around the Teghoria crossing. Neel looks amused with the proceedings but then his expression changes. He has seen someone at the other side of the road. He frowns and gets down from the taxi.

'What happened?' Nivrita inquires after him.

'Back in a minute…' Neel retorts and carefully crosses the busy VIP road.

Nivrita looks out through the taxi's closed transparent window. She notices Neel is standing behind a half-bent person on the opposite footpath.

The man is bent forward and is busy buying vegetables from one of the many roadside vendors. Neel taps on the man's shoulder who, in response, straightens up and turns to look at Neel with a blank face.

'Don't you recognize me, Arindam?' Says Neel.

The man looks at him with an open mouth now, and nods his head in the negative.

'We used to work together in Hindustan Bank.'

The man shuts his mouth and adjusts his specs a bit; conclusively.

'Sorry, you are mistaken,' he says and continues to select his vegetables. Neel keeps looking at him aghast. It can't be a mistake. Something dawns on him, and he pulls the man's shirt from behind and notices a cut on his neck.

'You are Arindam Dey! You have the cut-mark too. Why are you denying it?'

The man goes off balance because of the sudden pull on his shirt. He gets up and pushes back Neel forcefully.

'Get lost, you mad fucker!'

The push and the abuse escalate Neel's heartbeats. He hears Nivrita call out to him from the other end.

'That was strange. He is Arindam Dey. We used to work

together till last year. Then he left.' Says Neel once he is back inside the taxi.

'Are you sure?'

'I am. We used to be good office buddies. I saw the cut mark he had on his neck. It was a deep one. He got it when he accidentally scratched his neck with the sharp end of a compass. He'd told me so himself.'

'Then why didn't he recognize you?'

Neel shrugs and keeps looking at Arindam as he selects vegetables on the other end of the road.

Nivrita seems a bit ruffled by the sudden alteration in Neel's poise. She takes out a packet of cigarettes. In all these four days, this is the first time Neel notices the cigarette packet with her. It's Marlboro. By the time she brings out one cigarette from it, Neel blurts, 'If you don't mind, could you please not smoke while I'm around?'

Nivrita glances at him once, then at the cigarette, and keeps it back inside her bag babbling a soft apology. But she is not done. Neel sees her fidgeting with her bag and soon she takes out a photograph. She gives it to him. Neel checks it with a sense of scepticism. The picture looks old and has a boy in a white shirt and black jeans. Beside him in the photograph is a girl wearing a blue top and royal blue cropped trousers. The boy has one hand over her shoulder while the girl has her hand around his waist. Their smile looks forced, as if they weren't ready for the photograph. Neel finds something familiar about this photograph. But he doesn't know what exactly. He views the photograph up close just to look at their faces but cannot tell what is similar. Both the boy and girl are standing at a distance and the faces are not very clear. The light in the photograph isn't that good either.

'These are the characters of my story,' he hears Nivrita say.

'What do you mean by "your" characters?'

'It's a true story.'

'You mean whatever you are going to tell me has happened in reality?'

'Yes, but why do you sound scared?'

Neel does sound scared.

'Are you sure I'll be able to pull it off? I mean you haven't even read my writing. How come you trust me so much?'

Nivrita looks at him straight. 'I insisted you to write the story not because you are a bad or a good author.'

'Then?'

'Stop here, dada.'

'What?' He doesn't know what she means. A second later he realizes the taxi has stopped.

'I'll call you soon,' Nivrita says and gets down with her luggage.

As she waves at him, Neel waves back, and then at the next traffic signal asks the driver to take a U-turn from Ultadanga. It is evident he has lied to Nivrita. He doesn't live in Ultadanga. He lives in Lake Town with Titiksha. He didn't tell Nivrita the truth because he didn't want to take the risk of any sudden visit from Nivrita at his place, especially when Titiksha is around. He wants to keep Nivrita away from Titiksha for obvious reasons—he knows too less of Nivrita while he knows too much of Titiksha.

The taxi reaches the Lake Town footbridge and is waiting for the traffic ahead to clear. Suddenly two plain clothed men appear from nowhere, open the taxi doors, and get in.

'Are you Neel Chatterjee?' one of the two men inquires.

'Yes I'm. Who are you?' Neel is visibly unnerved. The taxi driver is about to shoo off the men himself when he hears one of the two speak.

'Kolkata Police. You have to come with us.'

Neel looks at the men, one at a time. Their eyes scare him.

Neel cannot believe his parents had filed a missing person report with the Kolkata police while he was in Jaipur. It was only when they left him at his place that he understood why the men barged into the taxi. They were following him from the airport. All through the Jaipur trip, he thought Titiksha must have told his parents about his trip. She often informed them whenever he did anything without telling them. He didn't like telling his parents everything himself because they didn't like Neel going alone anywhere. His parents love Titiksha though. From the time he introduced her to them they accepted her as their future daughter-in-law. Minor relationship hiccups occurred when Titiksha, being the woman she is, proposed to live-in with Neel for a year or so to see their compatibility, and then take a decision about staying together for the rest of her life. She has a thing against blind faith. At first Neel thought she may have been rejected by someone in the past because of which she has developed such preferences, but she has always told him that he is her first relationship. For reasons best known to her, she never used the term 'first love'.

Initially Neel was against the idea of living-in simply because he thought his parents would not accept it, forget allowing it. *Marriage is the only way a man and a woman can live together under one roof,* he thought. But to his surprise Titiksha managed to convince his parents. She never let him meet her parents since they lived abroad. Neel still doesn't know why she does not even let him talk to them over the phone.

In the bedroom of his rented flat in Lake Town, Neel patiently waits for Titiksha to come back from office. It is 10 pm. Normally she comes back by 8. He is worried about her and the wait is only adding to his worries. The surprising thing his parents have told him is that Titiksha hasn't picked up their call in the last four days. Not even once! That is strange considering the fact that Titiksha has always treated his parents like her own. And if she can book the hotel room for him in Jaipur, then can't she tell his parents where he was in the last five days? Alright, she can't even pick up their calls? And then it dawns on him that Titiksha is yet to respond to his messages as well. On an impulse, he dials her number again. He has by now tried her number several times but every time the number is busy. Who is she talking to all the time? He gets ready to message her again when he hears the door unlocking. He switches off the bedroom light to surprise her.

'It was great to be with you,' Neel hears her say.

Then come slurping sounds. It's too sudden for him to guess what those sounds could be. But chances are he knows what's going on in the drawing room. It's the same sound Nivrita and he made in Jaipur. Neel immediately stands up. He cheated on Titiksha because he needed something from Nivrita. Why would Titiksha cheat on him? Does she need something he doesn't know about? No way! It must be a girl who has come to drop Titiksha at home since he wasn't in the city. But nobody ever dropped Titiksha home. He holds his head and sits down on the floor. He can now feel a mild headache.

'Bye baby,' he hears her say next.

Titiksha is humming a song. She seems to be in a good mood. She comes to the room, switches on the light, and shrieks out loudly on seeing Neel inside.

'What the hell are you doing here?'

Should he ask her the obvious: was it a he or a she who dropped her? Or should he wait for her to clarify on her own? Will he able to take it if she says it on his face that it's a he? It can just be a friend. The slurping sounds hovered in his mind. *Friend? Really? Who is this new friend?*

'It's my place, remember?' Neel says with deliberate curtness.

'It's equally mine Neel, remember?' she says and and tries to calm herself down. The initial surprise in her eyes seems under control now. She keeps her bag on the bedside table and lies down on the bed to relax. Neel can feel a change in Titiksha. She didn't even care to hug him or ask how he has been and what all he did in Jaipur. Not that he would have told her what all he really did there, but still.

There's silence. Neel keeps looking at Titiksha who has her eyes closed. Something tells him that it's the lull-before-the-storm kind of silence. *A storm may happen anytime now,* Neel wonders with a dry throat. In a second or two she would say it's over—their relationship—their five-year-old relationship, which they were confident about till four days ago is now over. As if a relationship is one of those computer softwares which you install, enjoy, and then uninstall once you get bored to make space for another one. Why is Neel even thinking all this without crosschecking?

'How was Jaipur?' Titiksha says, her eyes still closed.

For a moment Neel feels maybe this sudden suspicion on Titiksha is because it's he who has cheated on his girlfriend and thus whatever she does now will be questionable to him, for he will see her actions through the lens of his choice. His own deficiency will make her strength look like her weakness. That's how the mind works. If you know you are dirty, the world around you smells dirty.

'Why?' Neel says.

'What do you mean why?' Titiksha gets up, switches off the light, and starts changing. 'You are my boyfriend. I have the right to know.'

'Sorry.' Though it is dark, his eyes are on her. The way she changes her dress has always aroused him. It's no different now. She always changes her lower first and then the upper. She wears Jockey shorts and a yellow spaghetti top.

She switches on the light and says,'It's been a minute and you still haven't answered me. What's wrong?' 'She walks to the kitchen. He knows her ordeal after returning home from office rather well: change, drink a glass of warm water with a pinch of lemon, wash her face, apply a moisturizer, switch on the television, and watch some stupid *saas-bahu* serial till it's time to prepare dinner.

As he follows her into the kitchen, he answers, 'Nothing. Jaipur was nice. Thanks for the hotel booking.'

'You knew I would do that, didn't you? Even after you fought with me before leaving.'

Neel has barely smiled when he notices her open the refrigerator wide and take out a bottle of cold water. As she gulps down the water, a stream of it trickles down her throat and onto her top wetting it in the process and making the top stick to her bosom.

'You always have warm water,' Neel says moving his eyes to her face.

'I have realized when you start using words like "always", "forever", or "never" for a person, then that person is sure living a boring life.'

This is not the Titiksha he knows. Four days back when he was adamant about leaving for Jaipur to get inspiration and kick-start his writing career, she was the one who gave him an hour long lecture on how important it was for them to settle down, to continue doing what they were doing in their careers without any change, and now she suddenly sounds like a nomad of sorts, shunning away emotional domesticity. How is it possible?

She goes to her room. He follows. Standing by the room's entrance, he watches her sit down with her laptop. *So she has stopped watching television as well?* Neel wonders trying to sit beside her. Immediately she shoots, 'Why don't you sit there? It makes me feel awkward with you staring at the laptop screen.'

Neel doesn't like her tone but he doesn't say anything. Once he is seated opposite her he asks, 'Why didn't you tell my parents I'd gone to Jaipur? They went ahead and filed a missing person report. It's unacceptable.'

'I'm not surprised. Your parents are way too possessive of you. Look at my parents. They don't even care what I'm doing in life. My life is my life, after all.'

'That's because your parents live abroad. Here in India, your life is everybody's, specially your parents' life.'

Titiksha doesn't respond but he notices her smiling looking at her laptop screen.

'What are you smiling at?'

'Nothing.'

'Then answer me first, why didn't you tell them I was in Jaipur. You didn't even pick up their calls.'

With the last query Neel hopes she would talk about what he assumes is the reason for the subtle changes in her: that she has another man in her life.

'Work pressure. I was not even in Kolkata.'

'What? Where were you? You didn't even care to tell me!'

'Did you care to call me from Jaipur? Only messages, huh!'

The most humiliating thing for Neel at this time is that she isn't looking him in the eye while talking. Earlier whenever she would get angry, she would look directly at him but not tonight.

'At least I cared to book the hotel for you.'

Neel is quiet now. Whatever she said is true. What about him? He even fucked a girl; a school friend of his in Jaipur. Does he even have the right to ask Titiksha if she is having an affair?

'One litre Pepsi. Please send it upstairs right now,' she orders on the phone. Neel guesses she must have called Ma Tara Stores—the local grocery store—downstairs.

'Since when did you start drinking Pepsi? Weren't you a Fanta lover?'

'I was, yes. Not anymore. I've realized you can't be too much into the "everything lasts forever" shit, or you'll miss out on various other tastes.'

What does that mean? That she is bored with him and wants someone else? Is she giving him hints so that he understands himself, and calls it quits without her having to explain much?

'Are you saying you are bored of me, Titiksha?'

'I'm saying I am bored of Fanta.'

'That's my favourite drink. Does that mean you are bored of whatever interests me?'

'Now you are talking like someone who has only been in one relationship all his life.'

'What does that mean?'

'Forget it.'

Just when Neel demands a clarification, the doorbell rings. He reluctantly goes to open the door, collects the Pepsi, pays the money, and brings it to Titiksha in the bedroom.

'What if…' Neel takes his time to phrase it in his mind, and make sure if he really wants to say it.

'What if' he repeats and continues, 'I tell you that I had a fling in Jaipur?'

There is no answer from her for few seconds. Then she looks at him. Eye to eye.

'I'll pluck one of your eyes with my own fingers.'

'What if I tell you that I suspect you are having an affair?'

Titiksha laughs out in an eerie manner as if Neel has just cracked a joke after a long time. Then she suddenly turns serious.

'I'll pluck both your eyes out in that case.'

⌛

Neel is waiting for Nivrita inside Flury's in Park Street. He has kept his laptop bag on the adjacent chair. It's a popular place but Neel is visiting it for the first time. He read Nivrita's late night message on his phone in the morning which stated she wanted to meet him here, for her office is nearby, and start narrating him the story. Neel too wants to start with the novel immediately—enough of inspiration.

He wonders if he should talk about Titiksha to her. The abrupt change in her has affected Neel so much that he couldn't sleep well last night. His eyes have dark circles around them and his hair—though he applied a lot of water—have funny curls, now that they have dried considerably. He has a faint stubble too. A waiter comes over and says, 'Can I take your order, sir?'

'Gimme a moment. I'm waiting for someone.'

'Right. And welcome back, sir. You have come here after a long time,' the waiter beams at him in a way as if he means what he said. He goes to another table.

After a long time? He must be saying this to every customer. Neel is pretty sure he has come here for the first time.

He looks at the entrance because Nivrita has just entered Flury's. She looks enraged. She sits down with a thud opposite Neel and holds her face as if she is trying to come to terms with something disturbingly important.

'What happened?'

'That bugger is having an affair.'

'Which bugger?'

'My boy-mate.'

What a coincidence! Neel wonders. Even Nivrita doubts her... wait, what did she say?

'What's a boy-mate?'

'He is the boy with whom I mate when I feel the need. He used to be my boyfriend initially, but with time we stopped being friends. Now we turn to each other only when one of us is horny.'

Neel tries to digest what Nivrita has just said. She makes sexual acts sound so casual. How can anyone be so casual about their sexual escapades? It's such a private thing. Neel has problems seeing himself naked in a mirror, so how can he not have a problem with the casual confessional tone of Nivrita?

'Are you sure?' he says.

'I was at home yesterday. He didn't know. And he came home with a girl. Damn, I'm sure about it.'

Neel's face flinches. He has a problem accepting the absurd similarity of the events he had had at his place last night. Even he was waiting for Titiksha and she came in with a guy. Or so he guessed.

'But didn't we share private moments in Jaipur too?'

By probing on her guilt, Neel is actually trying to calm his own guilt down.

'But he wasn't there in the hotel room while we were fucking each other.'

The way she puts it—blatantly straight—makes him feel uncomfortable. He would have liked it if she had put it the way he did—'private moments' instead of the crude F-word. The first thing Neel does after hearing the word is see if anyone is looking at them. Nobody is.

'Anyway, that's my shit. How is it going with your girlfriend? And yeah, please order something for me,' she says and snaps her fingers.

'Two cups of tea and a brownie,' Neel tells the waiter.

Titiksha is having an affair too. Should he tell Nivrita about his suspicion?

'Titiksha is good.' He chooses not to, but realizes, for the first time that he has shared his girlfriend's name with Nivrita. He notices her sharp glance suggesting she did register the name. It seems like she doesn't quite like it.

'You know, I think it's better to have an affair with a willing and committed person rather than an unwilling single one.'

'How do you know who is willing and who is not?'

A sly smile appears on Nivrita's face, 'Whoever comes to a girl's hotel room at night is willing.' The smile takes a caught-you-there form.

The waiter comes half a minute later and places the order on her side of the table.

'Have you ever been snatched, Neel?' she says looking at him obliquely while mixing the sugar-free in her tea.

'Snatched?'

'Yeah snatched. What if I snatch you from Titiksha?'

The sound of her statement has something deeply and dominantly sexual about it that he has to adjust his legs a bit in order to hide the instant erection. He blushes and ends up looking stupid in a cute way.

'Forget it,' she says judging his dilemma. 'Instead tell me what is sex according to you? And what is love?'

Neel sips his tea and thinks, *Why does she ask so many questions? Especially the ones whose answers are a far cry for him.*

'Sex is...you know what sex is. Love is...love is...'

'Love is...?' She licks the chocolate sauce from her lips which a brownie piece has left while she shifted it from the plate to her mouth. Neel can't help but think that now he knows her tongue is tastier than both the chocolate and brownie. He sucked it well that night.

'I can't articulate it well. Why don't you tell me about it?' Neel surrenders.

'Sex is when two bodies worship each other's hearts. Love is following the rituals leading to that worship and thereafter.'

Neel loses his erection. He gapes at Nivrita. She is one of those gifts wraps which, when opened, gives way to another gift wrap and another and so on, surprising you as well as arousing your curiosity to the hilt as to what exactly is it that is wrapped in the end.

'I'll have to scoot. But I'm free after lunch. I want to take you somewhere.' Nivrita is quick to gobble up the rest of the brownie.

'Where?'

'Many authors have told me that when you go to a place where the story actually begins in your novel, you write better.'

'Logical! So where does your story begin?'

'Our story. From today it's your story as well, Neel.'

Neel senses a longing in her voice which wasn't there before.

'Right!' he says.

'It's a school.'

'A school?' He remembers she did tell him that the protagonists are teenagers in the first half and then she didn't answer his query about the second half. 'Is it some fluffy high school romance?' he asks.

'Neel Chatterjee' the words slip out of her mouth in an overtly seductive manner as she leans towards him.

'Never' she now whispers, 'judge a story by its setting.'

He gives her a forced smile of acknowledgement.

For the next four hours, Neel kills time by browsing books inside the Oxford Bookstore in Park Street. He is amazed to see so many Indian authors' books. Eighty percent of them look and read the same. Replicating anything that is successful is a disease with Indians in every sphere. Twenty percent of the books are marginally better. He hopes to make it to the 20 percent soon. As he peruses the books, he overhears two youngsters talk.

'You don't see many foreign authors in the Indian bestseller lists these days. That's an amazing thing,' says one.

'Not really,' says the other. 'I think in five years' time, only those Indian authors will feature in the bestseller's list who have a dedicated PR team promoting the book on a monthly basis.'

'So you are saying if one wants to earn crores from a book as an author, he or she has to put in lakhs?'

'That's right. In fact I believe the term "bestseller author" will soon be extinct and it will be substituted by a more suitable and more practiced term like "best-branded" author.'

'Don't the publishers help?'

'They are the God. And God helps those who help themselves, if you know what I mean!'

The two youngsters break into mild laughter and move on to another book rack away from Neel.

Neel has absorbed every word they just said. He has money but doesn't have as much as they said one should to turn one's book into a hot property. His father has loads of cash, but he doesn't want to take it from him. It's now that he realizes how important Nivrita is for his dream to come true. She had said she would personally see that the book gets marketed properly. How many debut authors are given that kind of offer? For that if he needs to compromise only a bit and play on with Nivrita without upsetting her then he has nothing to lose but a lot to gain.

At precisely 1.45 pm he moves out of the bookstore and reaches the nearby Trinca's Bar and Restaurant. Nivrita eventually joins him. They cross the road and hail a taxi.

'Salt Lake, CA Block,' she tells the driver.

'Here.' She takes out two paper boxes and two plastic forks. She gives one box to Neel.

He opens the box and beams, 'I love Chinese.'

'I know.'

Neel's face stones up. 'You know? How?'

'I had a crush on you during school days. The first thing one does when one has a crush on someone is collect as much information about the person as possible.'

'But how do you know so much about me? I mean I rarely came to school.'

Nivrita takes a bite of the noodles and says, 'Tell me, lust is lust till it falls in love. But what's love when it falls in lust?'

Neel's mouth is stuffed but he doesn't swallow it. Instead he blabbers in a funny manner.

'I have no idea.'

Nivrita laughs. 'I was only playing with words. Don't look this serious.'

Neel relaxes. He swallows and asks, 'So what's the name of the school?'

⌛

They both are standing in front of a private school now. On the big rusty iron gate of the school entrance is written: Salt Lake International School.

'Just wait inside,' Nivrita says and walks towards a wretched looking shanty-shop on the far right corner outside the school. Neel doesn't mind entering the campus.

As he waits inside the campus by the main gate, someone taps his shoulder from behind. He turns to see an old man in a khaki uniform. He is clean shaven with heavily oiled but neatly combed hair.

'I couldn't believe but I was sure from the distance it was you. You haven't changed much Neel baba.'

Neel frowns. He is seeing the man for the first time in his life.

'I didn't get you.'

For a few seconds the man stands as if Neel has slapped him.

'Have you forgotten me?'

'You are probably mistaken. I never studied in this school.'

'I used to call you Neel baba and you used called me Abdul chacha.'

Neel shrugs saying, 'As I said it wasn't me.'

The old man is still not convinced. He also has a pronounced disappointment on his face as if he believes Neel does not recognize him intentionally.

'Baba, I have been working here for forty years now. By now may be forty thousand students, at least, have passed out but never before have I mistaken to recognize any student.'

A pause later he continues, 'I used to like you a lot and I still remember how I was suspended for a week, my only suspension till date, when you requested me for a smoke. I denied but you kept insisting, and I allowed you one puff from my bidi and the smoke choked your vocal cord, and you were hospitalized for a day. From then on you never smoked. Well, though I was suspended but I was happy at least the fear would never let you take up something as self-destructive as smoking.'

Neel recollects his freaky reaction to Lappan's cigarette. But how is it possible that this man knows him when he has never even been to this school before? He hears the old guard say, 'I understand. Maybe you are a big man now and don't want to recognize an old security guard like me. It's okay Neel baba.'

Neel feels bad. For a moment he wants to accept what the old man is saying. By then Nivrita arrives dangling a packet of cigarettes.

'Sorry, I always buy one from the shopkeeper there whenever I come here. Old ties never die.'

Nivrita doesn't seem to care about the old man. Neel doesn't say anything to him either and follows Nivrita inside. For once he does turn around only to notice the old man still gaping at him. Forty years of work he had said, the man needs a break for sure. He deliberately doesn't tell Nivrita about it, lest she thinks he has gone mad.

Few metres from the school gate is a white bust of a man at the centre of a small but well-maintained garden. It is of the man who built the school some forty-five years ago. The information is written on the marble slab below the bust.

On his left he can see a shade beyond which there is a basketball court. He follows Nivrita to that court. As he tries to keep up with her, he asks, 'Pretty big school. It doesn't look like it has such an expanse from the outside.'

Nivrita turns for once and says, 'The outside and the inside are two different things Neel. Don't try to guess the latter by studying the former.'

Neel wonders if she was being witty and there was more to what she had said. She doesn't clarify though. Neel soon forgets about it.

Midway through the basketball court, Nivrita turns right and enters a small gate and into the bigger building which is spread on either side of the bust from outside. Neel is right behind her looking around and taking mental notes of things.

'This is where the secondary classes happen from standard 6 to 12. Most of the story happens in this building,' she says.

Though there's a long corridor ahead but Nivrita takes the stairs to the immediate left of the small entrance. He follows. They climb up to the second floor. There is no sound which seems a bit weird since it's supposedly school hours. Finally they are on the second floor's corridor.

'Where are the students?' Neel inquires still looking around.

'It's a holiday today.'

'Why?'

'They had their annual sports event the other day so today is a holiday.'

'And they have allowed us inside?'

'I have the principal's permission with me.'

Finally Nivrita enters one of the classrooms. Neel follows close behind.

'This is exactly where the story begins.'

Something about the way Nivrita says it makes Neel wonder if it's her personal story. Then why didn't she write it herself if she wants to share it with readers? Why does she need a writer for it? And that too someone who has not written a single book! Seconds later, he thanks God for making her choose him to write the story.

'I would appreciate it if you write the story with a female protagonist in mind. It would be interesting: a male writer writing from the point of view of a female.'

Neel is considering her suggestion: a male writing from the point of view of a female. It would be tough for him, he feels.

'It may give us a marketing edge too,' Nivrita says next.

Hearing the words 'marketing edge' Neel says, 'Okay.'

'Great!'

'If you don't mind may I ask you something?'

'Sure.'

Nivrita now goes and sits by a bench at the back.

'Is this your story?'

'I told you this is our story.'

'No, what I mean is this your personal story?'

'This is Neel and Titiksha's story.'

For a moment Neel stands frozen. Then he thinks, 'Alright, she is joking,' he laughs out.

'It's not a joke. You can stop laughing.' There's intent in her voice.

Neel immediately closes his mouth tight.

'What do you mean?' he asks carrying a cocktail of incredulity and bewilderment on his face.

'What I really mean is the present English popular fiction scenario in India is such that people like reading about the writer's personal story more than enjoying a so called fictional story.'

'So even if it is not my story you want me to write it in a way as if it is?'

'Yes. You can say its reality fiction. There's as much reality in fiction as there is in reality television. Always remember, only two things sell in India—sex and sympathy. It's because there's a large, very large, number of Indians who are gullible, ignorant, and unaware. Hence, I think you should lend your and your girlfriend's name to the protagonists in the story. With that the chance of going closer to the readers will also increase. Secondly, if you write the story from the point of view of a female, it would tell readers how much you know women. Not every guy can write a touching story from a girl's point of view.'

Neel takes a few minutes to absorb what Nivrita has just said by pacing up and down the classroom. Only the ceiling fan's creaking noise is audible. Nivrita keeps looking at him, confident of his answer.

'Alright, the protagonists will have Titiksha and my names.' He slowly ambles towards the corner most seats in the classroom. *Just the debut book. Let me get published first then I'll publish what I want to write,* he tells himself and in the next instant he hears Nivrita speak.

'Great. So should I start narrating you the story? It begins in 1995.'

'1995? That's like quite a long time back. Can't we make it contemporary?'

Nivrita is quiet.

'It's fiction after all, so how does it matter if we change the year from 1995 to let's say 2013? The essence is important, don't you think?' Neel argues.

'Right,' says Nivrita. 'Moreover there are certain realities which no degree of fictionalization can change.'

Neel casually wipes a layer of dust with his fingertip from the last wooden seat and makes himself comfortable on it. There is quite a distance between the two since Nivrita is sitting at the left corner of the classroom by the wall while Neel is sitting at the right corner, where the windows are. He casually looks at the desk and at one corner he notices a word sculpted: Titiksha.

Before he can react to this absurd coincidence he hears Nivrita say, 'Let me start narrating.'

Not every Titiksha is the Titiksha he knows, Neel thinks quickly, and says, 'Wait! Let me bring out my laptop,' bringing out his Macbook Pro from his bag.

'One last request, Neel.' Nivrita puts her legs on one of the benches to attain a more comfortable position.

'What?'

'Write the story in past tense.'

'Past tense?'

'I feel there's this pain associated with past tense. It gives me a feeling that what had to happen has happened. Nothing can change it. The story I am about to tell you has already happened. Neither the lives the story has touched while it was happening can be changed nor the damage it has caused to its characters can now be undone. That's the power of the past. It can't be undone—come what may!'

Neel takes a moment to relax his mind. He has a feeling that it would be an interesting story.

'Or you can intersperse the past tense with abrupt conversations where the author seems to be talking to the readers. I won't mind that.'

Neel's Macbook Pro is ready now. So is he.

'Okay, I'm ready. By the way can you please tell me a name for the story; a working title of sorts,' Neel says waiting to type whatever Nivrita shall suggest.

Nivrita smiles at him as if she has been expecting this question.

'For the time being,' she says, 'Let's name it: Ex.'

WORKING TITLE: 'EX'
From Neel's Manuscript

1

Being Titiksha was never easy. But when I think back now, being easy was never being Titiksha either.

Where do I start? Introductions have always made me feel awkward for they lead to impressions. I was never fond of impressions. If I tell you that my age when this story began was sixteen, that I had a killer figure, cute smile, sexy eyes, sweet voice, and a frank nature enough to floor any guy, then you would immediately guess that I was a high school bombshell. Some of you will create an image of me and fantasize about me, wishing for my look-alike to be your next girlfriend. My thoughts would not let you sleep or allow you any inner peace. In short, my image will torment your mind, heart, and life—all in an enticing manner.

Hold your breath now. I was nothing of the above. Did your flight of fantasy just crash land? I was indeed sixteen but fat (never cared to weigh myself), regularly had pimples (one went the other appeared but thankfully they didn't leave much of marks), wore old fashioned thick specs, always kept my hair in a pony (I was never a shampoo model), reserved (I never mixed with people but observed everything from a distance), and no boy ever looked at me twice. And one more important and very real thing about me: I didn't give a shit about what people thought of me if they at all did.

Whatever I'll tell you is my life but not entirely my story. One's life cannot be one's story *only*. And if your life is only your story, it means it has surely been a waste. Even my life was a waste till I was sixteen. From then on, my story ceased being my story alone. What I'm trying to tell you is that post sixteen, I was royally and deliciously screwed by life.

Three important things happened the year I crossed sixteen.

The first important thing: My parents divorced.

For me it was an eventuality. I knew about this. I prayed for this. Why would a child pray for her parents' divorce? Oh, you wouldn't have asked this if you were in my place. I have grown up hearing what a mistake I was for my parents. They never told me this directly but whenever they fought, which was all the time, either mom said it to dad or dad told mom that they didn't plan and conceived me. I was an accident. Titiksha was an accident for them. I guess that explains why they never really cared for my needs and wants. I grew up the way I did because I had to. I soon understood everyone had issues, everyone had problems, and everyone came across a day when one's life's story ceases to be one's only. Life's best/worst trick, however, was that even after knowing well that everybody goes through similar shit, I felt my classmates, friends, or acquaintances were a tad bit better placed than me in life. It kind of made me feel better to be not better than people around me. An emotional paradox; finding happiness in the fact that I was facing bigger problems than others. In a strange way, it made me feel something worthwhile was happening in my life. More the shit, more the worth was what I concluded.

At nights before sleep took over, I always wondered if I would have been the same person if my parents had conceived me after proper planning. Probably then they would have felt responsible enough to care for me. And love me. Love! Till then I'd never known what love was. I only guessed it as some kind of a magic in a person which called for another person's emotional attention. I have craved to feel that magic in me, but have never come across anyone who made me feel that magic in me. If you plant a tree in the presence of high power lights from day to night, how does it matter? It will need sunlight to grow. I was not healthy. I felt like a weed which had grown because somewhere, someone forgot to clean up. I existed, I occupied space. That was about it. I didn't feel inferior, but I did feel unwanted. The saddest thing was I allowed life to convince me that I didn't deserve anything good. Till of course I crossed sixteen.

One of the reasons why I was shifted to my grandmother's place was to safeguard me from people who loved to poke into my life. Or so mom told me. I knew she was lying. That probably was another side effect of being an adult: nobody said anything straight. The truth was both mom and dad wanted to lead an independent life. When I complained to mom about how shifting school wouldn't help me since I was used to the school I was studying in from kindergarten, she only asked me to learn to live with things which I didn't appreciate. A happy life isn't the one where you got everything you wanted. A happy life is how well you accept the things given to you; she'd told me. I never complained to her again. I knew she was going through a lot of stress. I had seen her doing things which only dad used to do before—smoke and drink. She would also be in a ready-to-fight mood most of the times. Those were the days when whatever connections I felt towards her slowly diminished. I never understood dad so I never cared about what happened to him.

Mom got custody of me and left me with Yo-didun (I called my grandmother by that nickname because the first day she surprised me by saying her favourite TV channel was MTV!). Yo-didun lived in her house in Salt Lake. Earlier I was in Ballygunge, South Kolkata, in a two bed-room flat with mom and dad. I was comfortable living in a house with less people and more empty spaces. But at Yo-didun's place there were a lot of people; my maternal uncle, Ashok mama, his wife, Bijoya mami, his two sons—Sandip and Shib. I hated them all. They hated me even more.

Mama hated me because I was better than his sons in studies. Sandip was of my age and Shib was two years younger. Both had the brains of a donkey. I didn't exactly know why Bijoya mami hated me but she did. She always gave Sandip and Shib full glasses of milk during breakfast but not me. They had eggs regularly too. I got it only during weekends. She gave their clothes to laundry whereas I had to wash and iron my clothes myself. If I had periods, I was made to eat and stay separate from them. When Sandip and Shib studied, nobody was allowed to watch television at home. When I studied, the television's volume kept ascending at will. Every Thursday mama, mami, and their sons dined out but not me. That day Yo-didun prepared dinner for both of us. I helped her as much as I could.

'Shonamoni, you'll have the happiest husband,' Yo-didun always told me whenever I helped her with cooking. She thought my cooking was fabulous. Honestly she was the only person whose company I enjoyed. She never asked me much but answered a lot of my queries. I especially enjoyed the time when she oil-massaged my head at night. She knew I was being neglected at mama's place but she told me to focus on studies so that I could stand on my feet, and have my own life. She said women should always be financially independent. That was precisely my goal too. I didn't exactly know what I wanted to do in life but I knew I wanted to be financially independent, and not rely on anybody else for money. Another thing I was sure of was whenever I would conceive a child with a man, it would never be out of ignorance. My child would never be an accident.

The second important thing: I changed my school. Actually, I was forced into doing it.

My earlier school, Calcutta High, was in South Kolkata and since it was too far away from mama's place, I was admitted to Salt Lake International. I complained to Yo-didun about it. All she said was, 'Adults don't know how to decide for themselves, but they reserve the divine right to decide for their kids.' We shared a hi-five.

I accepted the change of school too just like the other changes in my life. Of course I was not an adult so I was not free to make an issue out of everything. I was never attached to anyone in my old school so in the end, I was okay with the shift. Yo-didun advised me to stay away from attachment.

'Attachment isn't everyone's cup of tea,' she'd remarked.

I was pretty sure that I would never be attached to anything. That's just the way I was. I enjoyed things till they were around me. Then if I had to go away, I went away. No fuss. No tears. Yo-didun thought it was actually a blessing in disguise which would come in handy for me later on in life. She was right.

Once, while I was oil-massaging her scalp, I asked her why she didn't marry post Dadu's demise.

She was just thirty-one when my Dadu died. She said it was because she was attached to Dadu. And when one is attached to someone, there's no room for anybody else. So for forty years following dadu's death, Yo-didun lived alone because she was attached to dadu. Forty years!

'A momentary presence of a person, at times, can comfortably numb his absence from your life,' she said. Attachment, indeed, was a dangerous thing—I made a note of it in my mind.

The third important thing: This is something confusing.

On the face of it, it seemed like a simple thing. Too simple to be significant. I later realized that's what most life-altering moments seemed like to begin with. As I dived deeper I knew it was anything but simple. Why or what made me dive deeper anyway? Why wasn't I happy with only the face value of the incident considering the fact that I generally was happy with the face value of most things? Reading between the lines, digging deep, and finding profound meaning to something otherwise stupid, bored me. But by the time I realized what had happened, I was already deep enough in it to let go of the feelings that mobbed my heart. When I narrated the incident to Yo-didun, she said, 'Did it feel like some electricity ran through you and lit a special bulb in your heart?'

I found myself nodding positively.

'How did you know this Yo-didun?'

'It happens. Especially when one is sixteen,

it happens exactly that way,' she said beaming from ear to ear as if it was a joke.

I relaxed knowing I wasn't the only one to feel the electricity Yo-didun talked about, or the special bulb in my heart she mentioned, at sixteen.

2

The 'special bulb' incident happened on a Friday which was also my first day at Salt Lake International school. The weather was hot and humid. It wasn't cloudy in the morning but it suddenly started raining the moment I stepped out of the house. When I requested Bijoya mami for an umbrella, because I wasn't able to find mine, she said there were three umbrellas all of which had been taken by mama, Sandip, and Shib. I had a raincoat too but after searching for it for ten long minutes, Bijoya mami informed me that her dear younger sister, Piyali has worn it to the vegetable market. When mami went away to the kitchen, I showed her the middle finger. I wanted to show it to her on her face but curbed myself from doing so. Piyali used to appear regularly at Yo-didun's place and at times even stayed over. She was a couple of years younger to Bijoya mami but was unmarried.

Finally, Yo-didun gave me her 20-year-old umbrella which was embarrassingly huge. I didn't have an option, but I still didn't take it. With a little money from Yo-didun, I managed to summon a cycle-rickshaw passing by which took me to my new school. I ran as fast as I could to a shaded enclosure inside the school campus where other students were gossiping among themselves. I guessed this was where the morning assembly took place. The rain had only increased its fury while I was running inside the campus. As I stood alone gasping for breath, I suddenly noticed everyone was looking at me mockingly. I was pretty sure I wasn't wearing any special newcomer's robe to my new school, so why were they staring at me? Half a minute later, I realized my blue bra line was completely visible through the white cotton school shirt, totally wet by now. Okay, time for a secret: at sixteen I had well developed breasts. Like a woman's.

With humiliation clouding my mind, I didn't know what to do next. The girls and boys were chuckling among themselves. My earlier school was a girl's school and now seeing the boys ogling at me and my bra-line got to me. I started crying. I had never cried in front of anyone before but that day was different. More so because I knew staring at me they'd also notice my fat, specs, pony, and what not. I was proud of what I was but for the first time their stares hurt me. I quickly covered my bosom with my school bag.

A girl came up to me. After I told her I was a newcomer, she showed me to my class: 11, Science. I scampered to the adjacent building. I may have looked funny while doing so, but I was happy to finally disappear from the sight.

The corridor was empty when I climbed the last step to reach it. Second floor, the girl had said, and then the third classroom to the left. I checked a brown coloured square wooden plate pinned above on the right corner of the door. It had '11-Sc.' written on it.

I was relieved to find the classroom empty. I closed the door, switched on all the fans, and stood under the one right at the centre of the room, desperately wishing to dry up before the assembly breaks and students began to pour into the classroom. All the cacophony coming from outside kept subsiding steadily.

A minute later it was all quiet. I heard a sudden noise in the classroom. I looked around but there was nothing. Something fell on the floor. I scurried towards the door stupidly fearing it to be some blood-thirsty-lost-soul. Shreya, a classmate from my previous school, used to share the stories of all the ghost/vampire/supernatural movies she had watched. Then I used to watch them, after which we freaked out together discussing it.

The blood-thirsty-lost-soul soon popped its head up from under a table. I could see its eyes; sparkling black. Its hair was slightly ruffled in the front. Slowly its face came up from behind the table. The blood-thirsty-lost-soul was a boy. If not a soul, I was sure he was a vampire. This vampire boy had a caught-red-handed look on his face.

'I'm sorry.' he said.

'What are you?' I asked.

'*Who* are you?' He stressed on 'who' as if to point out that my English sucked.

'Titiksha.' If he was really a vampire, I thought, it would be difficult to hide things from him anyway, and thus I decided to speak the truth.

'Why are you not in the assembly? And which class are you in?'

'Class 11, Science.' At that moment I realized he was yet to look beyond my face though he could have easily looked at my breast-hugging wet shirt like the others. Was he blind? Or, did my breast detest him so much that he was ignoring them? Or, was he really a vampire and only blood was his priority?

I'm a newcomer and...' I didn't finish my sentence because I suffered a loud sneeze.

'Sor...' Before I could apologize, I sneezed again.

'Sorry,' I completed quickly.

'If you don't tell anyone you just saw me having my tiffin here, then I think I can help you.'

Help me? By sucking my blood? 'I actually didn't see you have anything,' I said.

'Great.'

He almost jumped out of the last bench, wiping his face with a handkerchief. He was about the same height as me. As he came closer, I realized that the vampire boy was actually a couple of inches taller, with a healthy figure, a charming face, and a cute nose. Vampires around the world were cute. He was the first Indian vampire I had seen. Or so I thought.

'You said you could help me. How?' I was just

being curious. There was something about him—I don't know what—that compelled me to continue the conversation

'It's simple but you have to be quick. You game?'

He extended his hand towards me. Seconds later I understood I needed to hit it in order for him to speak further. I clapped his palm with mine.

'Cool! If you keep wearing that shirt of yours, you will fall sick on your very first day of school. So if you want, we can swap our shirts.'

I liked the way he relayed my problem to me; not with an indecent look or a smart ass comment but with a genuine solution.

'But won't you fall sick if you wear my wet shirt?' I asked stating the obvious.

'Trust me, I want to. Moreover it's raining so nobody will doubt if it is my shirt or not,' he smiled. This vampire boy was weird.

'Okay,' I said, confirming the shirt-swapping deal between us.

'Alright. I'll give you my shirt and stand outside the classroom, but be quick. The assembly,' he said and looked at his wristwatch once before continuing, 'will be over in two more minutes, max!'

I nodded suddenly interested in this ordeal. He moved out and closed the classroom door behind him. I would have never gone through such a ridiculous shirt-swapping deal with any other guy, on any other day. But was it any other day and any other guy? If life had a flash forward button, I would have pressed it then and there to find out who this guy was, would he ever mean anything to me, and if at all our roads would crisscross in the near future?

'Quick,' he quipped. I gave him my wet shirt. His shirt fit me quite well. Half a minute later, when he pulled open the classroom door from outside, I felt happy to see mine fit him rather better than I had imagined. For the first time, my large size was of some help. The bell rang again. The assembly was over.

'See you,' he trailed off and walked away whistling some tune.

Yo-didun was right. A special sort of electricity did run through me that day while watching the vampire boy walk away from me in the corridor. Somewhere within my heart, a bulb did light up. A bulb which I was ignorant of till then. Most importantly for the first time in my life, I felt connected to the magic in me. This boy had to be a vampire.

3

I washed the vampire boy's shirt the moment I came back from school. If you think that's funny, listen to this: I stood by the rope where I had placed it on the terrace to dry and, like a fool, kept staring at it till it dried in the evening.

I ironed the shirt, folded it neatly, put it inside a nice plastic bag, and then kept it beside my school bag to give it to him on Monday. All the while I kept asking myself, what the hell was I doing washing a stranger's shirt? Didn't he belong to the same species as dad who left my mother? The day dad informed me that he would go away and live with this other woman, I had promised him that I would never give any man a chance to reject me for another of my species or of his own. He said I was a kid and hence thought like an idealist just like he did at one point in his life. He said as I'll grow up, the idealist in me will die a slow and sure death. For it is life's incorrigible habit to take us to a point where we make certain decisions and swear to stand by it, and then it is life again that takes us to another point in time where in order to get what we want, we have to compromise that very decision of ours.

Post dinner, looking at my unusually lost self, Yo-didun told me about the lighting of bulb thing. I finally realized that I had washed the vampire boy's shirt not because he saved me from a possible Pneumonia attack. I washed his shirt, dried and ironed it for a different reason. I knew what that reason was but the point was the reason was in direct conflict with what I had decided the day the divorce was finalized between my parents.

I quickly copied certain important English and Physics notes from a fellow classmate's notebook, and then went to the terrace to ponder over the matter. For the first time, I felt an urge in me to be attached knowing well attachments were a dangerous proposition. But wasn't it attachment, again, that made people dare the impossibilities of their routine life?

I was finally summoned downstairs, and reprimanded by Ashok mama for being on the terrace for no business because according to Bijoya mami the neighbourhood is full of bad boys, and that girls of decent houses don't go to the terrace for no reason. I didn't react. When I told Yo-didun I wasn't hungry, she understood something was troubling me. She sat down beside me on my bed and stroked my forehead. It felt good whenever she did that.

'What happened, Shonamoni?' she asked gently.

'I'm feeling sleepy,' I lied.

Yo-didun's eyes shone with an amusing twinkle.

'Love is just like sleep,' she said. 'When it happens, you invariably close your eyes to the world and remain disconnected. You travel beyond time and space. You float in the river of realization, you climb the mountains of compassion, and you fly over the valley of emotions with the wings of faith. By the time you open your eyes again, you may have—just may have—missed out on a lot, but then it is okay, for by then you gain much more than you missed.'

It was evident she understood my problem. I was glad someone did. I was just having a problem accepting my problem. How could I fall for a vampire boy in just a few minutes of our meeting?

4

It was mandatory for us to change seats and partners in every period because our class teacher believed the worst thing we could allow life to do to us was make us accustomed to things. By changing seats, she said, we were embracing the concept of change so that we didn't panic whenever we encountered change of any sort—be it in a relationship, job, domestic life, or whatever.

Before interval, I was sitting with a weirdo who didn't talk to me at all except for asking me which deodorant I used. Post lunch break, I was sitting with a girl named Nisha who looked like a sweet person. She told me about all the subjects I was lagging behind in, and also which teacher gave private tuitions. I did ask my mathematics teacher, Rajiv sir, about it later, and he said I was free to join his tuition classes from that very evening. It was Nisha who told me about Neel. Finally I had got to know the vampire boy's name. Neel and Titiksha—the names sounded perfect together. That's how most stories start, isn't it? Something somewhere seems so perfect that the thought creates a rippling impulse within us and we start sleeping with its possibility.

In the evening, I went to Rajiv sir's house. Though Bijoya mami was against me taking tuitions since it would have given me a chance to better myself than her sons, she couldn't say much since it was my mom's money I was using to give the tuition fees. The truth of the matter was that I could tackle other subjects without private tuitions but mathematics was a bitch.

I was surprised to find almost half of my class at Rajiv sir's house. And one of them was the vampire boy: Neel. Though Rajiv sir was teaching, I was finding it difficult to concentrate. I kept furtively glancing at Neel. But he didn't look up at me even once. As if he wasn't interested in me. And why would he be interested? At that moment I wished something which I shouldn't have. I wished I wasn't me. I wished I was some hot-looking model who can make guys drool. Whatever nonsense people say, I think beauty is important. Who has the time to know a person and then fall in love anyway? Would I have glanced at Neel if he was obese, thick browed, and half-bald?

It was only after the tuition got over and we were about to leave that Neel gave me my shirt—washed and ironed. I was tempted to inquire whether he had washed it himself but realized how stupid it would sound and hence asked, 'How did you know I would come here?'

'Nisha told me.'

Of course! But why did Nisha had to tell you this specifically? Did he inquire about me? I wondered.

'What happened to you?' I said.

'What happened to me?' he echoed.

'I mean why didn't you come to school today?'

'Great, you noticed!'

'Yes. That's because I wanted to give you your shirt. I had brought it with me to school today. I don't have it now.' The justification was not required, still.

'You can give it to me tomorrow.'

'Okay.'

'Where do you stay?'

'Salt Lake,' I said. 'And you?'

'Paikpara. We can walk to your home if you don't mind.'

'Isn't Paikpara far from Salt Lake?'

'It is but I'm in no hurry to go home.' *So beauty wasn't everything after all.* I was supposed to take a cycle-rickshaw from the tuition back home but I gave him a walk-is-fine shrug even though I was screaming with joy from within.

He was traipsing beside me with his Hero Ranger cycle between us. It was a quiet night. But don't ask me about the noise I was experiencing inside. It was noise because I could hear it aloud but I couldn't make out what exactly it was telling me. There weren't many people on the road either. The area was much more lonelier than the one in which I used to stay in South Kolkata. We were just the two of us with a cycle-rickshaw or two passing by us with sometimes an indifferent, and at times an inquisitive looking passenger on it.

'I didn't come to school today because I had practice,' Neel said breaking the silence between us. I was happy for I feared we would end up walking home without saying a word. I was a bit nervous to initiate any talks. This was so new to me; walking alongside a boy. Correction: walking alongside a cute vampire boy.

'Practice? As in?'

'I play guitar.'

'Really?' I was into music myself; heavy metal, death metal, rock, jazz, R&B. You name it and I knew it. Though I was yet to learn a musical instrument but guitar was surely a musical turn on for me.

'Yes. We have a school band.'

Even better! 'Wow, great!'

'You like music?'

'Hell, yes! What's your band called?'

'Paintbrush.'

'Awesome. When do I get to hear some of your stuff?'

'Soon. We practised today. My house garage is our makeshift den. Would love to have you come and watch us play one day.'

'Deal!'

'Do you sing?'

'Oh no! I write.'

He gave me a surprised glance and said, 'Paintbrush needs a good songwriter.'

I smiled. My words, his tune. Never before had a thought given me the kind of chill like this one did. My heartbeats were sounding totally different that night.

We took a turn. With the road turning lonelier, I felt nosier inside me. I didn't know if the night was a figment of my imagination or reality. I prayed and hoped I wasn't in the middle of a dream. The gush of wind was pretty consistent. The moment I got used to it caressing my skin, I thought the breeze was sweet-talking to my heart, 'I know what's there inside you. And it's okay.'

'What does your father do?' Neel asked.

Whatever noise I was connected to vanished, and as if someone pushed me back to reality when

I was so ready to jump off from its edge and onto the oblivion of love with a faith whose name was Neel.

'He works in a real estate firm. And your father?' I said.

'Businessman. We have shops in Hathibagan, Ram Mandir, and New Market. We deal in clothes, especially Jaamdani and Toshore saris.'

'That's nice.'

'Nice? That's boring. You know my father has been sitting in the first shop—Hathibagan—since he was of my age. Now he shuttles between three shops. I don't want to waste something as precious as life running from one shop to another. Everyone seems to choose a specific coordinate in their life and remain there all through. But I want to live the life of a wind—shift co-ordinates continuously, go wherever I want to, and make people aware of my fucking existence.' A pause later he added, 'Sorry for the F-word.'

'Why the fuck are you sorry about that fucking word?' I quipped.

We laughed out aloud.

'What it is that you want to do? As in, do in life?' I asked curiously. I wanted to know more about him through his thoughts. His rebellious instinct was such an emotional turn on for me.

He kept looking at me as if he didn't get me.

'I mean…'

'I know what you mean. I want to be a rockstar. Travel to countries, continents with my music band. Sign autographs on fans' biceps and bosoms. Live a very unsettled and Bohemian life. Have sexy groupies following me. Do drugs. Do girls. And die by the time I'm thirty.'

'Thirty? Why?'

'If you don't die by the time you are thirty, you are so dead anyway after that.'

I couldn't stop laughing.

'Your smile is beautiful.'

I paused. Looked at him. There was something in his eyes that scared me. All the noise within me suddenly came forth with a greater gusto. Nobody ever appreciated anything about me. Never ever. And here was this supposed vampire boy who thought my smile was beautiful. This vampire boy was special. He was not sucking my blood, but he was slowly sucking me out of me.

'There's my place. I'll give you your shirt tomorrow,' I said and even before I could hear his reply, I walked towards my mama's house at a brisk pace. I wanted to turn back and see if he was looking but I didn't. I couldn't.

I didn't sleep that night. At four in the morning, I went to the bathroom and looked at myself in the mirror. I smiled. Was my smile really beautiful? Why had I never thought so before? Depressed, I went to bed and forced myself to sleep.

Next day as I stood under the shed in school, waiting for the assembly bell to ring so I could talk to Nisha about a particular problem in Physics, someone came up to me. She was fair, had a trendy haircut, and a slim figure. In short, she was everything I was not.

The next second she slapped me hard across my face and said, 'Miss newcomer, don't you screw with my boyfriend.'

I later learned the girl's name was Avni, Neel's girlfriend.

Chapter 6

WILL NEEL INTRODUCE TITIKSHA TO NIVRITA?

'How is it?' Neel asks Titiksha holding the printout of his manuscript with a sense of excitement. The four chapters, after all, are his first attempt at realizing his dream of becoming an author. And who better to share it with than his long-time girlfriend?

As Neel gives Titiksha the pages, he switches on the stopwatch. He is clocking her to divert his mind from his nervousness. He has an inkling Titiksha will praise and encourage him, but he wants to block the thought lest it makes him too excited too soon.

'What bullshit is this?' she says surprising Neel.

He presses his stopwatch. It reads one minute thirty seconds.

'Read it completely and then comment. Please.' Neel didn't want to use the last word but he does, like always.

'I'm done reading it,' Titiksha darts back.

It is 9 am. Neel and Titiksha are sitting in the drawing room. There is a small round table in the centre of the room on either side of which they are seated. Atop the table there is one Real fruit juice, two hard boiled eggs on one plate, and two separate plates containing a couple of grilled toasts. Titiksha has the printouts of the chapters Neel wrote last night, while she was asleep, though he knows she was messaging someone from inside her blanket because he did notice her mobile phone's light blink a few times. But if she has nothing to hide, why did she keep the mobile phone on silent mode? She never did that before. She was more open before he went to Jaipur. Neel thinks for a moment—even he was more faithful before he went to Jaipur.

'One minute and you've read all the four chapters? Am I supposed to believe that?'

'Doesn't that say something about your writing? And why have you given that protagonist bitch of yours my name? And it's I who play the guitar but in the story you show that Neel's character plays the guitar. What nonsense is this!' She has consumed the entire egg by now and is gobbling it furiously. She takes a sip of the fruit juice to shove the bolus further in.

'She isn't a bitch by the way.' Neel has half stuffed the hard toast inside his mouth and hence sounds funny.

'Why is she after someone else's boyfriend then? I anyway don't care what she is. And I don't care if you used your name for the protagonist. But why did you use my name?'

'Relax! These are not my characters, damn it!'

'Then?'

It is a slip, Neel is quick to realize. He can't tell her about Nivrita. Much like she isn't confessing about the other guy Neel thinks Titiksha is seeing. He isn't telling her about Nivrita because he isn't serious about her. He is only playing along to get himself published. But what are Titiksha's reasons of not telling him?

'Don't tell me you plagiarized someone's work,' says Titiksha standing up.

'Won't you have the toast?'

'Answer me. Don't avoid the question. ' She keeps her hands on her hips ready for a confrontation if need be.

'Do you think I would do that kind of a thing?'

Neel uses the following silent seconds to finish his breakfast.

'I don't know. Even if you have, it still doesn't change my reaction: bullshit is bullshit is bullshit.'

Has she even read any book? Ever? Neel wonders and says, 'I know why you are saying so.'

'Why?' Titiksha squints her eyes looking at him. She does so whenever she is ready to launch her angry self on Neel.

'You don't want me to become an author and hence you are intentionally discouraging me. But I won't give up.'

Titiksha comes close to him and laughs on his face.

'You are such a kid, Neel. I am telling you the truth. Of course I'm discouraging you because I don't want you to make a fool out of yourself in front of the whole country by printing this shit. Plus who will publish this shit anyway, my dumb teddy bear?' she says pulling his cheeks in a patronizing manner.

Neel can feel his rage rising inside. He decides to do what he always does whenever he is cross with Titiksha. He goes inside the bathroom, locks himself in, puts his head under the tap, and turns it on. The water slowly drenches his head and calms him down. A trice later, he smiles to himself in a sadistic manner wondering how wrong his girlfriend is about the 'who-will-publish-it' part.

The call bell rings. Neel shouts out and asks Titiksha to open the door. Titiksha shouts back at him to do so himself since she is changing. She seldom uses the word 'please' anyway. This is no exception. Neel, with water trickling down his head, reluctantly comes out of the bathroom, and goes to open the door.

Standing in a purple sleeveless kurta and a pair of black

jeggings is Nivrita. She takes out her black Ray-Ban and perches it on top of her head with a you-thought-I-don't-know-where-you-live smile on her face.

For the past few seconds, Neel has been simply gaping at Nivrita wishing intensely that her presence is unreal. He closes the door, opens it again, wishing there's no Nivrita. As he tries to close the door, Nivrita puts her leg forward and stops him. How the hell she came to know about his address?

'Water sports at home, huh?' Nivrita says noticing the water drops going southwards from his head.

'How do you know I live here?'

'I have been following you.' She suddenly lowers her voice and continues, 'From the day we landed in Kolkata.'

Neel doesn't know if she is speaking the truth. He hopes not. She raises her voice to say, 'Won't you invite me in?'

'Please come in.' An unsure Neel moves aside to make room for her. Nivrita gets in and he closes the door behind him. He can hear his heartbeats so loudly that for a moment he assumes the heart has popped up from his chest to his mouth.

'Small but a cute place nevertheless.' Nivrita looks around and sits on the half-folded mattress by the window.

'Who is it Neel?' Titiksha screams out from the bedroom.

'Give me a moment.' Neel excuses himself and goes inside the bathroom and locks it.

He doesn't reply to Titiksha because he doesn't know what he should tell her. For the first time, another girl besides Titiksha has come to his place. Running away from a situation has been Neel's hallmark way of handling anything. Inside the bathroom, he dries his head with a towel trying to listen if Titiksha has moved into the drawing room and discovered Nivrita for herself. But he can't hear anything. He is sure they are talking right now else Titiksha would have continued to shout till he replied, or would have banged the bathroom door, or had done something out of the ordinary. But there is only silence. Should he open the bathroom door and see what's going on between the two women? What if he sees a violent cat-fight between the two? He won't be able to handle it.

'Damn!' Neel punches the tiled wall of the bathroom hard. What if Nivrita ends up telling Titiksha everything? Neel turns and opens the door in a flash and pauses seeing Nivrita right in front of him.

'She is gone,' Nivrita says and pushes Neel inside the bathroom.

'You met Titiksha?'

'Yeah. Nice girl. Not the jealous types.'

Neel wonders how a smart girl like Nivrita can arrive at such a false conclusion about Titiksha. Only he knows how she has never let him meet, talk, or even see another girl right from the time they were in a relationship. And now he hears she is not the jealous types? What a joke!

'I told her we fucked each other real good in Jaipur, and all she asked me was if you had a protection on while doing me. That's a cool girlfriend you have.'

What should Neel do: smile, cry, or faint? Nivrita has told Titiksha about their fuck-session? And the latter didn't react? Really? Why? Is it because she already has someone more important than him in her life right now or she doesn't care what or whom Neel does?

'Chill dude! I didn't say any of that. She asked who I was.

I said I'm a junior where you used to work and need to get some papers signed by you. She said she was getting late for her office and excused herself.'

Finally Neel relaxes. He hates Nivrita's sense of humour, and that's the first thing he would tell her on her face once the book is published.

'Now get yourself a shower. You are stinking of sweat,' she says, and opens the knob. As the water cascades down Neel's body, she pulls up his T-shirt getting her arms wet in the process. Neel puts his hands up without resistance. She hurls his T-shirt at an empty bucket nearby, and runs her fingers from his throat down to his chest to his tummy and finally to his knickers. She pulls its elastic and releases it instantly. The elastic hits Neel's waist hard.

'I would love to watch you take a bath.'

No, I won't do that. Who do you think you are? I'm not your toy, okay? So please go out and let me bathe alone. Neel thinks all this but before he can put it across to Nivrita, he hears her say, 'When I told Titiksha you have some papers to sign, it wasn't a lie. Your debut book contract is waiting in the drawing room. I'm sure you won't waste much time now.'

The girl is a hunter and she knows exactly how to corner her prey. Neel wants to smell the book contract; pronto. He also would like to see Titiksha's reaction whenever he gets to show her the contract.

'I won't waste time,' Neel says and tugs down his knickers with his underwear. Nivrita sucks in her own cheeks slightly trying to focus her gaze on his groin. Neel turns around.

'That's a cute one,' she exclaims.

Neel takes the quickest shower of his life. He knows Nivrita is watching him, and he turns to see her every once in a while. The way she stares at him standing by the bathroom door is condescending. Her look says she owns him. For a total of three times she remarks that Neel has a soft and cute butt. And every time she does so, Neel's male ego feels challenged. He isn't enjoying it. He relaxes by reminding himself that the only weapon hapless people have is patience.

Once done bathing, Nivrita tells him she wants to take him to another place before letting him sign the contract.

When he inquires about the place, Nivrita replies with a counter question, 'Doesn't a kite belong to the thread that ties it to the earth as much as it belongs to the wind that wants to blow it away to unexplored spaces?'

Who is the kite? Who is the thread? And who the hell is the wind? Neel remains quiet wondering how a kite came into their discourse. Nivrita, thankfully, cares to explain as he dresses up in front of her.

'Meeting Titiksha I felt she is the thread you are tied to. And I'm the wind who will blow you away. Won't you like it Neel? To be blown off to places which exist within you but you have not had a chance to explore with Titiksha?'

Neel gives her a standard stupid smile, and puts on a shirt that she selects for him. If Titiksha is a control freak then Nivrita probably is her mother in that regard. Had it not been for the book, he wouldn't have agreed to anything this girl told him. But had it not been for the book, he wouldn't have gone to Jaipur either and got himself a publishing deal.

The moment he is done dressing up, she comes forward. Neel is serious while she has an odd smile on her face. He takes a step back and she takes a step forward. They continue doing so till Neel's back hits a wall. Nivrita takes a small step to reach him and raises his hands up, forcefully pinning them on the wall on either side. He isn't ready for anything physical at the moment. All he has in his mind is the book contract. He wants to make love to the bundle of paper than to her. Nivrita takes out a cologne from her sling bag and sprays it on his arm pit.

'When you are with me, you ought to smell my favourite.'

They are inside a taxi now. Neel tells her he could have asked his father to send their car, the one with black windows. He finds it difficult to travel in a car with transparent windows. He did so in Jaipur but that was an exception rather than the rule.

'Now you are with me Neel,' Nivrita replies. 'All the exceptions of your life will become the rule, and all the previous rules will simply have to fuck off.'

Neel is benumbed. Nivrita—there's something about her. He wishes he had the guts to fuck her then and there in the taxi. Like crazy-mad-hard. He thinks by doing so she will become submissive to him. Neel is unaware that it's his typical male chauvinist mentality speaking. To tame a woman, fuck her. To fuck a woman, love her. To love a woman, tame her. It is true he wants to control her the way she is controlling him. There's a sadistic pleasure he will derive if he can make Nivrita kneel in front of him, look into his eyes, and ask...no wait...beg, for sexual mercy. All this is in his mind. In reality, though, he knows he doesn't have an inch of courage to even touch her without her permission. She is as unpredictable as the weather and as unmanageable as nature.

The taxi comes to a halt near a bus stop. They get down. Though Neel insists on paying the fare, Nivrita doesn't allow him.

'Which place is this?' Neel asks looking around. There are not many people around. He can see a few shops, all shut except for a chemist shop opposite the bus stop. Neel takes a few steps and then realizes that he is walking alone. He turns to see that the taxi has left and Nivrita is standing on the footpath looking at him. Neel raises both his hands as if asking what the matter is. Nivrita walks down to him.

'I'm a bit lost. Can you tell me which way to go Neel?'

'What? I don't know this place. I don't even know why we are here! How can I help you? You're the one who brought us here, remember?'

'I know but...' Nivrita seems genuinely confused as she looks around. They are standing at a crossroad where four different roads lead to four different places. One of them would take them to their destination.

'Try your instinct,' she suggests. 'Till then let me ask the chemist.'

Neel gives her a helpless sigh. Nivrita goes to the chemist shop across the road while Neel stays where he is, staring at the four roads one by one. All of them look similar. As if out of four similar looking women he has to identify which one is his wife. And precisely then he pauses seeing a particular road. A boy and a girl are traipsing along. The boy is walking with his bicycle on one side and the girl on the other. This particular image does something to Neel. The feeling is too convoluted for him to decipher anything. He is sure he neither knows the boy or the girl. He hasn't even seen their faces and yet he thinks he knows where they are going. Why? It then strikes him that a similar scene has happened in the story Nivrita narrated to him. He wrote it himself in one of the chapters of his manuscript. Only it was night when Neel and Titiksha in the manuscript were traipsing along. Should he choose the road they chose in the story?

'Okay, I got it.' Nivrita has come back. Without even looking at her, Neel raises his hand aiming at the girl and the boy who by now have almost disappeared around the bend of the road and says, 'That way.'

'How did you know?'

Neel looks at Nivrita as if he has shit in his pants.

'I don't know.'

Neel walks ahead. This time Nivrita follows him. She stops him when they reach an old house. It looks like an odd place because most of it is covered with the branches of two huge trees on either side. The gate makes a terrible noise as she opens it and moves in. Neel follows visibly astounded as if he is dream-walking through all this. The place seems familiar, but ironically enough he doesn't know why is it so familiar. Is this what they call déjà vu?

When they reach the main door, he sees a lizard making its way out from the cracks of one of the windows. He doesn't look at it again but notices there are multiple cracks and black patches smudged on its walls. Nivrita has managed to open the wooden door with a key which she puts back in her bag. Before moving in, she switches on the lights inside from the switchboard beside the door.

As they enter, a pungent smell welcomes them. Nivrita is quick to open the windows in the hall. With sun rays entering scantily from one side, Neel can now see how the room looks—empty. There's a thick layer of dust on the floor. He can see Nivrita's footprints on the dusty floor wherever she goes. She takes the spiral stairs up. Nivrita turns to look at him once and says, 'Come along.'

Neel takes small steps and every time turns to notice the imprint of his shoes on the floor. There's something about the imprints. They add importance to a journey. Once a journey completes, people lose their importance. Sometimes even the journey loses its significance with time. But the imprints remain.

Neel takes the stairs and climbs up. The stairs lead him directly to the room where he has seen Nivrita go. He goes in and notices her sitting by a window with an old bass guitar in her hand. As he enters the room, she plays a tune on it to perfection. Neel stands mesmerized. He wonders: this girl is full of surprises. But there's something else that has caught his attention. His throat dries up.

'This tune...Titiksha plays this tune. How come you know it?' Neel sounds spooked.

'This was *his* tune.'

Neel comes close and looks at the guitar closely. There's a small 'paintbrush' painted on its face and immediately he recollects the school band's name he wrote about last night in his manuscript.

Titiksha's name was carved in a bench in the school Nivrita took him to the other day. Now Nivrita has brought him to an old house where she plays the same tune that Titiksha often plays in her guitar. And now the guitar has a 'paintbrush' painted on it! What's happening, really?

'Come, sit beside me. You can check out the book contract later.' Nivrita makes some place for Neel. 'Let me continue the story as of now...'

FROM NEEL'S MANUSCRIPT

5

It was during the Chemistry practical class in the laboratory the following day, after the lunch break, I found Neel standing right beside me performing the experiment that we all were doing. The echo of Avni's slap was still ringing loud in my ears. I wanted to wear my bitch-suit and slap her back harder but I couldn't because I didn't want Neel to think wrongly of me. But why did I care what Neel thought about me? This goody-goody-girl-nature never came naturally to me until that day. I held onto this new avatar of mine only because of Neel. One night of traipsing on a lonely road, and I was more concerned about his feelings than mine. Yo-didun never said love was also about digging your own grave with a stupid smile.

Between Neel and me there lay his notebook where he was noting down the details of his experiment. I had mine on the other side. For once I saw him tapping on the notebook as if calling for attention. I glanced at him and then on the notebook. It was written: *I am sorry!*

I took my notebook and kept it on his side

and wrote: *Why are you sorry? And* tapped my finger on it rather fiercely.

He wrote: *For Avni.*

I wrote: *She should be sorry not you.*

I know but she won't be. So I am.

What's her problem?

We are in a relationship.

So, what's that got to do with me? Everything, I confessed to myself.

Did you tell anyone you had my shirt?

Yes, Nisha.

She must have bitched you out to her.

The teacher was taking rounds. When she came to our end, we flipped the page. When she ambled away, we exchanged a furtive glance. His face was genuinely apologetic.

It's alright, I wrote. I didn't hit her back, only for you, I thought.

'Thanks,' he said aloud. The teacher turned immediately and barked out at us, 'No talking I said.'

I never spoke to Nisha afterwards. I hate gossipmongers. She must have known I had got to know about it. Neel and me? *Really?* Were we a threat to Avni? I don't know why but I felt happy. It somewhat numbed the slap for me. After the Chemistry practical class, we had to go to the library.

I was impressed with Salt Lake International's library. It was a huge hall and unlike my previous school they had a good collection of fiction, non-fiction, and academic books. Neel was sitting in a faraway corner with other boys while I sat by the table which had three girls with whom I had never talked before. I pulled out a Harry Potter book from a nearby shelf, and pretended to read it while the truth was that I was looking at Neel time and again. He did look at me once and smiled but I was so confused that I looked away. I repented it immediately.

Few minutes later, someone asked for permission to enter the library. The librarian allowed Avni to come in with a warm smile which I thought he could do without. The smile told me that the librarian knew her well. She spoke to the librarian for some time, walked to the last book shelf in the hall, and then disappeared behind it. I couldn't see her anymore. The bookshelves were placed in a manner which shielded the person behind it unless the books were pulled out of the shelf. And the one shelf she went behind was the last one adjacent to the bench around which Neel and his friends were sitting. I was about to look somewhere else when I saw the guys sitting with Neel nudging him with a naughty grin. I could guess what they were hinting at but I was not comfortable accepting it. Then the worst happened. Neel got up and, pretending as if he was searching for some book, went from one shelf to the other to finally behind the last one where Avni was probably waiting for him. What for?

I felt injured when I guessed the answer in my mind. It was then that I decided to get rid of the goody-goody-girl image. Good girls shouldn't be in love. I was. Was I? Why else had

I washed and ironed his shirt? Why else had I not complained about Avni's slap to the teachers? Why else was I feeling injured thinking about what all those two were upto behind that book shelf? It was time for a decision. Firstly, there was no denying the fact that I was in love. Yes! Maybe prior to meeting Neel, I was sure I would never be in love. It seemed like a waste of time to me. But I never thought this being-in-love thing would catch me unawares. I had to forget Neel. He was someone else's. I took a deep breath and made a decision: I won't come in-between Neel and Avni.

I saw Avni come out from behind the shelf with a book (as if!), wiping her mouth with the back of her hand. The next minute she moved out of the library.

I intentionally didn't come in front of Neel that day. It was only when everyone was dispersing after school that I saw him with his cycle alongside Avni, Nisha, and a few other students, ambling away towards the main gate. They seemed to be laughing at some joke. It was a hurtful sight. The more Neel and Avni smiled at each other, the more my heart was squashed. If I had not done what I did, then my heart would have died a certain death. And I was in no mood to witness such a private funeral for the rest of my life.

I walked straight towards the group and called out, 'Hey, Neel.' They paused. And turned. I went to him, put my arm around his shoulder, smiled at him, and kissed him on his right cheek.

'Thanks for offering me to write songs for Paintbrush,' I said.

I didn't care to wait for Avni's reaction. I didn't care to look at Neel's reaction either. They shouldn't have gone behind the bookshelf. That really pushed me to wear my bitch-suit.

I had started to love Neel not because everything was right about him. It was because something was wrong with me. And that wrong felt immensely satisfying. Once I reached the main gate, I turned to see Neel who was standing like a cuckold. Ditto for Avni. I wasn't sure whether I did the right thing or not. Maybe Avni did love him, but now that I too loved Neel there had to be some sort of a competition. Like uncle Darwin had said: survival of the fittest! *May the best win,* I thought, and walked out of the main gate showing my chubby middle finger to Avni. Little did I know I had just flagged a war of the bitches.

6

It was raining outside later that night. Standing by my room's window, I wondered if there were actually two kinds of rain: one, which you wish to simply admire from the safety of your house; the other, which compels you to move out of your comfort zone, go out in to the open, and get soaked. That's what Neel excited within me every time I saw him in school and tuitions. My world was full of craters until Neel decided to rain on them, filling them up and making it all appear as an ocean full of secrets. I wanted to get out of my emotional comfort zone and get soaked in him, and not merely admire him from a distance. And if that impulse was love, then probably I was in love with him. Don't you think our own senses conspire a lot against us and keep secrets? Falling in love probably happens when our senses share those secrets with us. It's like mini explosions happening in the mind, heart, and where not.

In the days that passed, after I kissed Neel in front of Avni, she made sure I suffered for it. Had I not kissed him, I could have seen Neel practising with his band. But Avni made sure I didn't. Neel liked me. I knew it, but he pretended not to. And because of his pretence, we were neither good friends nor lovers. He knew I had a soft corner for him. All through the following week, I made sure I glanced at him enough to make him realize he wasn't just another guy for me. If he still didn't get it, then he was an asshole, I told myself. But thankfully he wasn't one. I saw him catch my sharp glances most of the times. When he gave me his phone number, he asked me not to tell anyone. He was so scared of Avni! What's the point of a relationship when we do things out of fear?

I had no friends to share anything with. That's probably one of the reasons why thoughts about Neel gripped me emotionally more strongly than ever. When one is alone, the thoughts he wants to run away from are the thoughts which stays with him all the time. With time I lost touch with my only friend from my previous school—Shreya. When I shared this with Yo-didun, she said it's no big deal as people keep coming and going from one's life. The pain, she said, doesn't come from the fact that someone left us. We feel the pain of separation because of the intensity with which we try to hold onto those who are done with us or never had to do anything with us to begin with. I asked her whether wishing for someone is a good reason to get someone for real. She put forth a straight 'no'. I was shit scared. I wanted Neel the way Avni got him. I wanted to go behind the bookshelves of the library with him, and come out wiping my mouth like she did. I wanted to walk out of the school every day alongside him. And I also wanted him to laugh at my jokes. In simple words, I wanted Neel to be mine. Exclusively mine.

'What if someone loves a person but doesn't get him? Does that mean it isn't true love?' I asked Yo-didun. She laughed. I never liked it when she laughed at my queries. It made me feel like an ignorant fool.

'What do you mean by "get the person"?' she asked with a certain twinkle in her eyes which told me she was only testing me, and already knew what I was trying to ask her.

'It means to live with the person all your life, to be married to him, to admire the various sunrises and sunsets of your life with him, and to embrace him tightly during those sunrises and sunsets.'

'You are a true teenager now. Just like I was,' she said.

What she told me next was something important and true. She said, 'For all of us, the preference always is the physical expression of our longing for someone, the physical justification of our feelings, and also the physical manifestation of the desire we associate with the one we claim to love. There's always this craving for a physical proximity in everyone's idea of love if not in the definition of it. Hence the need to classify love into true, casual, and you know what all. Try not to restrain love by subjecting yourself to such baseless classifications. And try not to see your love for someone as something that you need, per se, even though it may sound great. That is because the need for the thing will always narrow your perspective of that thing and shall make you feel more miserable than happy being in love. That's one reason people undergo depression when they don't *get* a person they think they love.'

I tried to put what she said in perspective. I was not happy seeing Neel with Avni. Why? Because I wanted him to be physically there by my side. Then I asked myself: why I can't be at peace with myself knowing that he loves someone else? How was his love for someone else affecting my love for him? Funny, I realized the answer then and there—that Neel's physical proximity to me was important to me. I don't know why it made me feel as if my love for him wasn't true. Understanding my dilemma, Yo-didun said an epic statement which I shall never forget: she said love and lust are twins. Many a times they look similar and hence the confusion. But their traits are distinctly different. I obviously was curious to know how to distinguish between the so-called twins?

'By the feelings they generate in a person,' Yo-didun said. 'Lust generates pleasure. Love generates happiness. And no one but you decide what is pleasure and what is happiness.'

After the high dose of philosophy, I asked Yo-didun one simple question: Should I do something in order to draw Neel's attention or wish Avni and Neel a happy love life and part ways with him?

Yo-didun said, 'I won't suggest anything. But I'll wait to see if you really are my granddaughter or not.'

7

I had nothing to do with the fact that Neel was admitted to a nearby hospital that summer. He was admitted because he choked himself to an almost fatal level after smoking a bidi. I later heard that he didn't smoke for fun. He had lost a bet.

When I told Yo-didun about it, she was shocked. She said nobody under eighteen should smoke. I told her almost half the boys and girls smoke in our school. Yo-didun immediately grasped my hand and said, 'Promise me you will never do such a thing, Shonamoni.'

I promised her because I was sure I would never smoke. Yo-didun asked why their parents didn't reprimand them for smoking. As if they would tell their parents about smoking and drinking. Yo-didun complained that the connection between parents and children was getting diluted with every passing day. What she didn't know was that kids of my generation and their parents have a world of their own, and both, especially the kids, make sure neither intrudes into the other's life. I'm a prime example.

I also told Yo-didun about the virtual world, the Internet, where people often were what people weren't in real life. In response she asked if she could be a sixteen-year-old in the virtual world with such innocent fervour that I cracked up laughing. For lack of knowledge, she thought the Internet was a medium for time travel.

Later I informed Yo-didun that if a guy doesn't smoke in my school, he is nicknamed TGIF: The Great Indian Fattu. Students teased him stating that every TGIF had the same DNA which only meant they were a product of an intra-community fuck fest. I couldn't tell Yo-didun the last part. She asked me not to stay with such kids who smoked and consumed alcohol. I told her in that case I would have to go to school after school-hours and return before school-hours.

I don't know how were the times when she grew up as a school kid but since then times have changed for sure. My generation went to school but we were not merely school students.

There was nothing innocent about us. And we definitely weren't ignorant about anything. It was all there right in front of us: from the latest development in the cosmos to the latest adult MMS. With such information available to us 24X7, how could anyone be innocent? It was like how certain fruit sellers force-ripen the fruits and make them ready for selling. My generation was getting forced-ripened just like that. Growth-wise, our mind was ahead of our body. Hence our inner self was naturally a breeding ground for a lot of shit because everyone, including me, was a school going adult. At sixteen we behaved like twenty five, we said slangs with ease, we were casual and experimental with our sexuality, we searched for love because our hormones wanted us to and not because our heart felt the need to, we were selfish, we had no clue what our culture was all about, what freedom was for our previous generations, seemed like a cage for us because we wanted to leap ahead where our predecessors had stopped out of fear and shame. We didn't complain about each other to parents anymore, rather we showed middle fingers and bitched it out, we were ready to fight, we liked noise, we loved chaos, we kissed and smooched at the drop of a hat because the American television series told us that's the 'cool' thing to do. We watched porn more than we prayed. We were a group of attention-seekers and emotion-haters. So yes, our generation had come a long way from Yo-didun's. And the gap was so much that our elders, our education system, or our own morals no longer could teach us a better way to grow up into mature adults. And whenever they tried to change us, we had our middle fingers ready for them too. We were a fuck-all generation.

I told Yo-didun none of that. She wouldn't have got anything of this and perhaps would have cursed the world for turning worse since her youth faded. She would also have been tensed wondering how her Shonamoni would live in this bad world.

It was only when she asked how Neel was doing that I remembered I had to visit the hospital. The only problem was that hospital was at some distance from my place, and Ashok mama wouldn't have allowed me to go alone since I was a girl nor would he have taken me to the hospital himself since I was not his girl. Moreover, if I had told him I was supposed to visit a guy in the hospital, Bijoya mami would have triggered a soap opera at home. Instead, when I told this to Yo-didun, she asked me to visit Neel at least once in the hospital.

As a solution to the problem she said, 'I haven't gone out to shop for many years,' and winked at me. I kissed her so hard that we almost fell off the bed.

As we laughed, I hoped Avni had not visited Neel before me. How wrong was I.

8

Yo-didun and I, on the pretext of shopping in Haathibagan, took a taxi to Lake Town where the nursing home was. Yo-didun preferred to sit in the lobby while I checked with the receptionist, and went to the floor where Neel was. Thankfully I was there in the nursing home during the visiting hours by default. I soon found the room and saw Neel sitting on a bed. By his side was a woman helping him eat something.

'Hi!' he said on seeing me.

'Hi!' I said and smiled at him. He smiled back and introduced the woman standing by him as his mother. With an unsure smile, I folded my hands to greet her. She gave me a condescending look, and avoided looking at me, focussing more on helping Neel drink the soup. But I noticed Neel did not turn his eyes away from me even once. Whenever he looked at me, I wanted to get inside his head, into his heart, and read aloud whatever he was thinking and feeling.

His mother got a call on her phone and she stepped out of the room for a better network. She was about to call a nurse to help Neel have the soup when I volunteered. I think it was because of the urgency of the call that she gave me the soup bowl and left. I sat down where she was sitting, and helped Neel take a spoonful of the steaming soup. I had taken his mother's place. I don't know why but I loved the thought. Of course I didn't want to be his mother, but whatever motherhood stood for—care, love, nurture—I wanted to mean that to him then.

'Mom is always worrying. I am alright now and can have the soup myself.'

'It's okay. You should listen to your mom,' I said as if I was a middle-aged nanny myself.

'I heard you are here because you smoked? Why did you do that?'

'I got into a stupid bet. You know how it is. I had to prove a point or gift myself a stupid nickname for the rest of school life. Neel is a TGIF. That doesn't sound good, no?'

'And now you are here.'

'Yes. After I smoked the bidi, my vocal cord was choked.'

He said it casually as if it wasn't anything serious he had suffered. My cheeks flexed into a faint smile.

'Thanks for coming. I didn't expect you,' he said next.

'Why not?'

'I mean it's not a holiday.'

'I skipped school. And one second, I have something for you.'

I quickly flipped my bag, which I had slung across my shoulder, and brought out the get-well-soon card I had made for him the previous night.

'Get well soon, Neel!' I said giving him the card.

'Wow! Did you make this yourself?' he asked.

'Yes, I did,' I said with a pinch of pride. For the first time in my life I had myself awake to make something for someone.

He kept staring at the sketch I'd made on the front of the card which featured a boy and a girl holding hands and walking by a beach. Except Yo-didun, nobody knew I was good at sketching.

'It's brilliant. And the guy looks exactly like me,' he quipped.

'It's *you,* Neel.'

He immediately gave me a weird glance. It was weird because it did to me what nothing else ever did till then. I felt like I was dropping from a height, in slow motion, onto a velvet air-bed. I intentionally steered my words a bit in another direction.

'It's a card for you. So you need to feature in it,' I said holding another spoonful of soup to his mouth. He sucked it all in, glaring at me. I purposely looked elsewhere in the room and noticed a few bouquets and a card on the table where the medicines were kept. A specific heart-shaped card. He followed my gaze.

'Avni couldn't come yesterday, so she sent the Archies' card and those flowers for me.'

The fact that I had visited Neel in the hospital before Avni made me feel victorious in a stupid way even though her card had reached before mine.

'How is it going with Avni?' I asked deliberately.

'The usual,' he said. I kept the soup bowl aside since he was done drinking it. He wiped his mouth with a napkin. He could have said 'it was going great' or something like that, but he said a dull 'usual'. Was he trying to lead me somewhere?

'You guys are so much in love!' My tongue burnt when those words escaped my mouth, but I had to say it to get to where he was leading me, if at all.

'We are in a pact. Not love. We are family friends. And our wedding card was printed by our parents even before we were born.'

'You don't love her?'

'I was never allowed to experience love. In fact, I'm never allowed to choose things for myself. Things are accepted and rejected in my life according to my parents' taste. The only thing I truly relate to and have chosen for myself is music.'

I looked at him. He was staring at the ceiling as if pondering about something disturbing. The day we had walked together from tuition, he had sounded like such a rebel, but now he seemed more like a caged-rebel.

'Just asking, do you like anyone other than Avni?'

He looked at me. I was already looking at him. I died. He knew.

His mother came in hastily informing us that Avni had called and she was coming. She said Neel's dad was bringing her to visit him. 'Dear, Neel shouldn't talk much in this condition,' she said to me.

'I'm not sure. Maybe…' Neel suddenly said. His mother didn't know the context but I did. He was replying to my query now.

Do you like anyone other than Avni?

What did he mean by maybe? That I wasn't anyone else for him anymore? But he didn't take my name specifically. I felt as if all those nights I spent sighing and wishing for Neel hadn't gone to waste. Each moment was not just a vague fallacy but a solid prophecy.

I took my handmade card from Neel's side, and placed it right in front of Avni's heart-shaped card. I liked the way it eclipsed her card. As if her card never existed.

'Symbolic representation always goes deeper,' our English teacher used to tell us.

Chapter 7

IS TITIKSHA REALLY HAVING AN AFFAIR?

Neel switches off his laptop and retires to bed beside Titiksha who is sound asleep.

Before typing out whatever Nivrita had narrated to him earlier in the day, Neel was sitting with his book contract for a good three hours. Just caressing, flipping, and staring at it before finally signing on it. The front of the contract had the Word Tree logo which he had seen on the spine of all their books. Neel felt lucky to have signed a book contract this quick when a few days back he was in a dilemma whether to leave his job or not.

Before switching off the laptop, Neel had called Nivrita to request if the working title—*Ex*—could be the actual title because he believed it was an apt one. Nivrita told him that if he doesn't know the entire story yet, how could he say it's an apt title? Neel was quiet. Nivrita told him that she would take a decision once the manuscript is complete. Neel agreed even though he hated the way she said it. *She would take a decision!* For heaven's sake he was the one writing it (so what if it's her story?), and thus he should be the one suggesting the title, not her.

He has been trying hard to sleep, with Titiksha next to him, but it's as if sleep has eluded him. What would people's reaction be once the book is out? Neel tosses around the bed as winds of excitement play with the kite of his consciousness. Would his book be an instant bestseller? Would he be featured in the major newspapers and magazines like his favourite bestselling authors? How would Titiksha react when that happens? The wave of thoughts keeps his boat afloat. When more such waves are about to come up, his phone vibrates flashing: 'Nivrita calling'.

Neel picks up the phone, gets up, and goes to the drawing room to talk.

'Hello,' he whispers lest Titiksha wakes up.

'Don't tell me you've slept already?' Nivrita sounds conspiratorial herself.

'I was trying to sleep.'

'Good. I just did something and wanted to share. You may have a good night's sleep listening to this.'

'What is it?'

'My boy-mate and I were fucking. I blindfolded him and rode him.'

Nivrita's knack of getting to the details without any warning never goes down well with Neel. And why does she always have to use the F-word? Why can't she say 'making love' instead? Neel continues to listen projecting fake calmness.

'But after blindfolding him, I wrote your name on his forehead with my lipstick and then fucked him. Isn't that kinky?'

Which girlfriend would do that? Neel wonders. It's too disgusting a thought for his morality to digest.

'Of course I rubbed your name off before I opened his blindfold.'

'But why would you do that?' He had to ask her that.

'Why? That rat is having an affair, I told you. And this is how I get back at him; by humiliating his presence in my life.'

Neel's mind is too clogged to conjure up a reply.

'The bugger has gone to the bathroom now. By the way, did your girlfriend tell you about it?'

'About what?'

'Her affair. Shit, he is coming.' And the line went dead.

Neel shakes his head hoping this would help him forget what he just heard from Nivrita. He did tell her about Titiksha's affair, but he doesn't like Nivrita inquiring about it. It's his personal life. They should talk about it when he wants to and not when she wants to. He tells himself he would not tell Nivrita anything more about Titiksha's supposed affair.

Neel goes to the bedroom. He notices Titiksha. She is sleeping with her head turned the other way. Neel now tries to guess what Titiksha may have lied to him about, sacrificed, or accepted just to keep their relationship ticking. Even though he didn't listen to her and abruptly resigned from the job, she still hasn't left him. Maybe, with time, when his book becomes a bestseller, she will accept the fact that perhaps he was born to write. But to become a published author in a hurry, what has he done? Slept with a woman on the first opportunity he had? Neel feels sick in the stomach. For momentary pleasure, he cheated on his permanent happiness. Suddenly he feels Titiksha was right. He shouldn't have left his job to become an author. And even if he wanted to become an author, he should have not fallen for the temptation that Nivrita brought with her.

'I'm sorry Titiksha,' he says caressing her head. She budges slightly letting out a sleepy moan. The most atrocious thing however is that Neel suspects Titiksha of infidelity. He has no proof of it yet, and he still has thoughts of her cheating on him. Why? Just because a guy came home to drop her, just because she chats with someone over the Internet without telling him who it is, and just because she says she needs some space. Perhaps he is judging her instincts on the basis of his own impulse. The way he slipped in front of a temptation, he thinks Titiksha too may slip likewise if an opportunity arises. That being in touch with other guys would invariably bring forth such an opportunity one day or so he thinks. What should he do? Make her his pet and lock her in the flat. Ask her to resign from her job, and be his domestic slave for the rest of his life simply because he can't sleep beside someone who has slept with someone else? The moon of guilt is suddenly shining brightly in his dark sky of conscience. Should he wake Titiksha up and tell her everything honestly? What if she slaps him and leaves him in the dead of the night? He can take the slap but he can't take the break-up. Nivrita anyway never looks like the kind of girl who would like to be in a relationship. She is doting on him because of two reasons: one, he was her childhood crush and second, she said she loves to 'snatch', which in other words means she has a thing for other's belongings. Neel can't believe he just weighed the possibility of Nivrita and his relationship. Enough! He has to tell Titiksha everything. He won't be able to live with this guilt. Why should he anyway? He loves Titiksha, not Nivrita. The former is the one with whom he is trying to decorate his future. And the latter is only a tool to afford the decoration.

Neel turns on his side and wakes up Titiksha from her sleep. There's no response. He shakes her up vigorously.

'Get up. I need to confess something important. Please get up.'

Just then, his mobile phone vibrates with a message. He turns and picks it up from the side of his pillow. It's from Nivrita. *Don't feel guilty,* it says. Neel swallows a lump. It's as if Nivrita is reading his mind without really being there with him. He scrolls down his phone continuing to read the full message:

What I couldn't tell you over the phone was I saw Titiksha with a guy today in a mall. The fact that she is asleep and not interested in you tonight could well be because someone else has exhausted her. Good night handsome.

What if Titiksha is doing exactly what Nivrita is doing to her boy-mate—humiliating him by giving him clues that she is actually with another man?

'What is it?' Titiksha says, half-asleep.

'Nothing. Just move a bit. The bed is not yours alone,' Neel retorts.

⌛

'Are you sure you saw Titiksha?'

It's 7.15 pm. Neel and Nivrita are sitting inside the Cafe Coffee Day outlet of City Centre Mall in Salt Lake. It was Neel who requested Nivrita for a meeting. But he wanted to meet in some private place—where there would be no one but them. It was Nivrita who proposed the idea of meeting over coffee in a mall. Before this, Neel has been in a mall only a few times. The continuous noisy buzz triggered headaches in him. But he can't say no to Nivrita. Not yet. Moreover, it was him who set up the meeting in the first place.

'You have never been to a mall?' Nivrita's surprise is overt and justified considering the fact that most youngsters spend more time of the day in malls than their own home.

Neel only nods his head embarrassingly.

'Only three-four times.'

'Why are you so peculiar?' she asks to which he replies with a query, 'Are you sure you saw Titiksha?'

'Yes, I did. Yesterday, right here in this mall. At around 7.30 in the evening.'

'And she was with a guy?'

'That's what I saw. But tell me why it is a problem if she was with a guy? Men don't get it. We women aren't locks. We are key-rings. And a key ring has scope for a lot of keys, isn't?'

Seeing a perplexed Neel shaking his leg furiously under the table, Nivrita adds, 'Who knows, maybe they would be here tonight too.'

They! The mere mention of it drains all the blood out of his heart. It makes him feel as if he has been left out just like a piece of unimportant garbage even before Titiksha and he could talk about it and mutually break-off.

'Does a relationship ever break-off? And what does it mean really?' Neel asks Nivrita as a rebound to his inner turmoil.

For some time Nivrita looks at him mentally framing her reply.

'Before that we need to understand why does a relationship happen? It happens when you *want* to know a person, when you *want* to be with a person, and when you *want* the person to *want* you. When a relationship is about those wants, then it definitely can break-off. Or, should I say one fine day it can possibly vanish; all those vociferously felt *wants* can just vanish,' Nivrita gestures with her hand like a magician to make it sound more dramatic.

Those wants that Nivrita just talked about were there between Titiksha and him till last year. But truth be faced, Neel has come to realize more than being in love with Titiksha, he was used to her. He was used to her presence beside him in the morning and at night. He was used to the way they went about their lives. He was used to the fact that she was used to his shortcomings as a human being and that he didn't have to justify the choices he made out of his weaknesses in front of her anymore.

So many people remain with their partner simply because they are used to their relationship, and also because they have invested time and emotions to get used to that relationship. People don't usually understand it, but the investment of time and emotions do tire us in undecipherable ways. And flying out of that nest of exhaustion isn't an easy task. The least Titiksha could have done was tell Neel she is exhausted. Maybe he would have made a little hue and cry but in the end he would have accepted it and let it go. Everyone lets go in the end.

'Tell me Neel, is your love for Titiksha only love or true love?'

'All I know is I love her.'

'Why couldn't you tell her that we slept in Jaipur?'

'It's because I love her. If I tell her the truth it won't be good for our relationship.'

'People think true love is about loving the same person till their death. Bull-fucking-shit! Even liars and cheats can live with the same person all their lives. I believe true love is when you have the balls to say the truth to your partner without fearing the consequence. Hiding things is also compromising the relationship in your heart.'

'But I didn't tell her anything because I want to keep our relationship intact. You see, I care for it.'

'Relationship of convenience, I see,' Nivrita smirked. 'Human beings are too complex to carry out something as simple as love in an uncompromised manner. Would you forgive Titiksha if you discover she slept with a guy and later she tells you she didn't inform you because she cared for your relationship?'

Neel can't believe how cold Nivrita sounds. He wants to know what has turned her into someone like this. Or was she born this way?

'If she is serious with the other guy, she will have to tell me. Like what we did in Jaipur was not serious. So why should I tell her and jeopardize my relationship with my girlfriend?'

Nivrita doesn't speak anything for a few seconds. She looks around and then suddenly says, 'What's the time?'

'7.25.' Neel glances at his watch. 'Why?'

'Did Titiksha wear a grass-green top and a pair of white jeans?'

'I don't know. She was gone by the time I woke up today. But...wait a second...' Neel turns around in a flash and says, 'Did you just see her?'

'Them. I saw them. They just went by,' Nivrita gestures with her eyes towards the escalator.

Neel immediately dashes out of the coffee outlet. Nivrita follows. Their coffee remains unfinished.

Neel looks down. Nivrita joins him from behind and says, 'Come on.' They take the escalator together and get to the first floor. Neel is yet to see *them*.

'There by the bookstore,' Nivrita says.

Neel has no idea where the bookstore is but simply follows Nivrita into the escalator and reaches the ground floor.

'This way!'

They take a left and pass by the small bookstore and eventually move out of the Block A of the mall via a glass door and are now into the open.

Neel looks to his left and sees the entry of a Shopper's Stop store. He ambles ahead trying to look inside the store. Nivrita meanwhile looks to her right.

'I think I just saw her grass-green top.'

'Where?' Neel turns and comes close to Nivrita and tries to follow her gaze.

'They just took the stairs to Block B.'

Neel thinks he saw a glimpse of the grass-green top. Without waiting for Nivrita to move, he scampers ahead. This time she follows him. They have difficulty running at full speed because of the crowd. After crossing three-four stores on either side they reach the Block B stairs. They climb up. Ahead of Neel is a KFC outlet and to the left is a Club bag store.

Breathing fast Neel is feeling desperate to see if Titiksha is actually roaming around with a guy.

'Were they touching each other?' Neel shoots at Nivrita. She turns at him.

'Touching?'

Neel shakes his head slightly. 'I mean were they holding hands or something like that.'

'He had his hand around her waist.'

Patience is history now for Neel.

'What do we do now? I can't see anyone in a grass-green top.'

'Let's split up. Call me if you see them. I will do the same.'

'Okay.'

Nivrita takes the left towards the bag store while Neel goes ahead towards the KFC outlet. He carefully surveys the inside through the glass door outside. A guard opens the door and says, 'Please come in sir.'

'No, it's okay.' The outlet is crowded. Neel feels better outside.

'Neel!'

He turns in a flash and sees Nivrita gesturing him to come up. He does. They take few steps crossing the Club bag store when Nivrita shows her thumb toward the left and says, 'In there.'

Neel looks up. Gents washroom.

'I want to see Titiksha not the guy.'

'They are both in there.'

Inside the gents' washroom? What the fuck! Neel doesn't know if he is simply angry or feeling devastatingly humiliated.

'I think you should go in. I'll wait for you here,' Nivrita suggests.

With bated breath, Neel slowly approaches the gents' washroom. He pauses, turns back, and sees there's no one around except Nivrita. Few people go past the washroom on either direction but nobody goes in.

Neel enters the washroom. There's nobody inside. Apart from the urinals, there are two toilets. Neel goes ahead and opens one of the two toilets' door. It's empty. He is about to unlock the other toilet door when he hears a sound. As if someone hit the door from inside. Suddenly he hears a girl moan out with pleasure from inside the toilet. Next he hears a male groan. Neel shuts his eyes tightly. He can't take the moans anymore. He feels weak in his knees. Neel wants to die. He feels he shouldn't have listened to Nivrita and tried to follow Titiksha. He will have to live with these moans haunting him for the rest of his life. Neel's head is aching hard. He opens his eyes unable to bear the on-goings but sees nothing.

There's a sudden power cut. The disturbing rhythmic noises coming from the toilet stop with the power cut. Neel feels someone groping him all over. It's too dark to see who it is. He wants to retaliate but can't. He is pushed and he falls down. He feels weight on his lap. The lights come back on. He finds himself inside a toilet, sitting on a sink with Nivrita sitting atop him. She has her mouth pursed with his while one of her hand is pinching his nose. Neel is unable to breathe. He starts moving his legs vigorously, thus hitting the toilet door.

The disturbing rhythmic noise starts again similar to how it was before the power cut, till Nivrita releases his nose. Neel is gasping for air now. He coughs feeling choked. He looks up at Nivrita who is standing now panting and adjusting her dress.

'Wash yourself Neel. You are sweating way too much. I'll be outside.'

She unlocks the toilet door and moves out. Neel still sits on the toilet sink. Is Titiksha still there inside the other toilet? He somehow manages to stand up only to realize that his pants and underwear are tugged down till his knees. When did he strip? He quickly pulls up his pants and underwear feeling stupid.

As he moves out of the toilet, there is still nobody in sight. He notices a mobile phone on the floor. The phone set has split itself open with the battery lying under one of the urinals. Neel picks it up. It's Titiksha's. So she indeed was inside the toilet fucking some dude! He wants to throttle Titiksha to death right now. If she is done with him, she should have told him. Nobody has given her the right to humiliate him the way she is by being involved with some other guy and giving him clues about it.

This has to end. This will end! Before Titiksha terminates their relationship, he will do it himself. Neel decides.

He goes to the washbasin and splashes his face with water. He pulls out some tissue paper and is about to rub his face when he notices something written on it with what looks like a black eyeliner.

It says, *If you are accustomed to see only black and white then you'll never see me.*

'How did I get into the toilet with you? Why were my pants down? When did Titiksha move out?'

It's 9.05 pm. Both of them are on a boat floating on the river Hooghly. Nivrita has intentionally got him here because the first thing Neel told her after he came out of the mall washroom was, 'Take me to a lonely place.'

Thus they are here—at Princep Ghat—and she is rowing the boat herself. They are sitting by the edge of the two ends of the boat. Above them is the majestic looking Vidyasagar Setu.

'Don't tell me you don't remember!' Nivrita replies. Neel, perhaps for the first time after he came out of the washroom, looks at Nivrita.

'I only remember that the lights in the washroom went off.' His claim sounds genuine. 'What happened next?'

'As I entered the washroom, there was a power cut but thankfully I got to you before you got to the door behind which Titiksha and the other guy was. In fact, they too came out of the toilet when the power cut happened.'

'You mean the four of us were there in the washroom when the power cut happened?'

'That's what I said.'

Neel thanked his stars. If the power had come then, what an awkward situation it would have been: Titiksha with the other guy and Neel with Nivrita—all inside the washroom looking at each other, clueless what to talk about.

'You pushed me inside the other toilet. I think it was then that the two escaped,' Nivrita says letting go of the oars. The boat now floats on its own in the river.

I pushed her? Neel tries hard to think what really happened and says, 'They escaped.'

'Only you are to be blamed.'

'Me?'

'Yes. Who asked you to be horny at that time?'

'What?'

'Why else do you think your pants were down?'

'I tugged my own pants down?'

'That you should ask yourself. All I would say is I enjoyed it. It was unlike you, I must say.' Nivrita has her eyes fixed on Neel. He averts his eyes to the horizon ahead as if he is trying hard to remember what Nivrita implied, but in vain.

'Can you for once tell me something directly, without puzzling?' Neel is a little loud than he should have been. Even he knows it. To neutralize his supposed inappropriate behaviour, he says, 'Please?'

'How do I know why you tugged your pants down, forcefully stripped me half, and fucked me in the toilet? My guess is you got aroused listening to the moans.'

What rubbish! Neel can't believe what Nivrita just said. She is lying. Why? He doesn't know. He would have never done something as wicked as that. He clearly remembers he was burning alive with anger and jealousy after he heard Titiksha's moans. How can he make love to Nivrita in such a mental state? Neel is sure it must have been Nivrita who forced him to fuck her. And it was her, not him, who was aroused by the moans.

'Did you…' Neel pauses and then as if summoning some energy says, 'Did you see the guy?'

'Yes. Just a flash though because it was dark in there,' Nivrita is quick to respond.

'Was he good looking?'

Nivrita picks up the oars again.

'Why do you want to know? And how does it matter to you if the other guy was handsome or not?'

'I don't know.'

Neel knew why exactly he inquired about the other guy's looks. Being a guy he can't bear the fact that Titiksha is going around with someone better than him. It's a below-the-belt blow for his ego. Neel laments the fact that he should have talked to Titiksha on the first day when he suspected her of having an affair. At least he would have spared his ego from suffering this incurable hurt.

'Just tell me, was he smarter than me?'

'Your ego is hurt, isn't it? ' Nivrita says.

Neel feels enraged. Why does Nivrita have to be right every single time? Yes, his male ego is hurt. So what? On the contrary, if he was told that the guy isn't better than him, Neel would feel happy for Titiksha in a sadistic manner.

'Alright. Could you please row us back now? I want to go to my flat.' Neel is already having a slight headache. He doesn't know why his parents have not taken him to the doctor in the last four-five months. He doesn't have the medicine which he used to take for his headaches.

Neel decides to spend some time alone and think about what he should do next. Talking to Nivrita seems pointless since she never answers anything the way he wants her to.

Nivrita starts rowing the boat back towards the shore now.

'One can't love and be egoistic about it Neel,' she says.

'I am not being egoistic,' says Neel half-truthfully.

'Jealous?'

'No!' Half a lie this time.

'Then?'

'Even my parents know Titiksha. We were supposed to get married.'

'So?'

'What would I tell my parents if she leaves me now?'

'I think you are more worried about what you would tell *yourself* if she leaves you now.'

This damn woman always gets it right! Neel thinks and says, 'Maybe. There has been an emotional investment of five years. I thought I knew everything about her. I thought we were meant to be together, forever.'

'You know why people say "will you be mine forever"? That's because deep inside we all are insecure. We are a lump of fear. We are shit scared of being so much in love with this one moment when the person we love is there with us. So we want to multiply the moment, fearing the unknown moments that will follow the special moment. Hence, we ask if we will be together forever knowing well 'forever' can't be real. Tell me, do you know everything about yourself, Neel?'

'Yes, I do.' It's more of a stubborn stance than an assured one. He knows nobody can know everything about oneself. Hence, we need to fall in love and give ourselves a chance to know ourselves more deeply. And Neel is still in love with Titiksha.

Is he?

'Really? Everything? You knew you would sleep with a woman the moment you get a chance?'

Neel's lips are zipped now as he swallows a lump and listens to Nivrita.

'If you really knew it and still continued to be with Titiksha, then I think you know who the real culprit is.'

Neel crosses his hands placing them on his knees and digs his face deep in them. A moment later, his body subtly shudders as if he is crying.

'Tears won't help Neel. Tears never help.'

'Then what will?' Neel asks without lifting his head. His voice is broken.

'Apologize to Titiksha.'

It's now that Neel lifts his head and asks himself: is he that brave?

'Why do people cheat, Nivrita?' he asks with a gaze of a sinner down with guilt.

One look at him and Nivrita laughs out. The sound of it disturbs Neel as its echo hovers over the lonely river.

'First tell me why do people love Neel?'

Neel can't take it anymore. His head is aching way too much for comfort now.

Nivrita keeps rowing the boat with a still face, without poking Neel any further.

Neel is back in his flat, waiting for Titiksha to arrive. He wants to talk to her about where their relationship is headed, and then take a decision. It can't go on like this with her going around with another guy right under his nose. If she has to stay with the other guy, she better get out of his life. In fact Neel decides that the moment she comes, he will initiate an emotional battle, and charge her with infidelity. He will not tell her anything about Nivrita. He slept for business purposes but she slept for pleasure, and that's why it's Titiksha who has cheated on him and not the other way round.

Neel's conscience knows it's a lie. He knows he's being a hypocrite. His conscience knows he has committed something which is unpardonable. Infidelity anyway is a thin line between a physical act and an emotional one. He can't deny that he is attracted towards Nivrita, and if she says he would again sleep with her. But knowing this, he still thinks Titiksha is to be blamed? Who is he trying to kid?

The doorbell rings. Neel turns to look at the wall clock. 10 pm. He lets go of a conclusive sigh and gets up, goes and opens the door. It is Titiksha. She is wearing the same grass-green top he saw her wearing in the evening. No, Nivrita saw her wear.

Titiksha doesn't even care to look at him. She leaves her sandals by the door and enters the flat exercising her neck as if it's hurting. Neel can't guess if it's intentional or not.

'Who gave you the top?'

Titiksha stops and turns to look at him.

'What?'

'This grass-green top. I never gave it to you. Who did?'

'What's with the attitude, Neel? Who did what?'

'Don't you dare talk to me like that.' Neel has his index finger pointing at her. 'Just answer me.'

Titiksha comes to him in a slow but sure pace and, placing her hands on her hips, stands looking intently at Neel.

'Okay, I shall answer. But first tell me what were you doing with that girl in the hotel room in Jaipur?'

Neel's index finger slowly curls back to its original position.

'Don't think I don't know anything,' Titiksha says with a mocking smirk.

Lappan! That scoundrel must have told her everything, Neel infers from the confidence oozing from Titiksha's face. He should have bribed Lappan more. But it's useless to think about what he could have done in the past. He can't change it. But if she knew it all along, why didn't she question him on the first day itself?

'I didn't go to any hotel room with any girl.' Neel's voice has zero conviction.

'You are such a...' Titiksha turns and walks towards her room. Neel follows her.

'It was a business deal, Titiksha.' Neel finds her standing by the window with her back towards him, furiously arranging a Rubik's Cube. That's another thing she likes to do whenever she boils inside with rage.

'Business deal?' Titiksha pauses. The Rubik's Cube is solved. 'Go fuck yourself with a lighted candle.'

'I'm serious, Titiksha. It indeed was a business deal.' Neel is surprised to hear himself talk in a negotiable tone now. This is not how he had imagined the discussion to go.

'If you were not in it with your heart, you would have told me the moment you were back. You hid it from me.'

'And that's why you are punishing me by screwing a random guy?'

'Have you been following me?' Titiksha asks and hurls the Rubik's Cube at Neel, taking him by surprise. He ducks in reflex; it would have hit his forehead otherwise.

'You dog! You have been following me!'

'Yes I have. You compelled me to!' This is the right time, Neel feels, to start the emotional blame game and turn the tables in a way that Titiksha feels she is sorry for what she did, and guilty too, and then perhaps she would do things the way he wants. For any relationship to flourish, one of the two has to be the emotional slave. 'The day I came back, I saw you being dropped by a guy. You guys even kissed standing by the main door. Standing right by the main door of our flat! Don't tell me you got a boyfriend after I slept with a girl. You were actually having an affair before I had even met the girl in Jaipur. And by the way, you have no right to be angry for you too have had me followed around Jaipur. I know Lappan is your man.'

Titiksha comes to Neel and starts hitting him.

'You idiot. I had asked Lappan to take care of you because you had gone out of station for the first time.'

Neel knows Titiksha is speaking the truth. But he can't get himself to accept it, because then his argument would have died a certain death. Instead he now knows Titiksha is totally caught in his emotional trap.

'Stop it!' he holds her hands. 'I don't want to live with a person who cheats on me. You have to choose either the other guy or me. It's your decision,' he says heaving a sigh of relief. Finally what he had been waiting for since he came to his flat is done. He has successfully made her wear the guilt-jacket and from now on, Neel knows, Titiksha will forget the other guy and be his emotional pet. That's what people really like to do, isn't it? Make their loved ones their pets though they never have the balls to accept it lest their egos get deflated. Neel has a problem with Titiksha dating another guy because she is his 'thing'. If he considered her as a person who has the same needs and desires as him, then he probably would have understood that our heart is not a locality. It's a world. And every world—*every* fucking world—has its continents, countries, oceans, mountains and...is it really love if it binds you to one country or ocean or mountain specific? For lack of better options, probably it is. Sometimes love is the most comfortable apparel to cover up the most uncomfortable rashes of desires.

Neel waits for Titiksha to respond. Titiksha hugs him. Neel knows the hug is a clue to what she may be thinking.

'I choose your parents,' Titiksha whispers.

Neel breaks the hug and looks at her.

'What do you mean?'

'What I mean is I shall go to your parents and tell them that you slept with a random chick in Jaipur and hence I am breaking up this relationship.'

Neel feels agonized.

'You won't do that.'

'I will.'

'No, you won't.'

'I will. If you try to boss me, Neel, I definitely will.'

She will. Neel can read her resolve clearly in her eyes.

'Why are you dragging my parents into this?'

Titiksha leaves him and picks up her laptop. She sits on the nearby chair keeping the laptop in front of her.

'They should also know what a cheat their lovey-dovey son is.'

Titiksha averts her attention to her laptop. Her indifference, and an unprecedented arrogance has been the hallmark since Neel's return from Jaipur.

For some time Neel stands like a bird who is busy hatching while dreaming about her egg's future only to turn and realize that there's no egg. Frustration forces him to storm out of the bedroom and into the kitchen. He takes out a freezing cold bottle of water from the refrigerator and gulps half of it. As the cold water gushes down his throat, Nivrita's way of humiliating her boyfriend reverberates in his mind. The frustration slowly gives way to an evil grin. Neel takes some time to calm down totally and prepares his mind for the humiliating assault that he will be having on Titiksha.

Neel stands by the door staring at Titiksha. It takes some time for the latter to avert herself from the laptop screen to him.

'What now?' she asks.

Neel tries to look seductive and says, 'I am sorry baby. I want to make up for whatever bad I told you.'

He comes close, shuts the laptop screen, and kisses her on the cheek.

'Let's sort it out the way we did in college?'

Titiksha seems a tad surprised.

'Well, I don't mind.'

She was fucking in the toilet and she still doesn't mind doing it. In a way, Neel is happy because it only means the other guy didn't satisfy her thoroughly, and hence her yes to him at this hour.

He takes her by her hand and together they kneel down on the low lying bed.

'One second.'

Neel stands up, switches off the light, and takes out his handkerchief from his pocket. He kneels down once again and tries to blindfold Titiksha with the handkerchief. She stops him by holding his hand.

'What's this?'

'It will help sort things out better. Trust me.'

Titiksha slowly lets go of her hand as Neel blindfolds her. She tilts her face expecting a kiss but instead of complying, he breathes on it; in a circle from her left cheek to her forehead to her right cheek to her chin. It's only now that he kisses her on her lips slowly sucking on her lower lip. It's a soft pursing of lips which soon grows into an uncivilized smooch. He stretches his leg and reaches out for her purse lying on the side table beside the bed. He brings it to him with his leg. Then taking the purse in his hand, he unzips it, continuing to smooch her, and turns the contents of the purse upside down on the bed. He picks the lipstick up. Titiksha isn't able to breathe properly because of the way Neel's face is covering hers. She pushes him and breathes hard.

'Take it slow.'

Neel holds her face and writes on her forehead with the lipstick: NIVRITA.

'What are you writing?'

'You will know.'

And when you will know, you'll also know what humiliation is. Neel pushes Titiksha on the bed. She lies down. Neel lies on top of her pressing his lips on to her throat. As Titiksha parts her legs, he adjusts himself well between them and soon is inside her. Seeing Nivrita's name on his girlfriend's forehead gives him an unprecedented kick. He mauls her breasts, and fucks her with a virility he had never shown before. Titiksha starts butt-slapping him pleading him to slow down. But he doesn't. The moans he heard in the toilet, Nivrita's name right front of him, and Titiksha's infidelity all has made him a monster. After a good five minutes long sexual assault he collapses on Titiksha; done for the night.

It's morning now. The call bell rings three times at one go. Then stops. It awakens Neel. He feels a mild headache. The bell rings again. Once. Neel sits up and turns to his right. Titiksha isn't around. Probably she is in the toilet, Neel thinks, and gets up.

While going towards the hall room, he glances at the toilet. It's locked from the outside. The bell rings again.

Wasting no time, Neel goes ahead and opens the door to see Nivrita. He isn't able to decipher the weird look on her face. A moment later she bursts out laughing.

'What?'

'Who did this to you?'

Again the indirect talks!

'Who did what?'

'Who wrote my name on your forehead with a lipstick?'

FROM NEEL'S MANUSCRIPT

9

Till I crossed sixteen, I would regularly be depressed because I felt unwanted. Then Neel came into my life and gift-wrapped it with his love. This was what came to my mind when Neel invited me to his birthday party at his place. Till then I had never attended any birthday party before. Not even mine. I remember whenever my birthday arrived, my classmates used to wish me but not my parents. I never asked about it either for I assumed that was the norm: on birthdays only classmates wish you and not parents. By the time I realized the assumption was wrong, I didn't really care much because I was used to it and my own birthday, or for that matter anyone else's, lost all its significance for me. Whenever I was invited to any fellow classmate's birthday party, I used to miss it out of vengeance against my bad luck. It was a silly thing on my part but I used to feel like a winner by not availing the opportunity to enjoy myself only because whenever I wanted to enjoy before, I wasn't ever given the opportunity. Hence when Neel requested me to be there at his birthday party I was instantly in two minds.

We were standing by the water cooler filling up our bottles with cold water when Neel told me about the party.

'Won't Avni have a problem if I come to the party?' I wasn't scared of her. I only cared about Neel and didn't want to put him in any awkward situation like I did the last time by kissing him in front of Avni. Though the fact that he never confronted me about it meant he perhaps liked it.

'I have invited most of my classmates so why would she have a problem?'

Honestly I was expecting an answer like: I don't give a damn about Avni. I hid my disappointment well.

'But I don't go to birthday parties.' It was the truth but I said it to see his reaction; to see whether he would pester me to attend the party or not. Instead I saw his face turn sad and he become quiet. I wanted to pull his cheeks real hard for I thought he was looking at his cutest best.

'I will come,' I finally told him without considering the feasibility of it.

'Great! Any time after six. See you.' He went back to the class.

The problem was I wasn't allowed to go out of my mama's house in the evening except if it was for tuitions, and he knew well that I had my tuitions only on Tuesday, Thursday, and Saturday. Thankfully Neel's birthday was on a Friday. I consulted Yo-didun. Even she was quiet for she couldn't take me out late in the evening. Moreover, it was a birthday party, and not some shop where I could just pop in and out within minutes. I was in a fix. But this wasn't the only problem. Of all the days, the morning of Neel's birthday, I had to have my periods as well. There were dark circles around my eyes. And my lower abdomen suffered acute spasms. I didn't freak out because without those dark circles, I wasn't much beautiful anyway. But Yo-didun neutralized those dark circles by applying Kajal on my eyes. I saw myself in the mirror and for the first time I thought I had nice eyes. In the evening, the spasms relaxed. I lied to mama that Rajiv sir had some work on Saturday so he was having a substitute class on Friday instead. Fortunately he didn't dig further because Bijoya mami seemed convinced. That's the way it worked between them. If Bijoya mami had a doubt, mama would have one as well.

Yo-didun gave me her old earrings to wear but I politely told her that I was going to go without them. I was never into accessories. As I walked out of the house, I saw Bijoya mami gape at my dress. I was wearing my favourite salwar suit which was a touch better than the other dull salwars I used to wear on most days. If she'd asked, I would have casually told her all my other clothes were unwashed. But she didn't ask anything. I gave her a sly smile. I didn't care even if she understood that I was up to something for I knew she wouldn't be able to prove it.

Neel had given me proper directions to his place on a piece of paper which I kept referring to while directing the taxi driver. It was a huge house in Paikpara. I knew the party had already started because I could hear loud music blasting from the house. The guard showed me the way inside the house.

An old man-servant opened the door, followed by a brown Doberman who, I later learnt, was his dad's pet. It barked at me but the servant silenced it by repeating the word 'bondhu' (friend) a few times.

'Kokhababu is upstairs,' he said with a benign smile.

I was inside the hall but there was nobody there except me. One look at the spacious hall and I knew Neel hailed from a rich family. Not just a well-to-do but also a rich family. It was evident from the way the room was kept—the branded furniture, curtains, carpet, showpieces, paintings, and what not. Maybe his father's business was running really well. I remembered how Neel had told me that his father kept going from home to shop to home. If his father didn't work hard at the shop, then his birthday party wouldn't have happened. When one gets too much too easily, one overlooks its worth. How true! I could also guess Neel's family had travelled around the world from all the framed photographs of the three of them. I recognized his mother immediately. Soon I saw a man stepping down from the staircase. I recognized him from the photographs. He was Neel's father.

'We all have been waiting for you,' he said and then looking up, raised his voice as if calling someone, 'She is here!' He then came down to the hall room.

I was a bit surprised to hear Neel's father was waiting for me. I could sense a nervous feeling perpetrating in me. It meant Neel must have told his parents about me. I was curious to know what all he had told them.

'I'm sorry,' I said. 'I couldn't come earlier.' Next, I saw Neel's mother, whom I had met in the hospital before, appear by the staircase looking worried.

'Oh! She is just another of Neel's classmate. Not from the pastry shop. I don't know when you will learn to distinguish people,' she bellowed and disappeared.

Neel's father immediately gave me a condescending look, perhaps wondering how the hell could I be Neel's classmate? It was the same look his mom had given me in the hospital. I didn't quite understand why they did that. I understood Neel had not yet told them anything about me. But was it a reason for him to presume I was some pastry shop girl?

'The party is upstairs.' His father's voice was strict.

There they were—some of my classmates and many of whom I didn't know at all. Nobody noticed me. It was nothing new for me but I felt a bit odd being there. From the dresses they wore and their body language, it was obvious that most of the other girls hailed from affluent backgrounds. They looked much younger than me. It was then I realized why Neel's father had looked at me like that. With a demure middle-class attitude, no makeup, or trendy clothes, I was probably not even looking their age. I would have turned and moved out of the party and later lied to Neel I couldn't make it, if at that moment Avni had not called out to me.

'Hey newcomer!' she said. The fact that I wasn't a newcomer anymore and Avni still termed me so, told me that this party won't be what I had hoped it would be.

'Hi Avni,' I replied.

She was wearing taut pink shorts with a white off-shoulder top. L'Oreal was evident in the streak of her hair which was coloured purple in front. She came up to me along with her silly groupies.

'Where exactly are you coming from?' She looked at me from top to bottom. 'Fish market?'

I knew my world was different from theirs but at that instant, I wanted to belong to that world of Avni in order to prove that I too could belong anywhere. I coveted the world where people like Avni and Neel belonged. Not having to wash clothes themselves, no tension of scoring high marks all the time, and no feeling of loneliness during birthdays. So much for wishful thinking!

'Where's Neel?' I asked.

'I will tell you but you've got to promise me one thing.'

'What?'

'You won't embarrass him or anything the way you are embarrassing yourself standing here?'

There was further laughter from her silly groupies. I wanted to scratch Avni's face with my long, dirty, and uncut nails, but I saw Neel in the distance and stopped myself.

'Oh don't worry Avni. That's your speciality. I'm no match for you on that.' I walked away from Avni towards Neel. He was genuinely happy to see me. So was I.

'Hey, you are late. I've already cut the cake. But good that you came.'

I took out an envelope from my tuition bag and gave it to him.

'Happy birthday, Neel!'

'Thanks. You have a thing for making cards, isn't it?'

It's not a card.' I had known he would think I am a card-making-freak, and hence I had intentionally not made one for him.

It piqued his interest and he immediately took out the piece of chart paper from inside the envelope. I was good with paper and had made him a paper cut out of a lips opening. There was something written on it. He read on. Perhaps it took him some time to understand what it actually was.

'It's a song!' The smile he had was exactly the one that had encouraged me to write it.

'My first,' I smiled, 'for Paintbrush.'

'This is my best...'

I wanted him to complete it, and he would have actually said whatever he wanted to had Avni not barged in.

'So miss newcomer has written a song. Let me see.'

Even before Neel could say anything, she snatched the chart paper cut-out from his hand. She then called out for everyone's attention.

'Listen everyone! Someone has written a song. It's called Shit.' Everyone in the room looked at Avni with interest.

'Switch off the music please.' I exchanged a worried glance with Neel. 'There's no need to...' he started but by then Avni was reading my song out aloud.

She read all the three verses I had written with perverse animation. There was pin drop silence as she read the song lyrics. I wanted to vanish into thin air.

The silence persisted even after Avni finished reading. She looked at everyone with an amused face. I knew the room was about to burst into a roar of laughter. I was ready to rush out but I heard claps instead. And words like 'cool', 'sexy', 'beautiful', 'killer'. Words which I had never heard for myself before, but my creation for Neel did. I smiled at Neel. He was looking at Avni who dashed towards another room throwing the piece of chart-paper on the floor. Her attempt to belittle me had obviously failed. Neel picked up the paper cutting. I took few steps towards him and requested, 'Could you please give the song a tune?'

'If you've written the song, the tune shall appear too,' he said. The warmth with which he said it had so much romance infused in it that I fell in love with him again.

Neel's mother came out from the room where Avni had disappeared and asked him, 'Neel, why is Avni crying?'

'Ask her,' Neel shot back.

'I did. She said you were rude to her,' she said accusingly.

'I was?' Neel had the right to be irked. I was only looking alternately once at Neel and then at his mother.

'Where's the girl who made fun of her?'

'Nobody made fun of her mom.'

'Where is the girl, Neel?'

I had to step in.

'I had written a song for Neel. And...'

Before I could finish she assigned me a job.

'Go inside and apologize to Avni.'

I gave a what-the-fuck-is-that look to Neel. He returned the same look to me and then to his mother.

'What should Titiksha apologize about?'

'I won't listen to anything Neel. Please ask your friend to do what I asked.'

'But mom this is completely bullshit.'

'How dare you use that word with your mom?' She darted a filthy glance at me and said, 'I think you should choose your friends carefully, Neel.'

'I'm sorry mom but Avni is at fault here.'

'Her parents will be here any moment now. Your dad is downstairs waiting for them. I don't want them to see her crying.'

I don't know what happened to me at that instant. I simply went inside the room where Avni was sitting, apologized, and moved out.

Did I choose to bow down because I saw Neel's helpless situation and did not want him to suffer because of a song written by me? Love makes you do stupid things at times.

Neel's mother was busy briefing the servant. 'I have done what you wanted aunty,' I said. She looked at the room's entrance, and saw Avni there, smiling.

'Good. You aren't as disobedient as you look.'

'You are wrong aunty. I'm disobedient. But my obedience to you is because I love your son.'

I was sure Neel's mother was surprised at my sudden audacity for I was the girl who had, a minute before, done exactly what she wanted. I didn't wait for anyone anymore. I didn't even look at Neel. I simply reached the stairs, and as I was about to climb down, I heard my name being called out.

'Titiksha.' It was Neel.

I paused and looked at him with tears in my eyes. What had I done to deserve such humiliation? Just loved someone with all my heart?

'I love you too,' Neel said. It was loud enough to qualify as an announcement.

Chapter 8

WILL NEEL AND TITIKSHA SORT OUT THEIR RELATIONSHIP?

This is the least Neel has written since he began writing the story as narrated to him by Nivrita.

As he shuts down his laptop, he feels the story is taking a toll on him. In fact, from the time he started writing the story, nothing has gone right in his life. He wants to finish the story as quickly as possible. But even after asking Nivrita to tell him the entire story in one sitting, she keeps slicing it up, God knows why.

The laptop's display goes blank. If Nivrita had not told him about the scope of 'reality fiction' in India, and how a fictional story promoted as a true story helps one sell more because of the presence of a huge number of gullible readers, Neel would have requested her to change the names of the protagonists. It's weird to write about something with your own name. Neel gets up from his chair and stretches himself. While drawing the curtains of the room, he is amazed to see its dark outside. He doesn't seem to keep a track of time these days.

Nivrita had come in the morning and narrated the story further. And then she had left. After her departure, Neel slept for some more time and had then started writing from early evening. It's 10.30 pm now. *What the fuck!* Titiksha is still not home.

When Nivrita laughed at him in the morning, standing by the door stating her name is written on his forehead, Neel thought she was joking. When she couldn't stop her laughter, Neel ran inside and looked at the mirror. Nivrita's name was indeed written on his forehead. Neel was devastated. He thought he would humiliate Titiksha but she had got up earlier than him, probably saw Nivrita's name on her forehead, and had written Nivrita's name on his forehead instead to mock him and get even. As Neel washed the name off his forehead, he swore he would not let Titiksha go away with it. He intentionally didn't call her up throughout the day.

Let her think I'm okay with what she did and when she's back, I shall show her what real mocking is all about.

Neel had drowned himself in the story after that. And now it is way beyond Titiksha's normal time of returning home.

He calls Titiksha. A voice tells him that the number is unreachable. He tries a few more times. Unreachable. Neel is now anxious. Could she be in the metro? But she never takes the metro to come home from office, assuming she was in office all day.

Neel searches the contacts on his mobile phone and gets Titiksha's office number. There aren't many contacts in his phone anyway.

'Hello.' A man speaks on the phone.

'Hello. This is Neel Chatterjee. Could you please tell me if Titiksha has left or not?'

'Yes, yes. Titiksha ma'am has left on time.'

'At what time?'

'On time. Titiksha ma'am has left on time.'

'Could you please tell me at precisely what time? I'm her...'

Neel was a bit cautious. Live-in partner may not go down well so he says, 'I'm her husband.'

'Titiksha ma'am has left on time.'

What's wrong with this man? Is he a robot?

'Thanks.' Neel cut the line, a tad disturbed as well as frustrated. If she has left on time, then she should have reached home by now. Or is she with the other guy, hatching another scheme to humiliate him?

Neel's gut feeling says she won't be back for dinner. He searches for one of the Domino's Pizza pamphlets which someone keeps dropping at his doorstep time and again. He finds it, dials their number, and orders a Pizza, coke, and chicken nuggets for himself.

Let her come when she wants to, Neel tells himself.

The pizza comes in within thirty minutes. Neel takes another thirty minutes to finish it, and then sits in his balcony looking at the distant silhouette of the city, thinking nothing crucial. He is feeling sleepy as he yawns three-four times within a span of few seconds. What if he falls asleep before Titiksha comes in?

He reluctantly goes to his table in the bedroom, tears off a page from a notepad, and goes to the hall. With a cellotape he sticks one end of the paper on his door and the other end on the wooden frame beside it in a way that if someone opens the door, the paper will get torn from the centre. It's his way of knowing if Titiksha comes and leaves without his knowledge. Impressed by his intelligence, Neel goes to the balcony again. He falls asleep in no time.

It is morning now. Neel wakes up with a start when something hits him on the face.

'Sorry dada, by mistake,' Shouts the newspaper boy from below.

He has thrown the newspaper to the wrong floor.

'Please throw it back,' the boy requests.

Neel gets up and hurls the newspaper back. He goes inside and is surprised looking at the main door. The piece of paper is intact. That means Titiksha has not come back all night. Something has to be wrong with her.

Neel dials her number with his heart beating faster than normal.

The number you have dialled is unreachable, says a female voice in Bengali.

Neel wastes no time and dials his parents' number next.

'Hello Babushona, good morning.' It is his father on the line. It always is his father on the line whenever he calls.

' Did Titiksha call?'

'No. What happened?'

'She has not come home last night and her phone is unreachable.'

'What? Why?'

'How do I know? I'm a bit worried now. Should I report it to the police?'

'No!' The response is instant. Neel is taken aback. 'Not the police.'

His father sounds overtly concerned as if the first thing the police would do, if called, is arrest his father for the sudden and supposed disappearance of Titiksha.

Neel has gone to his parents' place. His father is at the breakfast table, eating.

'*O-go shuncho, Neel is* here. Give him breakfast,' he calls out to Neel's mother.

'I won't eat anything. Titiksha is missing.'

'How can you say she is missing? It hasn't even been 24 hours yet.'

'How do you know?'

'You told me over the phone Babushona that she didn't come home last night. Now it's daytime. Hardly twelve hours.'

'Hmm. But why did you ask me not to report it to the police?'

'They will also ask you to wait for 24 hours, that's why. Moreover, reporting it to the police may take the matter to everyone's drawing room in the neighbourhood. You understand what I am saying?'

'I do. But what else can we do? Her phone is not reachable. I don't even know if she is alright or not.'

'She is alright.'

For a moment their eyes meet. Neel doesn't look in to his father's eyes often.

'Breakfast is here for my Babushona.'

Neel's mother comes in the dining space followed by a servant who has a tray with a plate full of delicious fulko-luchi and another plate of alur-dum. She places a glass of Apple juice beside the two plates in the tray.

'Mom, Titiksha is missing and dad doesn't want to file a police report.'

His mother momentarily pauses, glances at her husband once, and then looks at her son.

'He must have good reason for that.' She pulls a chair and sits in between her son and her husband by the dining table.

It's now that Neel considers his father's reason. He understands if he files a police report, and even if they accept it, they would keep coming to their house to update them or gather more information, thereby letting other people know about the matter. People have a special power of sniffing other's problem, and relaying a distorted version of it to the world.

Neel quietly has his breakfast against his wish, pondering about what he should do if not report to the police. One reason why he wants to involve them is because he needs someone to conduct the search for him. Now he will have to pursue Titiksha else he won't be able to rest in peace. But for how long?

'What if Titiksha doesn't return even today?' he asks.

Instead of his father, he hears his mother say, 'Another *luchi,* Babushona?'

'No. I have a meeting.' He looks at his watch and realizes he is already five minutes late. He quickly finishes the remaining luchi and alur-dum.

It takes Neel a little more than twenty minutes to arrive at one of the exits of the Park Street metro station. He stands at a corner, watching the sea of men and women moving out with the clutches of impatience and indifference. Neel would have taken his father's car but it has been in a service station since a day before. A taxi would mean reaching where he wants much after the scheduled time because of the peak traffic hours. Hence he reluctantly took the metro from Belgachia metro station.

Neel moves out of the metro station only when a majority of the crowd has pushed themselves out.

As he comes out, he takes a sharp left turn, and a few steps later he crosses the main road and takes a right on the footpath to go towards the Apeejay House. He is supposed to meet Nivrita there.

He waits for a minute by the Kotak Mahindra Bank inside the Apeejay campus after which Nivrita comes out. Just like the other day, Nivrita is in Indian wear. It's a white and blue figure-hugging salwar suit this time.

'You look fucked up. What happened?' she says continuing to walk. Neel tries to catch up with her.

'Titiksha didn't come home last night.'

Nivrita stops. So does Neel.

'Let's celebrate!' she says with a brio that doesn't go well with Neel.

'What do you mean?'

'I don't even have to snatch you from her now. She herself withdrew from you. So let's celebrate.'

'Titiksha is my girlfriend. And I'm serious.'

'Don't expect me to find her for you. I am not a detective.'

Neel hasn't even made such a proposition.

'Can you at least accompany me? I have no friends. My parents also don't seem much interested. They say I should wait till night, but I won't be able to. And I don't like going around alone searching for her.'

'Okay. I will accompany you.'

'Thanks Nivrita.'

'Thank me when you find her.'

She begins to walk again. So does Neel.

'Now tell me,' Nivrita says, 'Have you been to her office?'

'No.'

'Chances are if she went on her own, then she would attend office. If not, then at least we can know she applied for leave or not.'

And she just said she isn't a detective? She certainly thinks like one. First her figure aroused him, now her intelligence does. He wonders in how many other ways will Nivrita arouse him in the future.

'Do you even know how many illicit couples go to Digha and Mondarmoni citing office work and have fun there?'

Neel doesn't know. He hasn't even heard the names of the places.

'Where does she work?' Nivrita says.

'Cintus Finance.'

'Have you been there before?'

'Yes.'

Neel thinks a little and then says, 'Once.'

'Good. Where is it?'

'Infinity Building, Sector 5, Salt Lake.'

'Let's take the metro till Shova Bazaar and then we will take a shared-auto from there to Ultadanga, and change in-between to Karunamoyee and then to Sector 5.'

Nivrita starts scooting towards the metro station. She suddenly pauses and turns to see Neel standing still. She shrugs at him.

'Can we please take a taxi?' He has already dared a crowd once in the morning. Twice in a day will be too much for him to handle.

'Sure!'

In the taxi, Nivrita takes the opportunity to narrate a bit more of the story to him. Though Neel's mind is on Titiksha, still work is work. He listens carefully. Due to heavy traffic, it takes them two hours from Park Street to the Infinity building in Salt Lake Sector 5—the IT hub of Kolkata.

'Third floor,' he tells Nivrita who waits for him to pay off the taxi driver.

As the taxi speeds away, they enter the Infinity building, which, if Neel is to believe, has leased out one of its floors to Cintus Finance where Titiksha works. There weren't much people going inside or coming out at this point in time.

Together they go inside the giant building, take the elevator to the third floor, and move out to see the entire floor getting renovated. There is no proper entrance.

'Is this where she works?' Nivrita is as dumbfounded as Neel. There's a continuous noise of hammering which disturbs Neel. He keeps blinking involuntarily with every hammering.

There's also too much dust in the air. Both Neel and Nivrita cough together. Nivrita covers her nose with a handkerchief.

Neel excuses himself to a worker who is skinning a wooden frame.

'Excuse me dada, this is Cintus Finance, right? Where are all the employees?'

The worker looks up at Neel continuing to skin the wood, 'I don't know babu.' He is talking Bengali with a Bangladeshi accent.

'We have been working here for the last two weeks. I haven't seen anybody except our sahib who comes from time to time,' he adds and shifts his focus to the wood again.

'Two weeks?' Neel first darts a look of disbelief at the worker and then at Nivrita. Even she seems surprised.

'But I called the office last night,' Neel declares. Though he is looking at the worker, he is actually telling that to himself.

'Why don't you try the number again?' Nivrita suggests.

Neel takes out his mobile phone from his jeans' pocket and dials the office landline number of Cintus Finance that he has saved since the time Titiksha joined the firm.

'Does the office number even work?' Nivrita speaks with her handkerchief pressed against her nose.

'Of course! I dialled it last night itself. A man answered it.'

As the call matures, Neel puts it on speaker.

'This number has been temporarily suspended', says an electronic voice out aloud.

Neel gapes at his phone for a moment and then looks at Nivrita.

'What the…' he starts.

'Fuck!' she finishes off.

They quietly move out of the Infinity building. Nivrita spots a roadside tea stall on the right side of the building.

She goes up to it and orders two cups of tea to the lady running the stall. Her kid whispers something in her ear looking at Neel and they together laugh. Nivrita lights a Marlboro for herself. Since it's an open area, Neel doesn't mind Nivrita smoking. He just makes sure he is at a safe distance from her.

'I'm sorry. Smoking helps me think better, so do excuse me,' she says and takes a long puff. They are given tea in a small earthen tea pot by the tea-stall lady.

Neel sips his tea and looks at few guys looking back in his direction. All of them are checking out Nivrita. It makes Neel feel uncomfortable. He goes around and stands in front of her, blocking the other guys' view of her back.

'Why would she lie to you about a fake office?' Nivrita asks almost done with her cigarette. One small puff and she throws it down, stamping it with her foot.

'It wasn't a fake office. I have been here before with her.'

'Once,' she stresses on the word.

Neel is trying to recollect something.

'I think I never went inside the building. Or did I? I'm not too sure.'

'Titiksha brought you here herself?'

'Yes.' This he clearly remembers. They had come together after she was selected through a campus interview.

Nivrita continues to sip her tea. Once finished, she turns to throw the tea-pot in a dustbin, when she notices the other guys at the tea stall. They have tags of their respective companies around their neck. Nivrita walks up to them, surprising Neel.

They are four of them in all. All brace themselves seeing the girl whom they had just mentally undressed approaching them.

'Hey brother!' she says. Three of them instantly relax as if they don't want to hear anything more from her. She looks at the fourth one who still looks eager to talk.

'Do you work in Cintus Finance?'

'No. I'm in CTS.' The guy adjusts his tag so that Nivrita can see it properly.

'Okay. Could you please tell me what happened to Cintus Finance. It used to have its office in the Infinity building.'

The guy thinks hard for a moment and then says, 'I don't think I have ever heard of that company.' He looks at the other guys for some clue but they too nod their head in a 'no'.

'Thanks,' Nivrita says curtly and goes to Neel who has now finished his tea.

'He has not even heard about the company, wow.'

'He probably doesn't know.'

'I have been working here for the last three years,' says the guy raising his voice from behind. 'I can bet my life there's been no company's office with this name here in the last three years at least.'

'Thank you,' Neel tells the guy.

'When were you here?' Nivrita asks Neel.

'Almost four years back.'

'The guy may be right in that case,' Nivrita says with a frown.

'You mean for the last four years Titiksha has been telling me that she is going to office but she isn't?'

'That or she never told you about the new address. Or she just told you about a different office from the beginning. Or maybe she changed in between and never told you about it. Or...'

'It's okay. The bigger question is why would she do that?' he asks.

'It's useless to stand here and guess a girl's intention. Find her. Ask her.'

Both cross the road to reach the opposite side from where they will get a taxi to wherever they decide to go.

'How about going to your parents and…' Nivrita proposes.

'Not my parents,' Neel blurts out instantly. There is no way that he will present Nivrita in front of them. They will pose unnecessary questions because except for Titiksha, Neel has never introduced any girl to his parents. In fact they may even guess because of Nivrita that Neel and Titiksha have had a fight and now she is missing. His parents are good at guessing things about him.

'I mean, I'll see what to do next.'

'Fair enough.'

A taxi goes by. The driver slows down seeing Nivrita wave at him.

'Park Street,' she says getting in.

'I think I will go home. Can we please do the rest of the story narration tomorrow?'

Nivrita takes a few seconds to think and then says, 'Okay.'

The taxi moves forward, takes a turn, and disappears. Waving off the smoke from the taxi, Neel coughs mildly. He gets a call on his phone. It's his father. He picks it up.

'Babushona, can you come home? We need to talk about Titiksha.'

Neel takes a second to respond.

'Is she back?'

'Just come home Babushona.'

Back at his parents' place, Neel sees his father sitting with a man who is in a police uniform. Neel stands frozen. He feels there's some bad news. Has Titiksha committed suicide? Or met with a fatal accident?

'Come Neel. Meet Inspector Parimal Biswas.'

The inspector glances obliquely at Neel and extends his hand for a handshake. Neel swallows a lump and then grabs his hand feebly. Inspector Biswas shakes his hand with confidence. The man looks too good to be a police inspector.

'Nice to meet you Neel babu,' Parimal says. The handshake tells Neel that this man could have rehearsed meeting him a number of times.

'I have told him about Titiksha's disappearance. He is going to be investigating the case,' Neel's father says.

Neel relaxes. It means they still don't know about Titiksha. He sits down opposite the inspector on the couch and looks at his father for some clue.

'After you moved out, I thought about it. You were right. It's our duty to involve the police.'

'Where are Titiksha's parents?' Parimal asks Neel.

'Abroad.'

'Hmm. Where does she work?'

'Cintus Finance.'

'Hmm.'

'But the office is not there anymore.'

Both Biswas and Neel's father stare at him.

'I am coming from there. The place where the office used to be has been under renovation from the past two weeks. I called the office landline number which Titiksha had once given me but that too isn't working since morning.'

'Since morning?' Parimal repeats after him.

Neel nods.

'Hmm. It does seem like a missing case. Anyway...' Inspector Parimal Biswas stands up. So do Neel and his father.

'I shall see what I can do.' The inspector pulls up his trousers that has fallen a little below his protruding belly.

'And don't worry,' he says, 'Mr Chatterjee, all of it will be discreet. So when did you last see her?'

'Last morning. No, in fact I haven't seen her since I woke up yesterday morning.'

'Did you two fight over anything?'

The images of Titiksha mocking him and stating she would go to his parents flashes in front of his eyes. And then the kinky blind-folded sex session which he thought would humiliate her but something else happened. He can't say the truth, else the suspicion will fall directly on him. A boyfriend who fought with his girlfriend because he found out that she was dating another guy and she goes missing the very next day—a classic crime-of-passion case.

'No. We rarely fought.'

'They love each other.' Neel's father steps in. 'In fact his mother and I were thinking of getting them married this year itself.

The marriage bit is a lie but Neel keeps quiet.

'Hmm, okay. I shall call you Neel babu, if I get any information regarding her. Good day,' Parimal trails off and turns to leave.

'Don't you need a photograph of hers?' Neel interrupts the inspector's gait.

Inspector Parimal Biswas turns to exchange an uncomfortable glance with Neel's father.

'Thanks for reminding me. You have one with you?'

'Not here with me. Actually Titiksha and I used to click photographs very rarely. Only on birthdays or...' Neel tries to remember something. Parimal and Neel's father swap a furtive glance.

'Dad,' Neel turns towards his father, 'I think we did click a few photographs when Titiksha was here.'

'Did we?'

'Of course. Remember I clicked one of mom, you, and hers together and then you clicked one of Titiksha's and mine?

'I don't.'

Neel's father, it seems, knows what his son is talking about but doesn't want to show he does.

'One minute inspector.' Neel goes inside, calling out to his mother. Half a minute later, he comes out with a Nikon CoolPix digital camera. His mother has also come out following him.

'Wait, let me show you.'

'What happened?' Inspector Parimal Biswas asks as Neel stops surfing the photographs in the camera.

'All the other photographs are here but none from the day Titiksha and I were here.'

'I told you Babushona we didn't get enough time to click any photographs,' his father says as if making a point.

'Never mind. I'll get my own camera. It's kept somewhere in my flat.'

Neel takes his leave before the inspector does.

'Where are you going? It's almost lunch time. Stay Babushona,' pleads Neel's mother.

'I'll come back soon, mom.'

Neel leaves for his rented flat. All through the way, he keeps thinking hard about the day Titiksha and he had visited his parents' place. It was the day he had introduced her to them. They had definitely clicked photographs. In fact he remembers the positions too. In all, four photographs had been clicked: two of both of them together by the dining table and the couch, one of his parents and Titiksha by the couch, and one of Titiksha, his mother, and him in the balcony. Then how come those photographs were not there in the camera anymore? Has someone deleted them intentionally? Does he have a backup in his laptop? Neel isn't sure. He hasn't seen them since a long time now. Has he ever seen them? He can't recollect. Then he remembers his mother had not let him take the camera with him. He doesn't remember why.

Neel reaches his rented flat in Lake Town. He goes straight to the bedroom where there is a Godrej almirah. As he moves towards it, his foot hits something. The hit takes the object to someplace else. Neel looks around and notices the object is now lying under the table. He bends down to pick it up. It's a cigarette packet. Marlboro. Nivrita's brand. *What is it doing here*? Neel asks himself. Was Nivrita here in his absence? But how can she be here? Only Titiksha and he had the keys. The main door is locked properly. There is no sign of forced entry either. A pigeon flaps its wings outside the window where it has laid an egg on one of the empty flower pots left there by an earlier tenant. Neel never felt like removing it. Nor did Titiksha. Now as he looks at the window, and notices that it is half open. He guesses someone must have thrown the cigarette packet from outside. Why?

Neel opens the cigarette packet. He finds something has been stashed inside it. He brings it out. It looks like an old piece of paper...a cut out of lips...inside there's a poem written...or is it a song?

Just like it was in the story Nivrita was narrating to him. And the one Neel is writing.

FROM NEEL'S MANUSCRIPT

10

Love makes all of life's coincidences seem like real intention. My parents' divorce, my shifting to Salt Lake International School, getting drenched on my first day to school, Neel's presence in the class, the shirt-swap, and all of the subsequent events were no coincidence even though it seemed so when they were happening. Coincidences in life—they make our stories interesting.

I don't know much about what happened at the party after I walked out of it, after Neel's open confession that he loved me. Later Neel told me nothing much happened. Avni left the party citing a headache. His parents, more importantly, were not harsh on him. For the first time in his life, he said, his parents didn't make a fuss about his choice. I was happy to know that because it only meant they had accepted his choice—they had accepted me.

In school, Neel and I were given the couple-of-the-year kind of treatment. It's not that Neel and I talked much. But because all our classmates kept nudging us respectively all the time, we felt like we were in an affair which neither of us formally maintained. I kept stalking him in school and at times he stalked me too. The hide-n-seek we played gave me soul-orgasms. It was a game we both were participating but neither accepted it. He made me forget to keep track of time. And that's the best thing anyone can do for someone. It's because time brings the past and future into existence. With my mind off time, I was finally 'living' in the truest sense of the word.

I couldn't take Neel off my mind though. I felt like I was possessed by him. So much so that at certain moments it didn't even matter if I loved him or if he loved me for I knew he had consumed me, and I could live a life off that consumption.

A few weeks after the birthday party incident, and after a lot of thought, I finally asked him, 'Why did you say that?'

'What?'

'That you love me.'

'Why did you tell my mom that you loved me?'

'I felt like doing so.'

'Same here.'

'What did you feel?'

'That I love you.'

I blushed a little but didn't make it obvious.

'No, I mean what exactly did you feel and why did you say it only at that moment?'

Neel, with a frown, started looking here and there, as if he was desperately searching for an apt answer.

'I like your presence. And it does something to me. I don't know what.'

In that 'I-don't-know-what', I got to know a lot about him, about me, and about us.

'Tell me,' he said, 'When did you fall for me?'

'The day we swapped shirts.'

'You mean you wouldn't have fallen for me if we hadn't swapped shirts?'

It was my turn to surmise an apt answer.

'Why don't you see it this way: it's because we were supposed to fall for each other that we swapped shirts. Incidents are merely an excuse. A means to an end.'

'You know what I like best about you?'

I shrugged.

'Forget it. If I tell you, then you will consciously try to maintain it. I would rather love it if you keep doing whatever it is unknowingly.'

If that's what made you fall for me, I will...I wondered but we left it at that.

All through the night, I kept guessing what it could be. What could be that thing in me which was worthy enough for someone to love me? I was lying on my bed, smiling to myself, when Yo-didun came and sat beside me.

'So it has finally happened.'

'What Yo-didun?' I sat up on the bed feigning innocence.

'When a girl of sixteen years smiles to herself before going to bed, it means it has happened.'

'It has,' I said rather softly. 'Why, shouldn't it have happened?'

Yo-didun sighed touching my chin with her fingertips and then immediately kissed those fingers as if she stole a kiss from my chin.

'It's strange, isn't it? Falling in love eventually becomes the one big event of your life. I'm seventy-nine. And every night I keep thinking about the number of times I fell in love.'

'Did you fall in love more than once, Yo-didun?'

'More than once? I fell in love so many times that I have lost count.'

That was a revelation. Until then, I had thought Dadu was the only man in her life.

'If the one you love doesn't make you fall in love with him again and again, then you were never in love with that person to begin with.' I met your Dadu for the first time on the first of November 1955. He was my father's favourite student. The next year he got himself a job and we were married. He died sooner than I thought he would. In the days that followed I really thought I had lost him, but as I kept thinking about our times when he was there with me, I understood he was that kind of a novel which even after you are done reading it, stays with you. You keep wondering about its lines, certain passages, and then you realize that there is more meaning to them than you thought while reading it for the first time.

And thus even after your Dadu's death I kept falling in love with him again and again.'

She gave me an endearing smile.

I hope my love for Neel is something similar, I thought. I slept well that night.

Avni started avoiding me in school after Neel's birthday party, and her silly groupies kept looking at me detestfully whenever I passed by them. Not that I cared about them, but I never abused Avni or her groupies because I knew if I was in her place, I would also not appreciate someone snatching Neel from me or acknowledge if Neel willingly got inclined towards any other girl just like he did towards me being in a relationship with Avni. True, he wasn't in a relationship with Avni by choice, but then he could have told Avni about it rather than playing on with the relationship just for the sake of it. Maybe she loved him just as much as I did.

This negative feeling towards Neel disturbed me. I had never experienced anything like this before. I knew nobody was perfect but still I would have been happier if Neel had told Avni that he was in a relationship with her because his parents wanted him to be, and not because he was really in love with her. And what was that they did behind the bookshelf in the library? I had seen it only once but I was sure they had kissed a lot many times before and after that. It troubled me so much that I chose to become blind towards Neel's imperfections. For every imperfection of his,

I was churning out a perfect excuse to cover him. I wasn't comfortable doing it. I never talked to him or anybody else about it either. Since my parents were divorced, I had already seen how brittle relationships could get with time. I didn't want Neel and my relationship to ever reach that brittle stage where one of us broke it into pieces and told the other that it was for good.

From the very beginning, I had full faith that Neel would love me one day. But when he actually started loving me, I began feeling insecure about him. Maybe it was because before Neel I had nobody in my life, whom I could hold on to, whom I could call mine. He was my first emotional possession. People don't leave their house locked fearing their stuff would be stolen. They do so because they know they have something priceless with them which they can't afford to share or lend to others. But how could I lock Neel only to myself?

From the night this thought occurred to me, I started noticing weird things about Neel which I had never noticed before, or had chosen to ignore in love. Every time I met him in school or in tuition, I had a problem if he talked to a girl or laughed with her. If he didn't look at me when I was looking at him, I felt enraged. I started expecting things from him which I knew didn't matter, and yet those insignificant things would hurt me if left unfulfilled by Neel. Until one day he told me something after school.

'Mom wants to meet you Titiksha.'

I didn't know why but with those words I felt Neel and my relationship would never ever be brittle again, that my fears were uncalled for. To my heart's relief, I somehow convinced myself that no other girl would ever be able to snatch Neel away from me. Yo-didun was right. There's always this craving for a physical proximity—and physical ownership—in everyone's idea of love.

11

'May I please talk with her alone, Neel?'

We were in Neel's bedroom. Neel's mother was great to talk to, quite different from what she was on Neel's birthday. I had not slept the night before, wondering what was it that she wanted to meet me for. But seeing her favourable attitude towards me, I relaxed.

'Sure mom,' Neel said. He gave me an assuring look and left the room. As he went away, his mom smiled at me, stood up, and ambled towards the door to lock it. I kept looking at her as she picked up her costly-looking purse and rummaged through it. She took out a cigarette packet and a lighter. She lit the cigarette and put the packet and the lighter back inside her purse. She took a deep puff and came back to sit beside me. She suddenly made a face as if I was stinking.

'Neel told me that your parents are divorced and that you live with your uncle who works as an accountant in a college?'

'Yes. That's true.'

'You know that you don't belong to our financial class, right?'

I knew what she meant. By then I'd guessed the goody-goody attitude she had showed in the beginning was only because Neel was around. This was her real self.

'I know I don't belong to a rich family,' I said.

'Then what are you doing with Neel?'

'I love him.'

'That's what every poor girl says when she meets a rich boy.'

In that moment, I realized why Neel's mom wanted to meet me. She wanted me to move out of his life simply because I didn't belong to, as she implied, the same financial class as them. I also understood why she was so submissive in front of Avni all the time. She belonged to an even higher financial class than Neel.

'I'm not a poor girl. Both my parents work and they sponsor my studies. I am from a well-to-do family.'

'How very wonderful of them! Equally good is the fact that you are aware that they are working hard to educate you. So why don't you make use of this opportunity and study hard instead of loitering around with my son?'

'I study hard aunty.'

'But all this love business won't help your focus.'

'My love for Neel doesn't defocus me in anyway.'

My resilience wasn't helping her intention. She must have thought I was a TGIF when she called me here. Well, I was never a TGIF anyway. Finally she stubbed her cigarette in an ashtray and said, 'Forget Neel. Neel's dad and I have grand plans for his wedding with Avni. Now come out with me and tell Neel that you will never meet him again, and that he deserves someone better.' She held my chin roughly and pressed her fingers on my face hard. It hurt but I didn't budge except for looking at her straight as she said, 'Is that clear?'

A few seconds passed by. Her eyes were burning with contempt. I nodded in agreement after which she let go of my face.

'You are a nice girl, Titiksha.'

I followed her as she moved out. My steps were heavy for I knew this could be the last time I was meeting Neel. I knew I would continue to see him in school and tuition but with a sense of loss, knowing he would eventually be someone else's. His mom wanted me to tell him that he deserved someone better than me. But how could I tell him all that when I had desired and coveted Neel ever since I saw him, and also knew he did the same for me? Was this temporary life that I lived between seeing Neel for the first time to the day when he left his mom and me alone in his bedroom, an illusion? Yo-didun always told me life was one big magic trick and if one wanted to enjoy the trick, one shouldn't be too inquisitive about it. Otherwise the trick shall disappoint you. Was I being too inquisitive about my own life being in love with Neel?

As I reached the hall room downstairs, I found Neel flipping through a sports magazine, sitting by the sofa. The Doberman was sitting by his side. Neel stood up the moment he saw me. His mom was standing by the stairs looking at us. At me in particular.

'Hey, are you leaving?' Neel came up to me.

'Yes.'

'So early? Weren't we supposed to go for tuition together?' I stole a glance at his mom who was waiting for me to tell Neel whatever she had told me upstairs in his bedroom.

'I need to tell you something, Neel.'

He gave me an enquiring frown.

'Your mother told me something while you were here.'

Neel looked up once at his mom and then at me.

'What did mom tell you?'

'She said…' I raised my voice a bit and continued. 'She likes me a lot and never wants me to leave you, come what may. Actually she thinks we are a perfect couple.'

Neel beamed as he looked up again at his mom and gave her a flying kiss.

'I love you mom,' he said.

His mother returned his kiss with another flying kiss rather reluctantly, all the while looking at me with scorn.

'Let's go for our tuition now. And please, let's walk. No car this time,' I said to Neel. It was directed more at his mom, though.

That was perhaps the first time I had claimed my ownership of Neel to someone other than myself. If I ever deserved the Best-Bitch Award, this was the moment.

12

Yo-didun couldn't believe Neel's mom had told me such nasty things. But she was also proud of how I handled the situation. Although it was spiteful, his mom deserved every bit of it. Her words weren't exactly honey-coated either. After listening to me, Yo-didun also said that's how great love stories were created: when someone dared to do something unexpected or when someone decided to sacrifice something dear. I had done both that day. I had dared to disagree with Neel's mom and I had also sacrificed my self-esteem owing to my love for Neel. Stupidly enough, I was feeling happy even after I knew I had been humiliated like never before.

For the next few weeks, Neel would take a cycle-rickshaw and come to my mama's house to fetch me. The first day I was a bit nervous seeing him by the house gate.

'Please don't come here,' I told him fearing mama's reaction. If he saw a boy from my school at his place, he would have thought of all kinds of things. I have never had any boy calling me up, even on my landline number, ever, so a boy visiting my place would have been stretching it too far. Even the neighbourhood wasn't a good one. People noticed whoever frequented the neighbourhood, whose house they went to, when and why. Thankfully the first day nobody really noticed Neel.

From then on, Neel decided to wait for me at the bus stop close to my place. I too used to move out a few minutes before my normal time.

Bijoya mami said she wouldn't be able to provide me breakfast because I was leaving the house ten minutes early. I sacrificed my breakfast. When I told Neel about it, he solved my breakfast problem by bringing me breakfast from his home. I didn't like that.

'But the cook loves me. She gives me extra without telling mom about it.'

Sharing breakfast with him behind the bus stop together had its own charm, and I chose not to say anything to disrupt it. Neel would intentionally come to school early. After his car dropped him, he would take a cycle-rickshaw to the bus stop where I would meet him, we would share breakfast, and together take another cycle-rickshaw to school. Everyday seemed like a new life. We talked when we were quiet, we were quiet when we talked, we were happy when we looked serious, and we were serious when we were happy. Every significant exchange between us was special and every insignificant thing was magical.

It was while getting down from the cycle-rickshaw in front of the school one day that Avni saw us. Not that we cared. We were on our way inside the school premises when she came up to us and said, 'So Titiksha has brought you to the level of a cycle-rickshaw from your suave car? Good luck Neel for your future,' saying this she was gone.

What I never understood was why this world was infested with people who judged an individual on the basis of their possessions and not what was within them. Nobody, except Yo-didun, appreciated the fact that I loved Neel a lot. All people noticed was if my parents were divorced or not, if I lived in a big house or not. Going by Neel's mom, I would have deserved him if my family was richer than Avni's. Why this materialization of love? Yo-didun had once told me how Bijoya mami married my mama because he had a secure job then. But then so many people might have had secure jobs? Given a choice, would Bijoya mami live with all of them? Prior to that, I always thought it was simple: you love someone then you get married, and remain together forever. But seeing his parents' reaction as well as how my own parents handled their marriage, even when it was a love marriage, I was totally perplexed. I tried to share my quandaries with Yo-didun at times but instead of answering like she always did, she asked me to discover the answers myself as I moved along in life. I didn't know how Neel perceived this. If he thought my love for him was manipulating him in some way, and making him compromise the luxury he was born with, then my love for him was a failure.

I didn't react at Avni's words when she retorted about the 'car to cycle-rickshaw' thing. Neel asked me to avoid her for she was being plain jealous. I believed him. During recess, Avni came to me and said, 'In case Neel has not told you before, he and I have made out many times—sometimes at his place, sometimes at mine, and also in various corners of our school. So even if you guys are making out, just remember you will always be his second choice. I was and will be his first girl. And you won't ever know how it is to be someone's first.'

And then the image of her going behind the bookshelf, followed by Neel in the library during my first week in school, flashed in front of me. The image told me I would never be what Avni was for him—his first girl. Probably for the first time I understood what jealousy was and how quickly can it burn a heart in love into ashes.

Chapter 9

IS TITIKSHA HIDING, MISSING, OR...DEAD?

Neel feels like there's some weight on him. The weight seems to be shifting back and forth around his pelvis. As his conscious mind slowly flowers, Neel opens his eyes. He sees Titiksha riding him with her hands on his chest. When did she come in? He wonders and looks at her loose hair covering one side of her face. Her moans are just about audible. As she jerks her head back and straight, the hair shifts from her face a bit. Neel notices her eyes shut tightly, and she looks drunk with passion.

Neel has no time to question her. He can feel the carnal pleasure himself. He is about to raise his hands to support her juggling breasts with his palm when he hears a bark; a sharp and loud bark. Neel twists his head sideways and sees to his horror a cage inside which a Doberman is barking out at him. Its canines look razor sharp. The Doberman eyes him with such ferocity that given just a little opening in the cage, it will barge out of it and eat him alive. How and why did Titiksha do that; bring a dog inside his flat? What the fuck is wrong with her?

Neel hears another bark. He pans his eyes and notices there are two, three, four, five, six, seven cages around him in the room and each one has a shining brown Doberman locked inside it, barking away at Neel with darting looks.

And at the centre of the cages are Neel and Titiksha fucking away naked.

With every fierce bark, Neel's eyes flicker with fear. He is too scared to find his voice. He tries calling out to Titiksha but she puts her hand on his mouth and continues to ride him. Her moans and the dogs' barks make a scary yet wild sexual concoction for Neel. Before he can choose between pleasure and fear, Titiksha grabs his hands and pulls him forward, herself lying on her back. It happens so quickly that Neel doesn't get enough time to resist. In an instant Titiksha, from being on top of him, goes under him. They are in the missionary position now with Titiksha tightening the grip of her thighs around Neel's hips. But there is one problem. There is only a difference of fifteen inches between one of the Doberman's face and Neel's. He had not seen this particular one because it had been hiding behind Titiksha till then. Now looking at it eye to eye, he knows this one has to be the fiercest of the lot. It barks. Neel shuts his eyes tight. He feels a pat on his butt from Titiksha, demanding him to move his hips faster. But his focus is no longer on giving Titiksha what she wants. It's the dog. It's his fear. By now he has understood the dog won't come out of the cage. It helps him eye his fear better. And the more he gets accustomed to the fear, the more his pelvic thrusts increase in intensity. The dog isn't barking anymore but only eyeing him with a growl exposing its canines. The other dogs are surprisingly quiet now. The dog takes a backward stance and leaps onto the cage with full force. Neel almost feels its tongue on his nose tip. His thrusts slow down. Suddenly out of nowhere, Neel barks out loud at it. The dog mellows down. Neel has surprised himself by barking like a dog. He looks down at Titiksha. She is moaning in ecstasy. He hears the dog bark. Neel barks louder. The dog barks even louder. Before Neel can continue this barking contest, he feels something building up inside him; an orgasm. He fastens his hip movement and feels as if his thigh and hip muscles may suffer a spasm any moment. As Neel barks once more, his head goes closer to the cage. The dog instantly bites onto his hair and tries to drag him. Neel hollers in pain. Titiksha hollers in pleasure. The dogs bark out in chorus. Neel's heart is in his mouth. Titiksha's mind is numb.

'Help me, Titiksha. Help me,' Neel cries out. He looks around to see but there's no Titiksha. There are no dogs either. There's nothing in the room, in fact, except for haunting silence. *It was all a fucking dream?* Neel wonders sitting up on his bed. He is naked and has a full blown erection which dies quickly. He rubs his eyes wondering who sees such a weird dream; making out with your girlfriend with killer dogs around.

As he sits alone on the bed, it dawns on him that he has probably lost Titiksha forever. From now on maybe he will have to only dream about her to get to her. Neel feels defeated from within. He has always loved her from the time he met her in college. She may not be the most perfect woman, but he still loves her.

For the first time since Titiksha's sudden disappearance, Neel misses her. Till now he has only thought about her absence but the dream makes him miss her presence. He is emotionally low. He starts crying. Wailing, in fact. In a matter of a minute though he composes himself and gets up. He is about to move out of the bedroom when his eyes fall on the Marlboro packet he had found in his room last night. He picks it up from the table beside the bed. He had kept the chart paper cut out under the packet. Now holding onto the cigarette packet, he picks up the lips-shaped chart paper cut out. He re-reads the lines on the paper. He doesn't know if it's the same song that the character Titiksha wrote for Neel in the story on his birthday because Nivrita never told him the song. But Neel nonetheless feels an eerie similarity between the two. He casually flips it. It's a note of sorts stating: *remember where we met for the first time?*

We? As in Neel and...? Nivrita or Titiksha? He met Nivrita at the Jaipur Literature Festival. So what about it? And he met Titiksha in college. Maybe Titiksha wants to meet him in their college. Why? Maybe she will explain the mystery behind the disappearance when he meets her. But why the cigarette packet? Neel thinks for a while and then looks at his watch. It's 10 in the morning. He has never slept till so late. Whatever happened to his sense of time? He hurries to the toilet. At least he has got a lead now. His college. Maybe all his questions will be answered when he gets to college.

Neel quickly gets ready to leave. He takes a taxi to where his college is: Munkundapur. It takes him close to two hours to reach the place. He gets down from the taxi after paying the fare and looks around. This is the place where he met Titiksha for the first time. He still remembers that she was wearing a yellow salwar kameez and was carrying a bag. She seemed to have an aura unlike others. Talking of others, he doesn't know what happened to them. The ones he used to talk to most in college were Arijit Pal, Anirban Debnath, and Rohit Haldar. Neel has no idea what happened to them after college. He tried to keep in touch but they suddenly didn't seem interested. Then Neel too gave up chasing them.

Standing by the road opposite to which stood the college once, Neel finds himself staring at an open field which is fenced by barbed wire and in the middle of it there's a bamboo stick planted on the earth. On top of the stick a board hangs: Gemini Realtors Pvt. Ltd. The entire college building, which at the time of his graduation was expanding, is nowhere in the sight now. Neel's throat has gone dry. He is sweating a lot more than he usually does.

He notices a man walking by on the opposite side of the road.

'Excuse me, dada.'

The man stops to look at him.

'What?'

Neel crosses the road and comes to the man.

'Isn't there a college here somewhere?'

'Here?' The man looks at the direction Neel is pointing at.

'I don't see one,' the man gives Neel a are-you-mad look.

'I mean there used to be one here.' Neel reluctantly changed the tense.

'So?'

'What happened to it?'

'I don't know. I haven't seen any college here. How long ago was this?'

'Four-five years.'

The man's face twisted in a let-me-think manner.

'I think you should ask Madhu da about this. He'll know.'

'Madhu da?'

'Come.'

The man walked ahead and Neel followed him. They reached a small wretched looking motel by the road. Neel had not noticed it when he came to the lane in a taxi a few minutes ago.

'Madhu da, this gentleman wants to know if there was any college here four-five years ago.'

Madhu da is sitting on a raised platform behind a rickety desk by the entrance of the motel. Looking at his upper half, Neel is sure he is way taller than the normal Indian standard.

He looks like he has come straight from his bed to the motel. He looks up at Neel and says, 'College?'

Neel nods.

'Yes there used to be one. Students from the college used to come in my motel too.'

Neel relaxed. He couldn't have possibly handled a 'no' from Madhu da. Neel himself must have missed this motel during his college years because he was picked up and dropped right in front of the college in his father's car. And he didn't look around much during those days.

'What happened to it?' Neel inquired.

'I don't know. I think five years back, students stopped coming. Then one day the building was broken down.'

'Broken down?' Neel actually whispers it to himself but the two men hear it clearly.

'Was it an old college?' asks the man who brought Neel here.

'Not really. It remained for four years.'

'Four years? A college for four years! What nonsense! You can't believe anyone these days. Everyone is a scamster.' The man is visibly disgusted. 'I'm sure it must have been some illegal racket to lure students.'

Neel does a quick math. 'Four years' Madhu da said. It means the college was there only during the time he studied there. Neither before that nor after. Coincidence?

'Look gentleman,' the man says, 'Why don't you look it up on the Internet. The college must have its own website if they are genuine. Maybe they changed its location. My son says the entire world is on the Internet these days. You know Madhu da...'

Neel's mind is elsewhere. Why would Titiksha tell me if I remember where we first met when there's no college here anymore? Or is it the disappearance of the college itself that Titiksha wants me to know about? Is it a clue to her disappearance as well?

'Dada, khe jaben na?' Madhu da queries if Neel wants to have lunch at his motel. He looks at Madhu da and says, 'No, thanks.'

By the time Neel gets himself a taxi to go back home, he has a plan in his mind: he would go to his flat and check about the college on Google. Titiksha has left her Internet dongle at their flat. Its time he should forgo his usual boycott of the virtual world and for a change, make use of it.

Another one and a half hours later, Neel is there at his flat. The elevator is out of order. He takes the stairs and reaches his flat. There is a heap of clothes in front of his door. He is skeptical about touching them. He drops on one knee and picks them up: one grass-green coloured top and a white jeans. Both smeared with something red...blood. Neel instantly let's go of the clothes. They belong to Titiksha. That's what she was wearing when Nivrita saw her last in the mall. Even he had seen a glimpse of it. What the heck is this all about?

Neel notices the back of the jeans which is now on the floor again. Something is written in blood there. He picks up the jeans and unfolds it completely. He is now able to read the note clearly:

Neel is a murderer.

⌛

Neel doesn't know for how long he has been sitting by his rented flat's door, and crying holding on to the grass-green top and the white jeans, and sniffing it regularly as if that would make Titiksha appear in front of him. The worst has finally happened. Someone has killed Titiksha.

Neel notices a middle-aged woman climb down the stairs. She pauses seeing Neel. She senses he needs help but Neel quickly hides the clothes, wipes his tears and turns his head away indicating he isn't interested. As the woman climbs down the stairs, now with a suspicious gaze, Neel gets up with heavy legs and long-drawn breaths. He takes time to unlock the flat. The key simply isn't going inside the lock. His mind is unable to focus on anything. After a good minute of struggle he unlocks the door.

As he closes the door behind, feeling emotionally drained, he clips his nose with his fingers. There's a rotten stink in the flat. Neel looks around but there's nothing rotting anywhere. He is having trouble breathing now. He tries to follow the stink and goes to the small corridor connecting the hall and the bedroom. As he passes by his washing machine in the small corridor, he stops. The stink is the maximum in this area. Neel drops the blood smeared top and the jeans he is carrying on the floor. And with trembling hands opens the lid of the washing machine—the stench that comes up from it pushes back Neel. Then slowly he tries to look inside by clasping his nose tightly. What he sees makes him scream out with plain horror.

'Oh God. Oh God! OH MY frigging GOD!'

There are chopped pieces of flesh inside the washing machine stuffed up to the brim. Neel collapses on the floor. Someone has chopped Titiksha into pieces, and stuffed her body parts inside the washing machine is Neel's conclusion before he loses consciousness.

It's the icky stink of flesh that brings Neel back to consciousness after about an hour or so. He gets up with a start, holding his head. He has a mild headache. Neel opens the washing machine's lid. There are two pieces of eyes glaring at him. Neel immediately shuts it. He quickly examines the windows of the flat. All are shut tightly. Neel relaxes. If the windows were open, all the inhabitants of the building would have been here by now. And what would he have told them? His girlfriend was missing and now he has her chopped pieces inside the washing machine of his flat? The residents would not waste a second to call the police and hand over Neel to them; the prima facie murderer. What is written on Titiksha's jeans? That Neel is a murderer. Does that mean Neel has killed Titiksha? And he doesn't know about it? Wow! What does that note mean, really?

Neel has reached the washbasin of the kitchen. He washes his face properly. Still he can't forget the image of the chopped flesh pieces. He washes his face for few more minutes. And then puts his head directly under the tap. It relaxes him slightly.

He takes out a bottle of cold water from the refrigerator and gulps it down. Who could have killed Titiksha with such hatred? She didn't have many friends or enemies. The only person she used to fight with was him. And whatever may be written on the dress, he hadn't killed her. But then who did? Neel is thinking hard. Could it be the guy with whom Titiksha was going around? He must have killed her and has now pinned the murder on Neel? He has seen one such case in a crime show on television at his parents' place where an illicit lover murdered his woman. In fact only he could have got the flat keys from Titiksha and dumped the pieces inside. How very convenient of him. But what went so wrong between them that he had to do this?

I'll find out who that guy is and kill him with my own hands after he confesses the reason for killing my beloved Titiksha. Enough of emotions now, Neel tells himself resolutely, it's time for some action. He keeps the bottle back inside the refrigerator. He brings out his handkerchief from his pocket and ties it around his nose and mouth to negate the stink. He opens the wooden wardrobe under the kitchen sink and brings out three big plastic packets from it. He heads towards the washing machine. He stands right in front of it holding its lid. He closes his eyes and makes a mental count...1...2...3. And then opens the lid in a flash. He feels like throwing up but somehow doesn't. He picks up the chopped pieces, and transfers it onto the three plastic packets, one at a time. Once done, he ties the packets well and takes them to the kitchen again. He empties the refrigerator and stuffs all the three packets inside it. He has seen this in a movie Titiksha had forcefully made him watch once. He never knew he would be enacting the same scene in real life. He remains still for a moment after closing the refrigerator's door. Then he vomits his guts out. Sobs. Vomits again. Sobs again. Then he cleans it all up and puts the blood-stained clothes inside the washing machine.

As he goes to the drawing room with two room fresheners in hand, he notices blood patches on the floor which he had missed earlier. Neel first mops all the patches from the floor, and then empties the two room-fresheners in the flat. Then he opens the windows, takes a bath, and sits down to think what he should do next.

If Titiksha's guy is trying to pin him as the murderer, then first he will have to track the guy down. And if the other guy is innocent, then he can at least give him a lead to whoever else could have done this. Though Neel thinks the first one is more probable. But how does he get to the other guy? Neel thinks hard and recalls why he came home from Mukundapur in the afternoon. He had to check the college website. The college where he met Titiksha for the first time, the same college the paper note in the cigarette packet led him to, in an indirect way.

Soon Neel gets busy with his laptop and finally googles the college's name: Neelkanth College of Engineering. There's no link suggesting the college's website. Neel ponders for a while and then goes to the AICTE website—the body which labels every engineering college of its worth. He searches the list carefully but there's no mention of Neelkanth College. Neel shuts the laptop screen in disgust. How is it possible? He had been given a certificate from the college which he had later given to the bank as well during his appointment as an employee. Was that a bogus certificate? Was Neelkanth College a bogus college? In that case, even Titiksha's certificate would be bogus. Is that why, maybe, Cintus Finance had expelled her, and she didn't tell him anything out of embarrassment?

Nothing makes any sense to Neel except that things are not right. There's a major flaw somewhere which he now knows but can't put his finger on to just yet. And that's what frustrates him. He won't let Titiksha's killer rest in peace. But he can't even share it with anyone that she is dead. That stage is gone. He should have done that the moment he saw the clothes, but how would he know that she had been stuffed inside the washing machine? Should he simply tell his parents? They will understand he is innocent. No, wait. Will they? What if they tell everything to Inspector Parimal Biswas and he comes to find the body in the refrigerator. What alibi does he have? He doesn't even know the guy with whom Titiksha was in the mall's washroom. But...Nivrita may identify him. Yes, she said she saw him. So should he call Nivrita?

Neel's phone buzzes and he shrieks out in shock. It is Nivrita calling. Neel presses the green button and puts the phone against his ear.

'Neel, where have you been all day? We have to hurry up now with the story. I want to get it published this year. Do you get that?'

As Neel's heart beats chugs back to normal, he wonders how come whenever he thinks of Nivrita either her message pops up, or a call, or at times she herself turns up. Who the hell is she...the devil?

FROM NEEL'S MANUSCRIPT

13

Neel and I had still not kissed. I had kissed him once on the cheeks, but that was more of a peck and it happened so quickly that it seemed like it didn't happen at all.

From the time Avni told me about their make-out session, a fear of sorts had engulfed me. I understood why it was important to look good. Earlier I was arrogant enough to perceive external beauty as something unimportant probably because I didn't have it. What I was curious to ask Avni, but certainly I couldn't, was who initiated the make-out sessions? Neel or her? It couldn't be Avni all the time. Then why hadn't Neel ever kissed me till now or even talked to me about making out? Whether I would agree to it or not is a different issue, but he could have at least asked me. Did Neel not find me attractive enough? A 16-year-old fat girl who wears old fashioned clothes like an aunty; would she be attractive to any guy? They say if you don't like yourself, nobody else will. I actually started hating myself. Was it because Neel didn't try to make-out with me? Was it because I thought he never would because of my looks? Was it because he was in love with the concept that he didn't belong to Avni anymore and I was only the means for him to materialize the concept? Was I just an option he could hold onto to stay away from Avni? I had never had so many questions troubling me ever in the past. It could have also been that the people around me talked so much about sex and making-out that I was unnecessarily hyping these things in my mind when they actually didn't mean much in a relationship. I really hoped that was the case. I loved Neel, he loved me—it should have been the end of the story.

Growing up with an uncompromising loneliness nested within me, I had developed a block against physical proximity. On one hand I was worrying about why Neel hadn't shown any physical inclination towards me, and on the other, I wondered about what I would have done if he actually proposed a make-out session. I had never been hugged properly by my parents. Skin to skin touch gave me the creeps. Had I not been charged with humiliation, I wouldn't have pecked Neel either. All these queries were making life miserable for me. I lost my focus on my studies, and for the first time got below average marks in Physics and Mathematics in a unit test.

Neel had fought with his parents and now used to travel to and fro from school on his own. I loved the fact that materialistic pleasures weren't important for him. We had few extra classes one day, and by the time school got over, it was late in the evening. The sky was roaring with thunder since afternoon and it was unbelievably dark. Neel and I took a cycle-rickshaw to the bus stop. We were struggling to hold onto his guitar in the cycle-rickshaw, and trying to protect it from getting wet. Neel wanted to practice after school but the rain was playing a spoilsport.

The moment we got down from the cycle-rickshaw at the bus stop, it started raining heavily. We thought we would reach our homes before the onslaught started but we were wrong. I had an umbrella. But Neel didn't.

'You go ahead. I will wait till it stops raining and then go home.'

'Are you mad? It may be several hours before the rain stops. Plus we have a test tomorrow.'

'There's nothing I can do.'

In a split second, I took a daring decision.

'Come to my place. We can study together till the rain stops. Then you can leave.'

'Are you sure?'

'Of course!' Honestly, I was shit scared of Bijoya's mami's reaction, but I still didn't back track on my decision. *That's how great love stories are made*—Yo-didun's words reverberated within me—when you dare to do something unexpected and unprecedented. Neel and my love story had to be a great one.

As we walked from the bus stop to my mama's place, roughly five-minutes walk, it turned out to the longest walk I had ever encountered. I had opened the umbrella but I didn't know how exactly to get Neel under it. To begin with, he did come under it, and held it above our heads while I held onto the guitar. But I guess he realized I wasn't comfortable and thus he stayed a tad away from me, thereby getting soaked in the rain. By the time we reached home, he was partially wet.

To my surprise Yo-didun opened the door. One look at us and she knew who the boy was. Neel touched her feet and she hugged him tightly with a cute smile.

'Where is Bijoya mami?'

'She has gone to her friend's place. Your cousins are upstairs.'

I relaxed. Coincidences like these make life beautiful, I thought, and both Neel and I went to my room, the one I shared with Yo-didun. But she didn't come to the room. 'I have to watch my TV serial,' she said.

True to her name, she was a rockstar granny.

Neel eyed my room properly keeping down his guitar by the door. Obviously it was nothing compared to his bedroom, but he didn't let it show. And why should I hide or fake something in order to gain something as genuine as Neel's love? What I was, I was! I gave Neel a towel and asked him to dry his hair while I went to the kitchen to make tea for the three of us; Neel, Yo-didun, and myself.

Minutes later when I came back to the room, Neel was still fidgeting with the towel with a messed up hairdo. He looked funny in a cute way. I laughed keeping the teacups on the dressing table.

'You rich kids. Don't you do anything on your own?' I said teasingly and went ahead to snatch the towel from him and rubbed it on his hair in order to dry them properly. In one instance the towel fell not only over his head but also over mine. Our heads were under the towel at the same time. We giggled at each other. I looked at him once and then looked down. I didn't want him to understand my feelings at that point of time. The worst part was I was sure he did understand them. I knew what was about to happen but I didn't back up. I stood my ground. His lips slowly came near mine and rubbed against it. It wasn't a proper kiss but that friction seemed to wake me up to a myriad of realizations. The most significant of those realizations being that I belonged to Neel. The moment was too emotionally vibrant for me to withstand it for long. I soon removed the towel, and took a few back steps to move away from Neel.

'You are the best thing that has ever happened to me,' he said without moving an inch.

I looked at him with tears in my eyes. They weren't happy tears. They were tears of doubt. Did he say the same thing to Avni too? Wish I had the audacity to ask him that then and there.

'What happened?'

Am I better than Avni? I wanted to ask but said, 'I love you Neel.'

'I love you too Titiksha,' he reciprocated softly but he sounded very sure.

As I closed my eyes for a trice, the tears which were hanging on my eyelids fell freely onto my cheeks.

'But why are you crying?'

'Nothing.' I still couldn't tell him I was shamelessly comparing myself to Avni. When Neel was a stranger, I couldn't tell him certain things. When he came close—very close—then too there remained certain things which I couldn't share with him. Maybe everything is not meant to be shared.

'Do you trust me, Titiksha?'

I nodded.

'Then your trust on me will be my strength to fight all temptations.'

That sounded like an assurance. It helped me calm down.

'Excuse me,' I said and headed towards the washroom.

Once I was back, we studied together till the rain stopped. Yo-didun made us some hot and delicious pyaaji as well. Only when he was gone that I realized he had forgotten his guitar at my place.

14

The brief kiss sorted a lot of things in my mind. I felt more confident about Neel and myself. He had become this language I was learning every day, knowing well that I would never be able to unlearn it. No relationship can be unlearnt. But you can always start learning another language.

And it's up to the aura of the new language how it can compel one to forget the old language. I wanted to be that new language for Neel. And probably I already was.

Neel also opened up a new world for me which I wasn't much upbeat about, but being in love with him I had to pretend I was. He invited me finally to one of his band sessions. It happened in this huge garage which belonged to one of Neel's friend's, Hemant. He studied in a different school and had a band of his own. There was a third band also in the garage that night, but I didn't know who they were or which school they belonged to. Hemant's father was an IAS officer who was out of station for some work along with his mother. All he had was Pandeyji who was his assistant, bank, and partner-in-crime.

There were cartons of Budweiser beer for everyone. I tasted beer for the first time. I thought it tasted like horse piss though some other girls said that it was their favourite. Neel was busy setting up his band. He had purchased a new guitar for himself and asked me to keep the old one which he had forgotten at my place with me. He said I could play it whenever I missed him even though I didn't know how to play a guitar.

With Neel busy with his band pals, I was feeling like the odd-one-out in the crowd. I couldn't relate to anything or anybody there. There were youngsters like me who were not even eighteen but were doing grown-up stuff. They were drinking, I saw a few couples smooching in the open in one corner, 'smoke-kissing'—as in a boy and girl would take a puff each from a cigarette and then release it inside the other's mouth simultaneously. I didn't know why or how they could get pleasure in doing such weird stuff. And yet standing there I behaved as if I did like it all. The same thing I did at school too.

There was this invisible 'dress-code', I realized, which one had to adhere to in case one wanted to remain in any social group. One *had to* belong to a certain group. Standing out was sacrilege. Rebelling was considered arrogance, and as gutter stuff. I always felt an ineffable pressure to choose like my fellow classmates, talk like them, and behave like them even if I wanted to show them my middle finger most of the times. There was no room for individuality. The choice was simple: either you become part of a group and participate in whatever they do, compromising on your personal beliefs and tastes, or live a lonely life, a life of a social outcast. If I wouldn't have drunk beer that night, I too would have been termed a TGIF. There was this group of Avni-lovers who were always on the lookout for an opportunity to tag me a TGIF and humiliate me further in front of everyone all the time. Till then I had foiled all their attempts successfully. But I remained alert.

Standing amid the garage band get-together, with a beer can in my hand, my eyes were looking for Neel. The next instant a guy came forward, and called for everyone's attention by clapping his hands.

'Hey there, listen up. The lead guitarist of Paintbrush, our own Neel, is in a serious relationship for the last six months or so he says.' There were whistles and loud cheers from the crowd. 'But he is yet to make-out with her! Not even a kiss!' There was pin-drop silence. I didn't know what the guy was trying to say. He raised his voice again looking at Neel, 'Who is the girl dude?' All eyes were on Neel now. I understood why he was hesitating. He didn't want to drag me into this shit. I loved him for that. I chose to step-in myself.

'I am,' I said aloud and all the eyes shifted their focus to me. The guy stared at me for some time and then said, 'I don't blame Neel for not making-out with you.'

There was an outburst of laughter from all corners of the room. I couldn't stand it. I felt someone had stripped me bare in public. The way they were looking at me told me that I didn't have the right to be in love with a handsome boy like Neel. Before I could do something, I saw Neel punch the guy hard. The others, instead of stopping the fight, were cheering them to hit each other harder. I let go of the beer can and ran to the spot. I had never seen Neel so violent before. And even though I hated what he was doing to the guy, I knew he was right to stand up for his girl.

I somehow managed to pull Neel out of the fight. The others booed as I did so.

I pulled him by his hand and said, 'Let's get out of here Neel.' He complied. By the time we were out of the garage, everyone in the crowd was chanting: 'They are The Great Indian Fattu couple!'

After moving out of the garage, Neel and I stood by a lamp post which had a fused bulb unlike the other lamp posts in the street. I could see blood dripping from his eyebrow. I took out my handkerchief and tried to rub it off, but he withdrew. He was quiet and looked intense. I didn't know why he wasn't talking to me since I wasn't at fault. Or was he rueing over the fact that we indeed never made out or because he, Mr Popular, indeed deserved a better looking girlfriend? Suddenly I felt more insulted standing there beside Neel than I did inside the garage when people were laughing at us.

'What was the need to tell them about what we have done or not done?' I blurted out. It came out a bit rudely than I would have liked it to.

Neel kept looking at me. I had never seen him give me that look. It was so full of contempt, anger, and everything I never associated Neel with.

His car came and stood in front of us. He simply went inside it and sped away immediately. No words, no gestures. He didn't even care to ask me how I would go back to my place. Few minutes later, I found a taxi to take me home.

I later learned that Neel had casually confided in his friend about the making-out matter, and the friend had blown the matter out of proportion in front of everybody in the garage. But the real shocker was the guy who'd announced it was dating Avni so there wasn't any prize for guessing why the guy actually came out with it in public.

In the days that followed, Neel and I became the butt of all jokes. Every time we were seen together in school, we could feel our classmates laughing in a hush-hush manner. 'Mr Popular had become Mr Jocular' was what they had on their lips. And of course 'TIGIF couple' was our new name.

Honestly, I was used to those glances, name-calling, and back bitching but what disturbed me more was that Neel was slipping away from me. I could sense it. We hadn't said a single word to each other since he left me by the lamp post. He started avoiding me in school and tuition.

There wasn't anybody waiting for me either at the bus stop in the morning or near the school gate at the end of the day. When I initiated a conversation—be it during the recess or in between classes—all I got was cold answers in monosyllables. Why was he making me feel like a culprit? I never forced him to love me. I never asked him to leave his car and travel in a cycle rickshaw with me to school every morning. I never insisted him to lie to his parents about the fact we were actively involved in a relationship. Then if he did whatever he wanted out of his own free will then why was he pushing me towards an emotional abyss? As if all these months, his love for me was a mere charity.

And suddenly he had run out of his 'mood for charity'. After trying for a few times, I let him go. It hurt my self-respect to go and ask him every time 'what was wrong?' as if he was a customer care agent for me and our relationship was an out of order phone or something. There were times at night when I promised myself I won't crib over the fact ever and the very next day in school, one sight of Neel, and my heart was squirming with pain. Finally Yo-didun understood there was something seriously wrong with me. She enquired about Neel.

'What to do, Yo-didun, when you have to suffer for no fault of yours?' It was only when Yo-didun wiped my cheeks that I realized I was crying.

'What happened Shonamoni?'

'Is it my fault that I am not beautiful and sexy?' Never before did I utter that s-word before Yo-didun.

'What's sexy?' she said rather innocuously.

'Another word for being attractive.'

'Who said you are not sexy?'

'I know it Yo-didun, I'm not. Just look at me!' I got up and stood in front of the mirror. That was when I started sobbing uncontrollably. Yo-didun came to me and caressed my back to help me calm down.

'Did Neel say you aren't beautiful?'

'No.'

'Then?'

'His behaviour did. I didn't make fun of him. It was that guy.'

'Why did the guy do so?'

'It was because...it was because...' I checked myself. I couldn't tell her why the guy made fun of Neel and me. She kept looking at me expectantly.

'Nothing Yo-didun. You won't get it.' I went to bed, stretched myself, and pretended to be asleep. I was sure Yo-didun must have understood it was something I couldn't share, but thankfully she didn't pester me about it. That night I missed having a sibling, a best friend, a family, parents...Neel. When I told him I loved him, it wasn't a joke. As I slept with tears drying on my cheeks, I finally decided it was I who had to do something about my love story. I didn't know what Neel thought about us at that point of time, but I would apologize. I would, if that's what he wanted to hear from me.

'Are you still pursuing him?' asked Yo-didun.

I turned on my bed. It was dark so an eye contact was not possible but I knew she was looking at me.

'In a way.'

'Stop it from tomorrow.'

'What?'

'He should feel he has lost you. After then, if he comes to claim you, be his. Else don't. A palm can't hold on to something if the fingers decide not to curl up. If you need to hold onto your relationship, you both have to work for it.'

Yo-didun had a point. An instant ago, I was thinking of apologizing to Neel even though I had done nothing wrong, but now I was pretty sure I would do what Yo-didun said. There was a fear of losing Neel for I didn't know if he at all would care if I stopped pursuing him. But then if he didn't care my taking a back-step then what was the point of loving someone who didn't understand your feelings for him?

From the next day onwards, I started avoiding Neel. I didn't glance at him or even make him feel that I knew he existed. It was tough for me but as Yo-didun said, the palm alone can't hold onto something. The taunts from the other classmates continued but the intensity died down. I was sure if Neel and I came together, it would regain its notoriety once again. The point was: would Neel dare to accept me irrespective of the stupid TGIF tag, the taunts, the mocking? And by daring to do so, would he make our love story a great one? It was a test I knew whose result I wanted to see alright but I was scared too. For if the results were negative, then I didn't know if I would ever be able to fall in love with a guy again in this life with the same kind of passion and piousness I felt for Neel.

On the tenth day of my avoidance of Neel, I got a piece of paper in one my notebooks during the English class. Our teacher had taken our notebooks for correction after a class test and Neel had been given the responsibility of distributing the notebooks in class. Though I didn't see him do it, I was sure he must have slipped in the piece of paper while distributing the notebooks. The piece of paper read: *Want to talk. Please be here in the class after school.*

After reading the note, I looked at Neel for the first time after ten days only to notice that he was already looking at me. We exchanged a smile. The hiccups that my life was suffering till then had finally stopped.

I did stay back in the classroom after school. And so did Neel. He was half-sitting on the teacher's desk while I was leaning back on the adjacent wall. He initiated the conversation.

'I'm sorry Titiksha. I really am.'

'Sorry for what?'

'For behaving so weirdly with you after the garage incident. It wasn't your fault.'

'So why exactly did you behave that way knowing well that it wasn't my fault?'

'I don't know. Perhaps…' Neel lowered his head and was softer when he continued, 'I took what that idiot said that night a bit too seriously.'

'You mean you believe you deserve someone better than me?'

He lifted his face and blurted out, 'No! I didn't say that. But…' He again went soft. 'I did consider it.'

'And so you didn't talk to me.'

Neel nodded his head subtly with a guilty expression.

'Look at me Neel,' I said. 'If I looked anything like Avni, and you know what I mean, we would have had a make-out session already, isn't it?'

Neel was quiet. Since he was quiet, I had the right to decide the answer to my liking. And it was obvious.

'You can tell it to my face Neel that you don't love me. I won't mind,' I said after I had mercilessly killed something within me.

'I love you Titiksha and that's why I am talking to you today. In all these days that I tried to ignore you, you invaded me all the more. If that's not love then I don't know what is.'

I was happy to hear him. After a long time, I was happy. In fact I had rarely encountered that kind of happiness before. It gave me a feeling that if I didn't do anything in life anymore, I would have still lived it to its core.

'Thanks Neel.'

He came to me and hugged me tight. I could feel his breath on my ears and neck. It tickled my senses. He spoke maintaining the tight hug.

'But I don't like the way people talk about you and me.'

'Do you mean the TGIF tag?'

'Yes. It affects me, and I hate it. I feel like smashing their faces. The worse is it's not only about me. It's about you and me. And when something happens to you, and I am not able to do anything about it, I feel weak.'

I smiled. There was something emotionally arousing about the way he was being protective about me. I broke the hug and looked deep into his eyes. I noticed he didn't look totally happy. And I knew why.

The kind of background I came from didn't let me open myself up the way Avni must have opened up in front of Neel. I knew if we made-out, we could have connected all the more intensely, but

I couldn't pull myself to doing so. It wasn't a matter of moral courage. Had it been only about courage, I would have made out with Neel. I wasn't ready for it; that's all. I could sense Neel wanted to make-out. Let's say Neel would have been happier had I instigated our making-out session or was more frank about it like Avni. I wasn't. I couldn't be that frank just as yet, because there was so much emotional junk within me that I had piled on since childhood, that I had to clean them up before I took the step that I thought Neel and I deserved to take. I needed time for that.

Something struck me seeing Neel's upset face. 'I have a solution.'

'What?'

'Can't we just lie to everyone that we did make-out?'

My suggestion made him look slightly happier than he was.

Chapter 10

WHO KILLED TITIKSHA?

'I guess that's enough for now,' Neel says pressing the corner of his eyes on either side of his nose. He needs rest but he can't. He has to find the guy Titiksha was dating or, he presumes, has murdered Titiksha and left her pieces in their flat. With each passing minute, the presumption is turning into reality. He'll chop the guy into double the number of pieces the moment he gets to him. It's a non-negotiable resolve.

At the moment he is with Nivrita in a CCD outlet in Lake Town, the only time he has managed to write the last three chapters sitting in front of Nivrita. She had wanted to come to his place and narrate another portion of the story in the privacy he always asks for, but for obvious reasons Neel requests her to meet somewhere outside.

'That's so unlike you,' Nivrita had remarked.

Sitting opposite Neel and sipping the last of her strong Macchiato, she can feel something's wrong with him. On other days Neel is rather still in public places. But today he is moving a lot. Sometimes he touches his eyes, sometimes he looks around like a spy, or at times he cracks his fingers, or scratches the back of his head.

'You look a bit bothered and disconnected. Any news of Titiksha?' Nivrita says wiping her mouth with a tissue.

Neel moves his hand away from his face. There's a momentary uncomfortable eye connect with Nivrita after which he nods his head.

'Did you report a missing case with the police?' She takes out a small hand mirror and checks if her makeup is in place. She then runs her fingers through her hair.

Neel nods.

'What are they saying?' Nivrita puts the mirror back in her bag and sits in a laidback manner.

'Nothing. The inspector said he would get in touch the moment he gets something worthwhile. In fact…' Neel stops. He isn't sure he should say what he has in his mind to Nivrita or not. What will she think?

'In fact what?' She urges him to go on.

'In fact,' Neel reluctantly says, 'I don't think the police will ever be able to find her.'

'Why is that?' She folds her hand and keeps them on the table looking straight at Neel.

'I didn't give the inspector any photograph of Titiksha. How will they identify her?'

Nivrita laughs out. Neel doesn't like it.

'Dude, are you mad? Don't you want the police to get to Titiksha?'

'I don't have any photograph of hers.'

'You don't?' She is serious now.

'I do. But not at my parents' place. I had to check for photographs at my place, but totally forgot about it.' With the dead body thing, everything else had totally slipped from his mind. He makes a mental note to check for her pictures the moment he reaches his flat again. But what's the point now? Even if he gives a photograph to Inspector Parimal Biswas, how will he be able to locate Titiksha for him? She is inside his refrigerator, resting in pieces. Neel feels like throwing up. Neel gulps down a glass of water all at once and keeps it on the table. He notices Nivrita place her palm on her cheek and look intently at him.

'I think you have lost her.'

How right she is, like always; Neel wonders. He has lost Titiksha forever now.

'I know.' Neel is cautious about what he says. He can't tell Nivrita or for that matter anyone the heinous truth just as yet. Only when the guy who was dating Titiksha secretly, confesses the crime, Neel would be able to tell everyone how he panicked seeing Titiksha's clothes in front of his rented flat and what he did thereafter. God, Titiksha is no more. Neel feels like crying then and there but somehow holds back his tears. He doesn't have enough time to even rue over the fact that Titiksha is no more. He may have slept with Nivrita, but he loves Titiksha. He would have never left her for Nivrita. Never ever. Not even if she didn't help him publish his book. But then Titiksha herself would have left him since she was having an affair with someone else. It's such an emotional quandary—to love and cry over a girl who you know would have left you soon. Neel holds his head and looks down trying not to think too much about it.

'What is it that you are hiding, Neel?' Nivrita says gently caressing his hair.

Neel slowly looks up at her. She removes her hand.

'You saw the guy that day, isn't it?' Neel says slowly, weighing down each word. Neel was waiting for an opportunity to put it in front of Nivrita. The story narration is an excuse. Neel wants Nivrita's help in tracing the other guy.

'Oh, don't tell me you are still into was-the-guy-better-than-me and likewise nonsense.'

'Did you see the guy that day, Nivrita?' This time Neel is more assertive.

'You know it was dark inside the washroom. I only saw silhouettes and probably a glance of his face, but I have no recollection of it. Why do you have to know about the guy? You better concentrate on finding Titiksha.'

'Hmm,' Neel grunts.

Almost a minute goes by with no words spoken. Then Nivrita abruptly leans forward and says in an exited manner, 'I have an idea.'

Neel looks eager hoping Nivrita will let him know of a way to zero down on the guy.

'What if I shift with you now?'

If words were bombs, this was a nuclear blast.

'Why?' It's the loudest Neel has spoken today.

'Why not? Titiksha isn't coming and my boy-mate has gone mad. He keeps fighting with me. And we both like each other, don't we?'

Like each other? Is that a reason to live together under one roof? Whatever happened to the good old society! And this girl is calling him mad?

Neel needs to cite an excuse. In the current scenario, he can't even have Nivrita in his house for a minute, forget living together in it.

'What will I tell my parents?' Neel tries to sound nervous.

'The obvious,' Nivrita says with her usual sharpness. 'That you have found another girlfriend.'

'They won't like it. Please try to understand.' Neel is already pleading. Not a good sign when one is trying to negotiate.

'How did they accept your living in with Titiksha?'

She seems more of an advocate than a commissioning editor of a publishing house, Neel wonders.

'They have met her. They liked her.'

'Then make them meet me. They'll like me. I know it. You know it.'

It's an advantage for Nivrita now. Neel is losing this verbal-coaxing-match and is quiet. He looks around with resignation—the way one does when one has nothing left to tell the person one is sitting with. Had he not wanted to be an author, he wouldn't have tolerated the shit this girl was ranting now.

'What are you thinking? Call your parents and tell them you want them to meet your new girlfriend.'

'Okay, let me find out where Titiksha is first. After that I will talk to my parents about you.' Neel has thought of a stop-gap.

Nivrita glares at Neel.

'I get it.' Nivrita gets up, grasps her shades and wears them in a flash. 'You don't like me. Right, Neel? You don't want to accept me as your girlfriend. Fine. I take it that you only want to fuck me for your own good.'

Neel shuts his eyes in shame while Nivrita storms out. He knows she has said the last sentence aloud, and other people present in the coffee shop will now throw glances that says you-are-such-a-pig. He opens his eyes slightly to see people around him indeed giving him that sort of a glance. He stands up and rushes outside to find Nivrita as well as avoid being looked at.

Once outside CCD, Neel sees her walking ahead furiously. Something about the gait tells him that he will have to pacify her else his debut novel could be in danger. He scampers towards her, and catches up with her in sometime.

'I'm sorry Nivrita. Don't take me otherwise. It's just that I am upset.'

'And living with me will make you more upset? Is that what you ran up to me for? Fuck you Neel.'

How could he beat this woman at words? Neel is furious with himself for not coming up with a proper excuse. Standing by the footpath he watches Nivrita get into a taxi.

'Don't try to get in touch. Ever!' she says. The taxi moves forward.

What's that supposed to mean? Oh, whom is he kidding? He knows exactly what's that supposed to mean. His debut novel has just died. There's renewed energy in Neel. He wants to chase down Nivrita and apologize. He sprints towards the taxi's direction. Since the road is clogged with vehicles, he can still see the taxi behind a bus. He soon realizes he is no Superman and gets into another taxi.

'We need to follow a taxi.'

'Twenty rupees more,' the taxi driver says. It's Kolkata—extra labour, extra charge.

Neel gets in. He can't jeopardize his debut novel for twenty extra bucks. If he loses Nivrita's taxi, he will lose her because he still doesn't know where exactly she stays.

The taxi driver does a good job. Almost half an hour later, Nivrita's taxi stops by an old looking apartment. Neel's taxi also comes to a hault a few meters behind it. Neel pays up and comes out just when Nivrita too is coming out from her taxi.

'Nivrita!' Neel screams. She stops by the gate of the high-rise and turns to look at him.

'I'm sorry. Don't do this.'

'Every dog has an affinity for a particular bone that it will never let go of. I knew you would come running behind me because the one particular bone you desperately want is in my hands.'

Neel doesn't like the way she puts it. It has a dehumanizing tone to it. But it's a fact. His bone of getting published is in her hands. Or so she has convinced Neel. Hence, he remains quiet.

'When I said we can live-in, I didn't mean we have to shift to *your* place. You can stay with me.'

As they enter the apartment campus, he looks up and notices there's an arch over the gate and on it is written:

SHARADA HEIGHTS

Instead of the elevator, they take the stairs on Nivrita's insistence. Her flat is on the top floor—fifth—and yet they are taking the stairs.

While climbing one floor after another, Neel has the same kind of sensation he had when Nivrita, weeks ago, had taken him to the deserted house where she played the same music on a guitar similar to what Titiksha often played for him. He feels like he has been in this building before, like he has climbed these steep stairs before. Suddenly he has a feeling there should be a flat which has a Ganesha Idol atop its main door. Neel keeps an eye on every flat's door as they take the stairs. It's on the third floor that Neel sees a flat's door which has a Ganesha Idol on it. It looks old but it's there and weirdly enough Neel was expecting it to be there. 'Neel,' says Nivrita. He is on the third floor while she is in-between the fourth and the fifth floor.

'I may be reborn again. But I'll never change my love for you.' Saying so, she moves up to the fifth floor. *Why did she say such a thing all of a sudden?* Neel wonders. It's so out of context. Also, it's so not a place to talk about life and re-birth.

Neel hears someone unlocking a door on the fifth floor. He starts ascending the stairs once again. This time with a laboured gait. Every time Neel tries to uncover a thing, he feels something pushing him to shift focus. A day before he thought he would unearth why his college changed its location, and he stumbled on Titiksha's murder. Now a minute back he was desirous to know how and why did he expect the Ganesh Idol to be present atop one of the doors, Nivrita tells him something mysterious about her love for him. Her love for him? Love? Nivrita loves him? He isn't convinced. Nivrita never looked like she can love any one person in present life, never mind life after it.

As Neel reaches the small space between the stairs connecting the two floors, he notices Nivrita busy unlocking the door of her flat.

'But in every birth my love for you will be predatory,' Nivrita says and unlocks the door. *Predatory love,* Neel wonders, *that's more like Nivrita.*

'Welcome home,' she smiles as if she has been waiting for this moment since a long time. Next she disappears inside her flat. Neel climbs the rest of the stairs and comes in as well.

He didn't expect the flat to be as dark as it is. There are thick brown curtains covering the open windows. A 42-inch LED Sony Bravia beside the window and myriad books. Neel can't guess what those books are about since he doesn't go near the bookshelf. Their spine looks old and somewhat distorted, almost as if they have been read again and again. A commissioning editor for a publishing house, obviously, has to be a voracious reader. Neel goes closer to the bookshelf and caresses the books. There's dust on the spine. Some of it sticks to his fingertips. Seems like she hasn't read them in some time now. *Strange,* Neel wonders, and keeps searching for books by Word Tree publishing, the company where Nivrita works. There's none.

'Don't you keep any books from your own publishing house?' Neel says still trying to find Word Tree books.

'The latest ones are by the television. And the rest are in office.'

Neel turns to notice that by the television stand are kept two piles of books. He goes and picks one up. It's by an author named Maninder Jadeja and the book is called *Let's Play Bf-Gf*. He notices the other books; each one has a funny name.

'*My baby, my life*'.

'*She crushed my heart*'.

'*I'm sad, he screwed my love*'.

Neel doesn't even know when his lips have stretched into a smile. Soon, Word Tree would publish his book as well.

Ex by Neel Chatterjee. For a moment he forgets where he is and why.

'Why don't you change, Neel? You are spending the night here anyway,' Nivrita speaks up from the kitchen.

'Am I?'

'Of course. What will do in your flat alone?'

He thinks of Titiksha's pieces lying in the refrigerator and shrugs. He feels happy to have followed Nivrita to her place. Going to his parents' place to stay the night would have piqued their interest.

'Yeah, sure. I'll stay over. But won't your boyfriend have a problem if he finds out?'

'Boy-mate Neel.' Nivrita appears in the hall room with a Budweiser beer can.

'Sorry, boy-mate.'

'I told you he is acting mad these days. He hasn't been here since a week or so.'

'Okay. But I don't have a spare set of clothes.'

'You'll find a few knickers on the hook behind the bedroom door.'

Neel expects her to say more since knickers will only take care half of his physical privacy.

'What? You really want to wear anything else in this hot and sticky weather?'

As if Neel has a say when Nivrita has decided something one his behalf.

'I guess not.'

'The bedroom is that way.' Nivrita points with one hand.

Neel goes inside the bedroom. As he is about to enter the room, he notices another room adjacent to it. The door is slightly ajar. A quick peep tells him that there's a table on which there's a laptop and a lamp. Probably where Nivrita reads manuscripts and works, he thinks to himself.

On the hook behind the door, Nivrita had said. Neel locks the door and checks the wall behind it. There's a wooden plate which has four hooks pinned on it. The first hook has a tee hanging on it. The second has two knickers. The third has a trouser along with a kurta. And the fourth has...Neel can't believe his eyes. From the fourth hook hangs a police uniform. On it is a name badge on which is written: Parimal Biswas.

'After you freshen up a bit, we can continue with the story. What say Neel?' he hears Nivrita say.

For a moment Neel feels he has no voice.

FROM NEEL'S MANUSCRIPT

15

Neel didn't want to spread rumours about our intimacy but then he also didn't want us to be tagged as a TGIF couple. Neel agreed to my suggestion, even if it was reluctantly so. We decided to lie to our classmates that we had in fact made-out. Some of his friends knew that he was supposed to meet me in the classroom after school. So Neel decided to tell his friends that we made-out in the classroom itself. I was okay with it for at least we could be together in school without being mocked at. Maybe we were both too naive to gauge the ill-effects of the rumour. We only wanted to give our relationship some oxygen by shutting up our classmates.

Neel went ahead and confessed to Avni's boyfriend that we had made-out in the classroom itself. It was two days later that I saw the first ramification of the rumour. In the girls' toilet, just after the assembly, I saw it written on the wall in a very noticeable manner: 'Titiksha of XI science has a fucked cunt!' The statement was accompanied by a vulgar sketch. I immediately tried to scratch it out. I wondered if the same was written about Neel in the boys' toilet. I went to the class and told Neel about it. He said he hadn't seen anything as such in the boys' toilet but promised to check. During recess he said the same thing was written on one of the walls of the boys' toilet as well. What surprised me was even in the boys' toilet it was my name scribbled along with the vulgar sketch and not his. As if it was only I who had supposedly made-out. When I asked Neel if he had scratched it off, he said no. I told him he should have.

'But what's the problem? Let it be. Just because someone says something doesn't mean it's true.' He had a point alright but I would have liked it if he had scratched that disgusting thing off the wall. He understood my predicament and said, 'Alright I will strike off your name. Fine?'

I gave him a flying kiss.

After school when I went to the girls' toilet, I got the shock of my life. The same statement now was all over the wall. Somebody had replicated the initial statement and sketched a hundred times over. It seemed like a slap right across my face. Even if I tried to, I couldn't rub it off. The wall was full of them. I went to one of the maids working in the school, brought her in, and requested her to wash off the graffiti if possible. She agreed but asked what it was that was written on the wall. I made something up.

While I was waiting impatiently for Neel near the school gate, after school, trying to frame in my mind how exactly I should share the toilet issue and ask him if we should report it to our class teacher or not, I saw Neel waving at me. I waved back. As he came towards me, Avni stopped him. They were talking and I noticed Neel smiling about something and then Avni hit him on his shoulder lovingly. *Lovingly!* Here I was going to tell Neel that maybe Avni was behind the vulgar graffiti and there he was, smiling alongside her. I marched towards them and very stupidly caught hold of Avni's shirt collar and asked why she was doing it. She was obviously taken aback and so was Neel. He started yelling at me, saying that I was hurting her but I didn't leave her until Neel forcefully took off my hand from her collar. She feigned innocence. It irked me the way she was playing the sympathy game with him, as if I was the bitch breaking her life apart.

'You should learn to behave Titiksha!' Neel shouted. I stopped. I looked around to realize most of the students were gaping at me as if I was some crazy soul. I regained my composure and simply walked off from there.

At night when I had cooled down a little, I felt ashamed at my reaction. Whatever it was, I shouldn't have gotten physical with Avni. It must have given a very wrong image of me to Neel. I was sick and tired of acting abruptly like a possessed soul. The way Neel raised his voice against me felt worse than the graffiti on the wall. I wanted to apologize to both Neel and Avni. The whole incident exposed a side of me which I had only seen in Avni till then. When

Neel and I had just met, I couldn't grasp why exactly Avni was feeling jealous of me, and now seeing the two together in school today, I felt the same. Was I being possessive of Neel just like I had accused Avni of being the same once? Had I started to treat him as my property like Avni was doing when I stepped in? My worst fear at this point of time was what if Neel turned towards Avni because I was acting the way she was acting before? Love did the same thing to me as it did to her. Does it do the same thing to everyone? I tried to be honest with myself. I was being possessive and aggressive in school because I was still not sure about him. I mean I was sure about him but I wasn't sure if he was sure about me. Hence my insecurity kept me on my toes all the time and pushed me to stupidly grab Avni's shirt's collar that day.

'You can't hold onto anything; especially that which is not yours. And what really is yours, will remain yours irrespective of the fact you hold onto it or not.'

I turned on my bed to see Yo-didun reading aloud from a book. I didn't share the incident with her but maybe she had guessed it from my grim look what could be the issue. We shared a smile and I turned my back to her. I would apologize to Neel, and if he says, to Avni too. I couldn't afford to become another Avni and instigate Neel to get inclined towards someone else.

Next day I was ready with my egoistic guard down. I didn't see Neel though. Avni was there but I wanted to apologize to Neel first.

The assembly happened on time after which I reached the classroom. Everyone was laughing at me. I turned to look at the blackboard where it was written: 'Titiksha has a fucked cunt!' Alongside it was the same vulgar sketch which I had seen last day in the girls' toilet. Even before I could react, our class teacher was in the room. Everyone quietened. The next thing the class teacher noticed was the blackboard.

It was then that Neel came in. He was late that day.

It didn't take much time for Neel to understand what was going on. The class teacher shot the obvious to me, 'Titiksha, what's all this nonsense?

'I don't know teacher. Someone is spreading rumours about me.'

'Who?'

'Neel!' Someone spoke up from behind. We turned around but didn't know who it was.

'Who was that? Come on stand up.'

Nisha did; the same bitch who had once informed Avni about the shirt-swapping incident on my first day in school. I don't know what her problem was.

'What did you just say Nisha?'

'Neel told everyone about this.'

Neel shot a furious glance at Nisha, then a furtive glance towards me, and in the end he faced the teacher who was standing with a give-me-the-truth look on her face.

'Neel, did you spread this vulgar rumour about Titiksha?'

Neel stood still. I knew what he was going through. He was in a quandary. If he spoke the truth, the rumour would remain a rumour, alright, but the question would then be who spread it. Obviously it would easily be proven it was him who confessed to Avni's boyfriend. And if Neel agreed to the statement on the blackboard being a reality—that I indeed had a fucked cunt—it would put both Neel and me under strict disciplinary action. Before he could say anything, I spoke up.

'Teacher, I think Avni has done it.'

'Avni?'

'Avni Jain, XI Commerce.'

'Why would she do all this? Call her.'

I stood my ground while the monitor of our class went out to fetch Avni from her class. A few seconds later, Avni entered our classroom.

'What's all this?' the class teacher asked her gesturing towards the blackboard.

'It seems like someone by the name of Titiksha has lost her virginity teacher,' Avni said in her typical I-am-a-smart-ass manner. Most of the class burst out laughing. Only Neel and I didn't.

'Shut up!' the teacher said to the class and confronted Avni.

'Titiksha claims you have written this.'

Avni shot a surprised look at me and said, 'Why would I do that Titiksha? How would I know this fact anyway?'

There was further hush-hush laughter.

'Don't give me that shit,' I started but was cut short by my class teacher.

'What kind of language is that?'

'I'm sorry teacher, but Avni is jealous of Neel and me.' I was speaking the truth.

'Jealous?'

'Neel and Titiksha are having an affair,' Nisha butted in from behind. Of course she was on her queen-bitch's side.

'Do you students come to school to study or waste time on all this? All these nonsensical Hindi movies are eating your head out it seems.'

I glanced back at the class. Almost the entire class had a we-accept-the-truth expression hanging on their faces. The teacher sat down on her chair, opened her bottle of water, and drank some of it. Nobody talked in between. I thought it was the right time to squeeze in my request.

'May I please rub the blackboard now teacher?'

The teacher looked at Avni, at Neel, and then at me.

'No!'

My heart skipped a beat. She stood up.

'Monitor, rub the board first and look after the class.' She said and glanced at Neel and me. She said conclusively, 'You three follow me' and walked out. I didn't look at Avni but I looked at Neel who was looking at Avni. I didn't know why he wasn't looking at me. He seemed scared of something. Even I was. But one glance from him would have given me strength. Didn't he know that?

'Neel...'

He didn't listen and followed the teacher urgently. It was only when he was gone that I realized I was trembling with fear for I knew where exactly our class teacher must have gone. Avni came to me and whispered, 'Whore, I told not to screw my boyfriend the first day you were here. Now you will rot in hell!' She walked out too. As I stood there unable to move fearing the worst, the class started booing, displaying their middle fingers at me. I left hastily and stopped outside the Principal's office. The class teacher, Neel, and Avni were already inside the Principal's room. I stood outside gaping at the name plate: Dr Geetika Kumari Iyer. My heartbeats slowly ascended. I was too numb to think anything worthwhile. Avni came out and told me that the Principal was waiting for me to join the rest of them inside. I followed her inside.

Dr Iyer looked like she was in a bad mood.

'I thought you were a good girl Titiksha. What happened to you?' Dr Iyer spoke to me directly. I didn't know my gait from the classroom to the principal's office was so slow that everything had been relayed to her by then.

'It's not true ma'am,' I barely managed to speak in my defense, pronouncing every word with caution.

'Then what's the truth; tell me,' she said removing her glasses. She looked menacing without them. 'I'm all ears.'

'It's a joke.'

'It's not a joke ma'am. Neel told me about it.'

It was a rumour alright but Neel was not supposed to tell Avni about it. Never! He was supposed to tell her boyfriend only. But why was I believing Avni's statement? She could very well be lying to create misunderstandings between us.

'Neel didn't do anything like that,' I said.

'Titiksha please don't talk out of turn,' Dr Iyer said to me and to Neel she said, 'Did you tell Avni what was written on the blackboard?'

Neel remained quiet. He should have said no straightaway. But he didn't. Then I realized that maybe he did tell this to Avni. Maybe, I realized to my horror, Avni was right.

'Your silence tells me you did say this.' Dr Iyer continued, 'Why? Why did you initiate such a nasty rumour about a decent girl who is also your classmate?'

Neel was still quiet.

'Answer me Neel or else I will have to call your parents.'

'Ma'am please don't report this to my parents,' Neel pleaded.

'Then answer me with honesty.'

'Titiksha asked me to.'

I couldn't believe he had taken my name. And did he say I 'asked' him to?

'What nonsense are you saying Neel! I had only suggested it to you to make you happy. The final decision was yours,' I screamed.

Dr Iyer looked shocked beyond belief.

'Titiksha, you suggested him to write such a nasty thing about yourself?'

This time I was quiet.

'Alright I want to meet both your parents tomorrow first thing in the morning,' Dr Iyer declared.

'Ma'am...'

'Bring your guardians Titiksha. Avni. you may leave.' She had given the bitch a clean-chit.

I saw Neel almost pleading to Dr Iyer to take back her decision of summoning his parents but she didn't. And I didn't know how on earth was I going to tell Ashok mama and Bijoya mami about why they were being summoned to school?

Chapter 11

WILL NEEL GET TO THE OTHER GUY TITIKSHA WAS DATING?

What is Inspector Parimal Biswas's uniform doing in Nivrita's bedroom?

This is what Neel wanted to ask the moment he came out of the bedroom wearing one of the knickers which could have also belonged to Parimal Biswas. Not that he has any issue with Parimal, but somehow from the time Neel saw the uniform, he hasn't been able to take his mind off it. It would have been better if he had talked about it before Nivrita started narrating the story, but he decides against it and keeps his query for when they take a break.

Nivrita is in the kitchen preparing Spanish omelette for both. Neel stands by the kitchen door and asks, 'What's your boy-mate's name?'

'Huh?' Nivrita turns to look at him in a flash and then carries on making the omelette.

'The name of your boy-mate?'

'Parimal. Why?'

'I saw his uniform behind the door.'

'Oh okay.' Nivrita transfers the omelettes from the pan onto two separate plates. She picks two forks from a nearby stand and brings the two plates to Neel. He takes one plate, one fork, and together they head to the hall.

'I have met him.'

'You have? Where?'

'He came to my place. Dad had called him to investigate Titiksha's missing case.'

'What a coincidence!' Nivrita sits on the two sitter sofa, legs curled up, and switches on the television. She surfs the channels when Neel suddenly asks her to stop at one particular channel where a Bengali television serial is being shown.

'Hey, that's Arindam, my colleague,' exclaims Neel.

'The one you met while we were coming from the airport?'

'Yes. What is he doing?'

'Well, now you know why he left his job. He is an actor.'

'I never knew he liked acting.'

'We don't know a lot of things about others.' Nivrita changes the channel and puts on Discovery TLC (Travel and Living channel).

'You like this channel?' Neel says making himself feel comfortable; on the corner of the three-sitter couch where Nivrita had been narrating the story to him earlier.

'I always have.' Nivrita has her eyes fixed on the television.

'Even Titiksha liked it.'

'Liked?' She shoots a glance at him.

'Likes,' Neel corrects himself even though the correction is incorrect. Titiksha is now past tense.

'Hmm, I know.'

'You know?'

'I have met Titiksha once, remember, at your place.'

They discussed their favourite television channels on the first meet? Weird.

There is silence as Neel observes Nivrita digging into her omelette in total bliss. He came to her flat believing they would have a good sex session, but not for once did she give him a signal that she was interested in him sexually whereas the Nivrita he met in Jaipur seemed carnally possessed. Maybe Parimal has been keeping her satisfied.

'When will Parimal be back?'

'No idea. He never tells me. I never ask either. He has the key.'

'Don't you ever feel bad that he is cheating on you?'

Nivrita gives him a look as if she doesn't know what he is talking about.

'You told me once that you thought he was having an affair, right?'

'Maybe he does have a dozen affairs; how does it matter to me? Initially I was a bit pissed but then I thought he isn't my property. All I care is he is here when I'm horny.'

Neel feels disgusted by the way she puts it. How can sex be everything in a relationship? Sex may at best lure one into a relationship but it's love that decides whether the relationship shall sustain or not.

'Don't you have a heart?' Neel can't believe he said it aloud.

Nivrita looks at him sharply and says, 'Someone burnt my heart long back. Now I only have hormones. And whenever they flare up, I call up my boy-mate.'

I call up my boy-mate. I call up...Neel springs on his feet.

Finally he has got a way to get hold of the other guy Titiksha was dating, and who he suspects must have murdered her.

'I need to go.'

'Where?' Nivrita puts her legs down.

'I'll be back soon.' Neel sprints towards the door, opens it, and runs out.

It's only while calling for a taxi that Neel realizes he is in knickers and doesn't have his wallet either. More importantly, even his flat keys are in his jeans' pocket. He goes up this time in the elevator. As the door opens he sees Nivrita standing there with his jeans.

'What happened?'

'I think I know how to get to the other guy Titiksha was dating.'

'Was? How can you be sure she isn't dating him anymore?'

'I'll explain later.'

'You better be back soon.'

'I will.'

Neel grabs his jeans, goes inside, and comes back within seconds wearing it. He takes the elevator and disappears from sight.

Once there, Neel unlocks the flat in an uber-excited manner and saunters into his bedroom. On the table where he usually sits and writes, he finds the thing for which he has come rushing up all the way—Titiksha's mobile phone. He had found it in the washroom in a dismantled condition. It takes a minute for Neel to put the battery, sim card, and finally he switches on the phone. Neel's heart is galloping like a racing horse. He puts on the date and time and then after the phone has loaded properly, he checks the contacts. There are a total of only one contact.: 'Chocopie'. Neel checks the number. It's not his. Who else will Titiksha call Chocopie? He tries to dial 'Chocopie' but notices there's no network.

Neel dials Chocopie's number from his own mobile phone. It rings but nobody picks up. He calls again. No answer. Then again. This time someone cuts the line. Neel is sure someone has noticed his call. He tries again. The call is taken.

'Hello?' Neel says with an anxious voice. Nobody talks back.

'Hello?' Neel can hear someone breathe.

'I know you're there. So why aren't you talking?'

A hiatus later Neel adds, 'I also know what you did to Titiksha. But I will get you for this. You get it?'

The line is cut. Neel looks at the phone. And dials again. This time a mechanical voice says that the phone is switched off.

'Motherfucker.' He has the other guy's number now but still doesn't know who the guy is. Should he call the mobile company customer care service and request for the name of the owner of the number? Neel decides to try.

'Can you please tell me which network this number belongs to?'

'No sir. I don't have the liberty of telling you that. Can I help you with anything else?'

Yes, go fuck yourself Neel thinks, but says, 'No, thanks.'

It's then that Neel realizes that he is in his flat. The same rented flat where Titiksha too is present but in a different form. Neel suddenly feels fear chaining him down. He thinks Titiksha will call out to him from the refrigerator. He closes his eyes hoping to get out of this situation as soon as possible. He shouldn't be hiding Titiksha's body parts like that. It's not good. He should inform someone soon.

With steps made heavy with fear Neel goes to the kitchen. It's dark. He switches on the light. Then he approaches the refrigerator and with trembling hands slowly opens its door. The packet is still there. Neel sits down on the floor.

'I'm sorry Titiksha. I'm so damn sorry.' He sobs for some time. He then rubs his eyes and gets out of the flat.

An hour later, Neel is back at Nivrita's place. Looking at his swollen eyes she can tell something is terribly wrong.

'What is it that you are hiding, Neel?' she asks as they settle down on the couch. This is the second time in the day that she has asked him this.

'I didn't do it.'

'What?'

'I didn't kill Titiksha.' Neel says, his entire body shuddering. He can hide it no more.

'What are you saying?' Nivrita is shell-shocked.

It takes two minutes for Neel to relay whatever happened from the time he saw the blood smeared clothes in front of his rented flat till he found the flesh pieces in his washing machine.

'Someone killed Titiksha, chopped her into pieces, and left her remains in the washing machine,' Neel is surprised by h ow easily it all is coming to him unlike what he had thought.

'Calm down.' Nivrita goes close to him and takes him in her embrace. Neel holds onto the embrace and continues to cry.

'I loved her. I loved Titiksha. I wanted to marry her. Now I won't ever be able to get her.'

Listening to Neel ranting about his love for Titiksha, Nivrita doesn't budge. As if she has developed emotional insulation and that no amount of emotions can touch her. Her hand mechanically moves on Neel's back trying to calm him down.

'What did you go to your flat for?' she asks.

'I have the number of the guy she was dating.'

Nivrita breaks the embrace and looks at his teary eyes.

'You know his name?'

'That's the problem. I called but he didn't talk and then switched off the phone.'

'Give me the number,' Nivrita says and takes her phone in her hand and gives Neel his phone from beside the couch.

As Neel calls out the number, Nivrita punches the digits in True Caller, an Android app which displays the person's name on which a specific phone number is registered.

Once done, Nivrita touches the 'search' button on her phone and waits. Neel too waits with a blank face. A couple of seconds later Nivrita looks up at him with a bewildered look.

'What happened? Got any name?'

'Yes.'

'What?'

'Parimal Biswas.'

FROM NEEL'S MANUSCRIPT

16

I didn't talk to Neel the day we were summoned to the principal's office. In fact, he too didn't make any attempt to talk to me. We maintained a distance surprisingly with the same ease with which we used to be together on other days. It made me wonder what this relationship was. At times it seemed as unbeatable as time, and at other times, as manipulative as fate. It anyways was not the numero uno fear on my list that day. The primary fear was how Ashok mama and Bijoya mami would react when I tell them about the principal's summon.

I couldn't tell them in the evening after returning from school. I wanted to but whenever I passed by them, I felt so choked with fear and anxiety that nothing came out of me. And the more it stayed within me, the more it throttled me. During dinner, not a single bolus of food went down my throat, but still I pretended as if all was fine.

When Yo-didun enquired why was I holding onto a fake face all evening, I broke down. I finally confessed to her what the problem was. I couldn't look her in the eyes after my confession. She only asked me if it was the truth: if I had actually made-out with Neel? I rightfully denied it. She was quiet for some time and then asked me to be brave. It made me sob further for I thought she meant I won't get any support from anyone. She was right.

I thought I would first tell my mother about the matter but it was Yo-didun who prepared me to relay it to mama since I was staying with him. Moreover, I didn't want to bother my mother. Later that night, when mama and mami were about to retire to bed after dinner Yo-didun took me to their room.

'Titiksha wants to tell you something,' Yo-didun said. She took a step back and pushed me a little forward as mama switched on the tubelight.

'Yes, what is it?' he said.

I turned to look at Yo-didun. She gave me an assuring look. I looked at mama and said, 'Dr Iyer wants to meet you tomorrow.'

'Who is Dr Iyer?'

'She is the principal of my school.'

There was a momentary silence.

'I knew such a day will come!' Bijoya mami climbed down from the bed. Her tone told me she was all ready and charged up to make a hue and cry over it. But mama cut her short.

'One minute,' he told her. 'What is it about?' he asked me.

'Someone has spread a rumour about me and she needs to talk to you about it.'

'What rumour?' Bijoya mami was sharp.

'That I have an affair with a boy.' I couldn't tell him the actual rumour.

'Oh God! All our prestige will go to the gutters now.' Bijoya mami shouted. Mama looked at me with contempt for some time, and then slapped me hard across the face. I stood still. I had expected this.

'Is this why your parents have left you with me? To bring shame to me and my family?'

By then my two cousin brothers had also come to the room.

'Don't beat her. It's just a rumour,' Yo-didun protested but mama asked her to go to her room.

'There's no smoke without fire,' Bijoya mami chipped in.

Yo-didun took me along with her before mama could hit me again. I called up Neel but he didn't pick up the call. I desperately wanted to talk to him.

Though I told my mama and mami it was a rumour, he didn't care about it. He would have probably killed me if it was the truth instead of a rumour. According to them a mere rumour, a baseless accusation would bring shame to their household. Not for a single second did they behave as if they would protect me in case it's proved that I was right about it being a rumour. I was screwed both ways. I was sure that had it been his son, he would have said the other girl was at fault. At that point I realized why Neel didn't pick up the call. At his place his parents must have blamed me, the girl, for dragging him, the boy, and his family in the rumour-ruckus. His mom didn't like me anyway. I was sure she would hate me even more now. How this would affect Neel and my love story, I didn't know. I prayed hard at least he would understand me. I know Neel feared his parents a lot, but then I also knew he loved me a lot. Spreading the rumour was suggested by me, I agree, but only to get rid of the TIGF tag and the relentless mockery, bordering on harassment, we both were subjected to in school.

I kept thinking every possible shit that could happen to me. I didn't know when I slept. The morning arrived. I spoke absolutely nothing while going through my routine chores before going to school. Then I went to school with mama.

Chapter 12

IS TITIKSHA'S BOYFRIEND AND NIVRITA'S BOY-MATE THE SAME?

'He is not picking up my call,' Nivrita says aghast after dialling Parimal's number for quite a number of times.

'Is this the same Parimal Biswas? Your boy-mate?' Neel asked with a voice half dry with astonishment and half wet with curiosity.

'It has to be. The name can't be a coincidence. The son-of-a-bitch was fucking me at night and dating Titiksha during the day.' Even Nivrita looks shaken with the development.

'But why Titiksha? And you?' Neel is tense.

'What's common between Titiksha and me?' Nivrita looks at him for an answer.

Neel thinks for a moment.

'I am.'

'But why you?'

'Yeah, why me?' Neel almost echoes Nivrita.

'Do you know Parimal from before?'

Does he? Neel thinks hard. No! He has seen Parimal only once. At his place when his father had called him to investigate Titiksha's missing case. In that case, even his parents didn't know him. But if Parimal Biswas is Titiksha's boyfriend and Nivrita's boy-mate, does it mean even Nivrita's life is in danger now. Neel's heart skips a beat.

'But how do you know its Parimal who murdered Titiksha?' Nivrita says.

'C'mon. There can't be anyone else. She never mixed with many people. His number in Titiksha's phone can't be a coincidence. I'm sure he knew me the day we met at my parents' place. I could sense that he did. His body language was such that it seemed as if he knew me from somewhere. I'm sure he asked Titiksha about me. The only thing I need to know now is why did he do it? Why did Parimal have to kill Titiksha?'

'Maybe because she realized her mistake and didn't want to marry him after all?' Nivrita says.

'Enough of maybe's. There are hundreds of them. I want to know why exactly he did this,' Neel retorts.

A haunting silence follows. Neither of them is comfortable in it.

'You should have reported it to the police then and there,' Nivrita says sounding pensive. 'Now you don't have an alibi Neel. The police will think you are cooking up a story.'

'That's what Parimal's intention is. Unless we get him to confess.'

'Right. Let's get him.'

'Not we, I'll get him. You wait here and don't open the door till I'm here. Not even if Parimal comes. I don't trust that bastard.'

'I think I should let him in if he comes here. Let him not get the impression that I know what he has been up to. That way I can keep him busy and maybe I'll be able to churn out significant information from him. Of course I'll call you.'

It sounds better than his plan.

'Okay. But be careful. I don't want to lose you, Nivrita.' There's an innocuous genuineness in his voice that hits Nivrita hard. Even Neel is surprised. Does he really care about Nivrita so much?

'I will take care. And you too. But how will you get to him?'

'Leave that to me.'

The determination in Neel doesn't let Nivrita ask any further questions.

⌛

It does not take much time for Neel to reach his parents' place.

'How did you locate inspector Parimal Biswas?' Neel asks his father. They are in the hall.

'Why? I called Chitpur Thana.'

'Did Parimal himself pick up the phone?'

'No someone else did. The person said he would send an inspector to our place and inspector Biswas turned up. Why are you asking all this?' His father has sniffed some problem.

Neel doesn't want to involve his parents yet.

'I want to talk to him. I have Titiksha's photograph.' It's only a ploy.

Neel's father gives him a weird gaze.

'What?' Neel shrugs looking at his father's expression. 'I told you I have Titiksha's photographs with me.' He now realizes why Parimal never called him again for the photograph. He never needed one.

'Dad, please call Parimal and tell him you want to meet him.'

Neel's father looks at his son. With a sense of reluctance, Neel's father calls someone from his mobile phone.

'Are you dialling his mobile phone?'

'No, let me first dial Chitpur Thana.'

'Okay.' Neel waits to hear his father talk on phone.

'Hello. I'm Atul Chatterjee. May I please talk to inspector Parimal Biswas?' Neel's father says.

'I see. When will he be back? Alright, I will call then.' He keeps the receiver down.

He looks at Neel and says, 'Parimal Biswas is on a holiday. They don't know when he will join back.'

Neel holds his head and thinks hard. There has to be some way to reach Parimal Biswas without him knowing anything about it.

Neel feels his father's warm grasp on his hands.

'Is there any problem, Babushona? You can tell me.'

He feels good that his father has shown concern towards his problem after a long time. All these years he always felt distanced from his parents. They used to be caring, and also saw to it all his needs were taken care of, but he never could share any of his problems with them. He didn't know why. They always seemed welcoming in an unwelcoming manner. And add to it their possessiveness. Whatever he did, he had to tell them in advance until Titiksha and he started living-in together.

'The problem, as you know, is Titiksha is missing.' Neel couldn't tell his father the truth. And before his father can react, he says, 'Where his mom?'

'She is hosting a small party with her group of friends.'

Nothing new for Neel's mother. Preferring parties to her family has always been her hallmark. Neel gets a call. He withdraws his hand from his father's grasp and takes out his mobile phone from his pocket. It's Nivrita.

'Excuse me dad.'

Neel gets up and goes a little away from his father.

'Yes Nivrita.'

'I had a talk with Parimal.' Nivrita sounds excited.

'He picked up your call?' Neel is cautious.

'No, I messaged him that I wanted to meet him. His message just came in. He has agreed.'

'Great! Where are you meeting him?'

'I'm not meeting him, you are. There's a restaurant called Renuka opposite Nagerbazar petrol pump. Do you know the place?'

'I don't but I will look it up.'

'Good. Keep me updated. And Neel...' A hiatus later she says, 'Be safe. I don't trust that scoundrel anymore.'

'Thanks. When will he be there?'

'An hour from now.'

Neel takes his leave from his father. He lies to him, telling him he is going to his flat but he in fact is on his way to the Nagerbazar petrol pump. Neel doesn't have to ask anyone to get to the meeting spot. He climbs down the taxi and panning his sight locates the restaurant; Renuka. It is right opposite the petrol pump by the series of shops on the lane. Neel crosses the busy road and enters Renuka.

It's an almost empty B-grade restaurant. The ceiling is low. At one end is a middle-aged couple having noodles. They are the only customers. One of the boys in the restaurant is ogling at Neel as if he has no clue why he is here.

Neel makes himself comfortable in a corner seat which has a good view of the entrance of the restaurant.

The boy who was ogling at him seconds ago comes and puts a glass in front of him, pouring water in it from a jar. He puts a laminated computer print-out, with soft edges, on the table. It's the menu.

'The rates are old. Just add five rupees to everything. That's the new rate,' the boy says and waits for the order again ogling at him. Though he hasn't had a good lunch, Neel still isn't hungry. From the time he has seen the flesh pieces in his washing machine he has not been able to even think about food. He looks at the menu then at the boy and says, 'I'm waiting for someone.'

The boy almost snatches the menu from him with an I-don't-give-a-fuck attitude. Neel sips some water and keeps his focus on the door. He glances at his watch. Parimal should be here any moment now if he is punctual. What exactly should he do when he sees Parimal? Obviously he will recognize Neel. Should he catch hold of him and beat the shit out of him? What if he overpowers him? Parimal is a police man after all. He is a criminal too. Criminals usually have more muscle power than ordinary civilians like Neel. He hasn't even brought anything to beat Parimal with if need be. No, he would sit with him in Renuka itself, probably order some food, and talk about the murder. What? Talk about the murder? Is he here to date Parimal?Rubbish! Neel has to catch him and pin him down and beat him till he confesses to killing Titiksha. That's final.

Neel's impatience increases with each passing minute. He empties the glass of water. While keeping it back on the table, he notices Parimal step inside Renuka.

Neel impulsively stands up seeing him. Parimal notices Neel immediately since there are not many people in there. Parimal turns and runs out in a flash. Neel follows him. As he passes the restaurant boy who has been ogling at him, Neel hears him murmur, '*Boka choda.*'

Neel scoots out of Renuka. He notices Parimal cross the road and run towards the nearby flyover. Neel runs after him but isn't able to cross the road as quickly as Parimal. The honking of horns makes him emotionally unstable. Somehow he is able to keep his focus on Parimal and cross the road.

Running after Parimal for the next two minutes and thereby going into lanes and by lanes, which Neel has never been to, he finally is able to catch hold of him. Neel has surprised himself more than Parimal with the speed with which he has chased him down. Both are now gasping for breath, standing at the corner of a by lane. Parimal tries to run but Neel catches him by the collar of his shirt and slaps him hard twice.

'You swine. You thought you were going to meet Nivrita here, right? After killing Titiksha, you think Nivrita and I will let you live in peace?' He punches him hard. Parimal's nose is bleeding. The punch has hurt Neel's knuckles as well.

'Who the fuck is Nivrita?' Parimal says rubbing the blood off his nose. 'I don't know any Nivrita. It's Titiksha ma'am who asked me to go to the restaurant at that particular time.'

Neel stares at him as if he has just been backstabbed by his most trusted friend.

FROM NEEL'S MANUSCRIPT

17

As I sat behind mama in his scooter on our way to the school, I had pretty well guessed what would happen in the principal's office. But what actually happened that day was much worse than I could have ever imagined.

When Ashok mama and I entered Dr Iyer's room, I saw Neel with his parents already present there. To my surprise, even Avni was there with her parents. Both Neel and Avni stood in front of me like complete strangers. Neither cared to look at me. I introduced Ashok mama to Dr Iyer. There were four chairs in front of the principal's table and those were occupied by Neel's and Avni's parents. Ashok mama wasn't given a chair to sit so he stood nearby from where he could talk to Dr Iyer. I noticed Neel's parents eyeing my mama with the same condescending look with which they had eyed me before. Such megalomaniacs they were!

As mama greeted Dr Iyer, she wasted no time in accusing me of being a bad influence on both Neel and Avni. I was disappointed on hearing this. I had expected Dr Iyer to warn me, ask my mama to help me focus on studies, and leave me with a warning. But to be called a bad influence on Neel and Avni? No way was I ready for this! I was so blank that I didn't remember much of what exactly was said, but the basic gist of the matter was, I was tagged as a bad girl who wasn't fit to study in a proper school where people like Neel and Avni, hailing from well-cultured families and whose parents were educated people with a social stature, studied. Salt Lake International wasn't for someone like me whose parents, even after being in the same city, would only send the guardian to meet the principal. I felt bad for Ashok mama. He didn't do anything to hear someone's wrath like this. I don't think even at his workplace his superiors had ever talked to him like that. He could have been a wife-pet but he was a sincere man otherwise. I wouldn't have protested if he had killed me that day. I was the root cause of all trouble. For others and for myself too.

The meeting ended in fifteen minutes with Ashok mama not given a chance to talk and I not asked for any apology. Mama was simply handed a piece of paper in which my future had been typed on the school's official letterhead before I had entered the room that morning. It stated that I had been expelled from the school because, in the principal's words, Salt Lake International couldn't keep a student who spoilt other fellow students and distracted them from doing what they were primarily in the school for; getting an education. Neel and

Avni were asked to focus on their studies, and let off with a warning.

Mama didn't talk to me after the meeting. I didn't know about him but I had turned into a zombie. I had not only been expelled from the school but the transfer certificate mentioned such words that I had no chance of securing admission in any other good school elsewhere. It was obviously not the principal's decision alone. Neel's parents—especially his mother—had finally got a chance to take her revenge. She had tried to explain it to me before but I was too deeply in love to take anything seriously. And why were they to be blamed? What was Neel doing being quiet before the principal? Why didn't he tell her that all of it was a joke? That if someone had to be expelled, it had to be those students who were harassing us in school. Above all, it was only a goddamn rumour! And my future had been compromised by these so called 'harbingers' of good education. Neel's mother was right. There was a difference between them and me. They had the power to turn a wrong into right. I didn't even have the power to prove a right as right.

It was while moving out of the school gate that mama said, 'I'm going to work now. By the time I'm home in the evening, all your things should be packed. I'll talk to your mother.' And then he was gone.

When I came back home, Yo-didun was curious to know what had happened. I didn't respond. My actions did. I started packing almost immediately without shedding a tear. I didn't want to think anything for there was nothing to think about actually. The only thing that remained for me to see was what mama would tell my mother and whether she would give a damn about the whole thing or not.

In the evening, after mama was back from office, he unleashed himself on me. He said that he had told my mother that she had given birth to a prospective whore and asked her to fetch me from his place before I shamed them more. Yo-didun tried to intervene but he shut her up and continued to call me names. Every time mama calmed down, Bijoya mami came and put fuel to the fire. I didn't react; neither verbally nor emotionally. I was blank. Nothing mattered to me anymore. I knew I was doomed for life. I was only waiting for time to pass and the next day to arrive so that I could leave mama's house. I didn't have dinner nor was I asked to. Yo-Didun and I didn't talk much either. I had never seen her that quiet. I hoped she knew what the truth was, and that I hadn't let her down in anyway. I was her granddaughter. I wouldn't have done anything to shame her. After all she was my real and only companion at mama's house.

I skipped dinner. In fact I had skipped food the whole day. I felt nothing within me when I retired to bed early that night. No pain, no pleasure. No treasure, no tears. No chaos, no calmness. I was just lying there on the bed like a lump of mass. Strangely enough, I liked being a mass: nothing to think, nothing to feel, and nothing to say. I was awake but I wasn't alive. I was lifeless but I wasn't dead. Not yet.

Somewhere in the wee hours of the night, I saw a light shining on the window beside my bed. I could hear heavy rain beating down the street. Rain was a little odd at that time of the year. I must have slept without realizing because I didn't hear any thunder or saw any lightening. The light certainly wasn't just a lightening for it persisted on the window pane and was moving all over it as if someone was intentionally throwing light. Curious I got up from bed. I noticed Yo-didun was sleeping. The entire house had an eerie silence about it while outside steady wind roared. I peeped out from the corner of the curtain. I heard the loudest my heart could beat.

It was Neel staring at my window with a torch in his hand. He was totally drenched. I saw him waving at me.

Chapter 13

IS NIVRITA NOT REAL?

'What do you mean Titiksha asked you to do all this?' Neel has grabbed Parimal by his shirt's collar. Parimal's hands are atop Neel's hands trying to remove his grab.

'I mean I don't know anybody by the name of Nivrita.'

'This is the best you could come up with for persuading me, you asshole? Tell me why did you murder Titiksha?'

'Murder?' Parimal's eyes broaden. 'What are you talking about?'

'You killed her, and then chopped her into pieces, and stuffed it inside the washing machine in my flat so that I'm the one who gets caught for her murder—that's what I'm talking about.'

Parimal gives him a bewildered look and says, 'Now I know. You are totally mad and hence Titiksha ma'am wants to get rid of you.'

Again Titiksha *ma'am*?

'Weren't you guys dating?' Neel asks.

Parimal laughs and says, 'I am only working for her for some money. I'm not even a real policeman.'

'Aren't you Nivrita's boy-mate?'

'I don't know who Nivrita is.'

Nothing makes sense to Neel. Nivrita doesn't exist, Titiksha has hired this idiot to get rid of him by getting herself chopped to pieces, and the most bizarre thing is he is neither dating Titiksha nor has he killed her. All of it seems unreal.

'And what if whatever you are saying are lies? Why should I believe you?' Neel says.

'If I'm lying then, you can hand me over to the police. There's no hiding from the police anyway. I didn't know this will cause me so much trouble, else I would have never accepted Titiksha ma'am's offer.'

Yet again Titiksha *ma'am*!

Neel looks at Parimal's eyes. To his horror he reads nothing fake in them. He wants the eyes to tell him he is lying. Of course he has heard about Nivrita. She is his girl-mate. And what did he tell him; that he is totally mad? Alright, he will give this man a chance. This man who Neel firmly believes has murdered Titiksha, and has been sleeping with Nivrita, and is right now only bullshitting him, he will give him a chance. It's only because Neel wants to prove to himself that he isn't a crazy person. But before that, another idea strikes him. Holding onto the man with one hand now and taking out his mobile phone, Neel calls Nivrita. If she doesn't exist—like what the man is implying—she won't pick up the phone. As it begins to ring on the other side, Neel puts the phone on speaker.

'Nivrita will pick up and then everything will be clear.' Neel says.

He is expecting Nivrita to pick up while Parimal is confident it's Titiksha who will pick up. Both keep waiting but nobody picks up. The call ends. Neel and Parimal look at each other like fools.

'Can I take out my mobile phone?'

Neel nods. Parimal brings out his mobile phone from his trouser's pocket and in his contacts shows Titiksha's number. It's the same as Nivrita's.

'See it's the same number.'

Neel checks. Indeed it is the same. Neel lets go of Parimal's shirt's collar.

'Thank you sir. I swear I have got nothing to do with all this.' Parimal adjusts his shirt and runs for his life. Neel dials Nivrita's number again. There's no response.

Neel takes a taxi and goes to Sharada Heights. He takes the elevator and reaches Nivrita's floor only to see the door locked. On an impulse he dashes down using the stairs, takes the same taxi which luckily for him hasn't found another passenger, and heads to Park Street; to the office of Word Tree Publishing India Pvt. Ltd.

Neel gets down near Apeejay House in Park Street, the usual spot where Nivrita used to meet him before going to any other place.

He asks a couple of people about the exact location of Word Tree Publishers India Pvt. Ltd. They direct him to go to the first floor of the Apeejay House. Neel follows the directions and reaches the first floor.

The moment he moves out of the elevator, he notices a glass door to his right. Above the glass door, a big golden plate reads 'Word Tree India Publishers' in black bold letters. Neel relaxes. After the case of his missing college and the sudden vanishing act of Titiksha's office, Neel feels relieved to see that the Word Tree office does exist! He approaches the two uniformed security guards at the main door.

'Excuse me, I'm looking for the Commissioning Editor.'

The two guards look at each. The first one speaks, 'Megha madam has left.'

'I'm looking for Nivrita Roy.'

The two guards again exchange glances. This time they seem clueless.

'There's no one by that name.'

Neel feels a thud in his heart. Was that rascal Parimal right?

'Are you sure?'

The second guard speaks up, 'Why we would be lying? Everyone signs while coming in and going out. We know every employee's name here.'

The guards' look as genuine as Parimal's eyes did when he told him that he doesn't know any Nivrita.

Neel swallows a lump. His mobile phone rings. He takes it out from his jeans. The screen flashes: Nivrita calling.

Neel feels choked. He presses the green button and takes the call.

'Neel, help me...help me Neel. Parimal is here. He has gone mad...he will...he will kill me.'

'Nivrita? Where are you?'

'At my flat. Come soon,' The line disconnects with a shriek from Nivrita.

So that bastard Parimal had lied to him after all. But why aren't the guards recognizing Nivrita's name here? Well, he can take care of it later. He needs to go and save Nivrita first. She sounded extremely scared on the phone. He has lost Titiksha but he won't let Parimal murder Nivrita. Neel doesn't wait for the elevator. He rushes down the stairs, runs across the street, and takes a taxi for Nivrita's place. If he can reach on time, if he can save her from Parimal and catch him red-handed, then every piece of this confusing maze will come together. He asks the taxi driver to drive fast, even if he has to break a few traffic rules in the process.

Neel tries Nivrita's phone number a few times from the taxi but it is out of reach. It only escalates his anxiety.

As he gets down and pays the taxi driver, he gets a call from Nivrita again.

'Hello, where are you? I just reached Sharada Heights.' Neel says as he saunters inside the locality.

'I'm on the terrace Neel,' Nivrita whispers over the phone. 'Parimal is here too. Please come soon. I don't want to die.'

'I'll be there. In fact I'm climbing the stairs now,' Neel says. He is all ready to fuck the life out of Parimal—the man who chopped his girlfriend into pieces—and now is trying to kill Nivrita.

By the time he reaches the terrace, Neel is gasping for breath. He waits for a moment right outside the terrace door and takes in some air. Then he pushes open the door with caution. It opens with a creaking sound. A wild gush of wind hits him. A thunder roars in the sky. He looks up to notice the sky is abnormally dark. It may rain soon. He looks around. There's no life, no sound. Only darkness. Has Parimal killed Nivrita? Neel asks himself.

'Hey vampire boy!'

Neel turns around to see Nivrita. All calm and composed. Her face tells him her life was never under any threat.

'Vampire boy?' Neel mutters.

'Ever since you toyed with it, my heart still has your fingerprints.'

What's that supposed to mean? Neel wonders and looks at a smiling Nivrita.

'Ready to listen to the last chapter of the first half of Neel and Titiksha's story?' she asks.

Neel feels like he is confronting a ghost.

FROM NEEL'S MANUSCRIPT

18

Seeing Neel downstairs by the road in the rain, waving at me, I thought I was sleep-walking. He gestured me to come down. I closed the window. Neel was indeed there by mama's house at this hour. I glanced at the big watch on the wall adjacent to the window. 12.35 am, it said. What was Neel doing there? It was a day of unexpected turn of events. Forget about seeing him downstairs, I honestly didn't think I would even hear from him again. He flashed his torch light once again on the window. I impulsively gestured for him to wait. I had to go to him—even if we were meeting for the last time. A voice inside me said tomorrow is too fickle to be trusted. Today is everything. Tonight is the moment. If Neel was there downstairs at the dead of the night, and in this weather, there had to be a solid reason for it.

I dared to move out of the house. I didn't care to change. I was wearing what I wore after I was back from school—a royal blue cropped trouser and a blue top. I tiptoed to the main door, unlocked it, and cautiously, without waking anyone up, moved out.

It was raining hard then. The unexpected thrill of seeing Neel by the house made me forget the umbrella. I didn't care to go inside again lest I woke up anyone. I moved out in the rain and soon scampered to Neel, careful not to slip on the road.

'What the hell are you doing here, Neel?' I said and pulled him towards the chemist shop diagonally opposite my mama's house. Its shutters were down but its extended roof gave us enough shade to shelter us from the incessant rain.

'What if I tell you love itself is afterlife? From the time one loves someone, he or she transcends normal life as we all know it. And death is a means to bring someone back to that very life so that one can fall in love and transcend it yet again—a cycle of sorts?' Neel said. Something about him was abnormal.

'What nonsense are you talking about?'

'I ran away from my place,' Neel said. He was shivering.

'Obviously. Your parents would have never allowed you to come here at this time. But what's up, really?'

'No. I won't return to my home ever.'

I kept gaping at him for some time. He himself preferred to clarify.

'I have had enough, Titiksha. They want me to go to a boys' residential school somewhere in Dehradun now, and I don't want to. I mean what will happen to all my Paintbrush dreams? I tried to persuade them but they, as usual, aren't getting it. And more importantly, I don't think they will ever allow me to be with you.'

I could sense a pain in the way he said the last part. A certain pain I could well identify with. It was the same pain within me that I had chosen to remain ignorant about in the last few days. A pain which would soon become a way of life for me and control my choices, alter my perceptions, and slowly transform me into someone I never thought I could become. A pain which would invariably tease me every time I pretend about its non-existence. Most importantly, it was a pain that would never allow me to see anyone the way I saw Neel, never feel for anyone the way I felt for him, never belong to anyone the way I wanted to belong to him. This was the pain of getting separated from Neel forever.

'I can't live without you Neel,' I said stating the obvious.

He hugged me tight. But there was something more important that was getting aligned to the other—our souls. I wanted to disappear right into him.

'Please tell me we can be together always,' I said. He could tell that I was crying, and I could guess so was he.

'I'm sorry for being indifferent in the last couple of days. I was afraid. I was afraid if the real thing came out, people would make more fun of me, of you, of us. I was afraid you would have to undergo hell because of me. And the worst was even after knowing all this,

I couldn't stand for you. I was afraid of my parents. But today when Dr Iyer expelled you, and later when my parents talked about sending me off to a residential school, the fact that we may no longer get to see each other ever again struck like a blow. I rebelled. I have finally rebelled Titiksha.'

'You rebelled for me Neel?' This wasn't a real moment anymore. Neel and I standing by my house under the chemist shop's roof in that rainy night and confessing our feelings; I bet my life that night wasn't real.

'I rebelled for us. I fought with my parents. They said you have poisoned my mind, and if I don't forget you, they will kick me out of their house. I told them I wouldn't mind walking out of a house where nobody cared about what I want. I want to be with you, near you always, Titiksha.'

There was silence except for the rain which was now falling with renewed intensity.

'What do we do now Neel?' Holding onto him I spoke into his ears. 'My mother is coming tomorrow morning to fetch me from here. I don't know what her plans are for me. Maybe she too would send me to some boarding school. I don't want that.'

Neel broke the hug, looked deep into my eyes, and then hugged me tight once again. The way his body shuddered, I could understand that he further broke down.

'There's nothing we can do,' he spoke in my ears. I could feel his breath as his lips moved. 'I have thought about it enough since evening. We don't have options Titiksha. If we choose each other, then there's no option left for us. If we elope, my parents will get to us sooner or later. Eloping is improbable. If we follow what they want, then we have to forget each other. Forgetting you is impossible. And if we follow what my heart says then...'

'What is your heart saying?' This time I broke the hug. I looked at him. He looked at me, caressing my cheeks.

'Let's end it Titiksha for a better beginning.'

I knew exactly what he meant, but I wasn't sure if I had the audacity to do it. I had to take a decision. What was the life I was living? Parents who never cared for me, mama and mami who despised me. Yo-Didun was the only one I cared about but she was old and hence wouldn't be there by my side always. The only person I really loved was there in front of me. And he was as helpless as I was. Had Neel not come there that night, I wouldn't have dared to decide what I did in that instant being in his arms. I convinced myself Neel was correct. We had to end it for a better beginning. There comes a time in your life where to commit to something, you don't ask yourself whether it's right or wrong. The only thing you ask yourself is can you or can't you. I asked myself the same thing: can I or can't I?

'I'm ready,' I heard myself say. Neel continued to gaze deep into me. Then he pulled me out in the rain. We ran across the street for a good five minutes and reached Sharada Heights where Neel's friend lived.

The friend was waiting inside the apartment campus under an umbrella. Seeing Neel, he waved at him. As we approached him, Neel's friend said, 'Guess what dude, I got a new camera tonight.' The friend asked us to stand straight as he took a picture of us with his new camera. Neel and I exchanged a glance. I kept my hand around his waist while he kept his arm around my shoulder. We complied lest the friend suspected anything. The moment he clicked our picture, Neel asked for the terrace keys.

'Are you guys sure? It's bad, bad weather tonight.'

If only he knew what we were up to. Neel took the keys to the terrace. The friend asked when we would be back. Neel lied to him and said in an hour. As we were climbing up the staircase, Neel relayed to me that he had told his friend that both of us needed to go to the terrace because we wanted some private time together. His friend had bribed the security guard and fetched the terrace keys for us.

It was dark when we opened the door of the terrace. A cold wind was blowing amid the rain. It was there before too but now the wind had a foreboding chill. I was too emotionally numb to give words to what exactly I was going through. Everything seemed to be happening slowly. When I tried to feel it, all of it started happening too quickly for me to register. Neel and I kissed, we smooched—for the first time to our hearts content. It must have been special but

I wasn't myself anymore. I was doing it but it wasn't happening to me. We sat for some time on the edge of the cemented barricade of the terrace contemplating life and feeling our fervour for it slowly evaporating as our craving for remaining together forever took over. Sitting beside Neel, I realized every one of us had something special to lose. In Neel's case it was me. In my case it was Neel. And if one wants to hold on to that thing one never wants to lose, then one has to surpass life. Neel was right. If we could not choose each other, then there were plenty of other options we could go for. But since we did choose each other, there was no other option than the one we had chosen for ourselves. I was happy.

The moment finally came where we had to execute our decision. Both of us stood on the cemented barricade of the five-storey building and jumped off.

Only one of us died.

Chapter 14

SHARADA HEIGHTS
NEAR TANK NO. 4, SALT LAKE, KOLKATA

The Present

'That's where the first half of Neel and Titiksha's love story ends; Sharada Heights.' Nivrita pauses and then says, 'That's where we are right now as well.'

Nivrita is standing on the terrace. Neel is standing right in front of her, by the stairs leading to the water tank above. He doesn't care about what happened to the fictional Neel and Titiksha. Whether they jumped off the terrace, survived, or died. Neel wants to know something else.

'What's going on, Nivrita? Where is Parimal?' Neel says doubting if Parimal was ever here. It's now that Neel feels a cold wind blowing. It is getting fiercer each second.

'Nivrita?' Neel can't see her clearly. A torch light is switched on. Nivrita keeps the torch on the ground. The wind subtly moves the torch alternately towards Neel and Nivrita. He can see her whenever the torch light falls on her.

Nivrita ambles to the nearby cemented barricade which marks the limit of the terrace and facing Neel, makes herself comfortable on it.

'Have you ever been to a posh hotel room, Neel? Ever drawn the curtains of one of the windows in it and stood by it only to realize the view outside is of a filthy, poverty-stricken and worn-out part of the city? At that point in time, I'm sure you must have felt happy because you were inside the posh hotel room, away from all the social garbage that nauseates you all the time. But at the same time, my guess is, you might also have been sad because you knew it was a hotel room after all. And hotel stays can never be permanent. Sooner or later, one has to return to the ugly city outside. Neel, your love for me was one such hotel stay. And you never had the balls to turn the hotel that I was for you into your home.'

The wind tilts the torch partly towards Neel. Its light falls on his face.

'What do you mean?' he says.

'Let me now narrate the second half of Neel and Titiksha's love story,' Nivrita says. Though Neel can't see her face now, he guesses she will have a loose smile on her face suggesting she is making fun of him by unnecessarily testing his patience.

'Can't you first tell me what's all this about? Can't you tell me the second half of the story later?'

The wind tilts the torch towards Nivrita now again.

'Certain choices in life develop thorns with time. But since they were *your* choice, you got to hold onto them even if it means your emotions continue to bleed. Tell me Neel, what do you think happened next? What happened to Titiksha? What happened to Neel? Did they both die? Did one of them die? Or did they both live?'

Neel glares at Nivrita. He understands he'll have to hear what she wants to share first, and then she'll tell him what he wants to know. Like always.

'Alright, my guess is both Neel and Titiksha jumped off the terrace as per their plan. And then maybe one of them is born again because you said only one of them died.'

Nivrita is quiet.

'Who was it? Who jumped?' Neel says.

'The one who kept the promise, jumped.' Nivrita's voice was turning graver with every word she was speaking.

'Who kept the promise?' Neel sounds eager now.

'Titiksha did. She was the one who died that night Neel,' she says. 'Titiksha jumped off. Neel didn't.'

Neel is sorry to hear that. He remembers Nivrita telling him the story she narrated to him was true. It had happened to real people. With his real life girlfriend Titiksha gone, he can understand how cruel death can be.

'I'm sorry to...' he starts but is cut short.

'Just sit tight and listen,' Nivrita says.

'Hear me out Neel.'

Neel swallows a lump sitting by the water tank. He takes a deep breath and braces himself. His gut feeling tells him Nivrita has something more discomforting to share. And he wants to hear it, after which the first thing he will ask her: 'Why isn't her name on the Word Tree office's register?'

'Around seven months back,' Nivrita begins, 'a rather worried looking couple came to me. They only had one request for me: to take care of their son; their only child. Like every other parent, they too seemed concerned but felt helpless about his situation. In my profession, it was my duty to accept their request. But they said they couldn't bring him to me because they had kept his condition a secret from him from day one. While they were talking, I had a feeling I'd seen them somewhere. A few minutes into the conversation and I knew where exactly I'd seen them. Obviously after a gap of almost fifteen years, they didn't recognize me. I didn't care to clarify who I really was. Just to confirm my hunch, I requested them if they had any photograph of their son. They showed me a photograph. One look and I knew it was Neel Chatterjee—the same Neel who had subjected Titiksha to hell only because she loved him with all her heart and soul.'

Nivrita gets down, picks up the torch, and keeps it at an angle from where Neel can see her from head to toe. She turns to show her back to Neel. Then pulls up her tee. On display are the burn marks on her back.

'The skin will only tell you about the marks. The pain is now a part of my existence..' She pulls down the tee, turns, and looks at Neel with such intense hatred that it unnerves him. She takes the torch, switches it off, and slowly ambles towards him. Neel can see a subtle silhouette of her, against the not so dark sky, approaching him. She stands close to him now and switches on the torchlight on her face. She looks menacing.

'I'm the one you ditched that night, Neel Chatterjee, 15 years ago, on this very terrace.'

What? No, he didn't hear her correctly. Or did he? Neel's entire body stiffened.

'What are you talking about Niv...Nivrita.' Neel has difficulty pronouncing her name.

'I'm not Nivrita. There was, there is no Nivrita. I'm Titiksha Roy, the one who loved Neel Chatterjee of Salt Lake International School.'

Neel's eyes broaden with shock and horror. Nivrita or Titiksha—Neel isn't sure anymore—she switches off the torch and in the darkness goes back to where she was sitting a minute ago. Neel can hear his heart beating the fastest he has ever felt. Titiksha aims the torch straight at Neel and switches on the light. It falls on Neel's face and he has problem keeping his eyes open. He blocks the light with his hand.

'I used to burn myself every time your memory haunted me Neel. I wanted to punish myself enough so that never ever in any other birth, in any other form, would I repeat the mistake which I committed in this birth—to fall for you.'

Neel wets his dry lips absorbing every word deep into his conscience.

'I accepted your parents' plea. I had to. I'm a psychiatrist by profession and treating patients is my moral obligation. But for this particular patient—that's you Neel Chatterjee—I wanted to get to your heart first. I wanted you to know what happened to us, to me, what I went through, because I remained glued to that one moment when I fell in love with you even after you ditched me. Making you the author of the story I wanted you to feel Titiksha's pain; *my* pain. Forgetting is easy Neel. Living with memories is difficult, especially those which enrich your soul by injuring your heart. Do you know your real age is thirty-three Neel and not twenty seven? And I'm thirty-two.'

I'm thirty-three? Is that why I always looked older compared to the students I studied with during school? But why this six years lag, Neel wonders feeling heavy. In the last few seconds, he seems to have gained weight. Even a simple hand movement demands a lot of energy from him.

'That rainy night I jumped first, Neel, whereas we were supposed to jump together, and end our futile love story for a "better beginning", or so you had told me. But unfortunately, I was the only one who dared to jump. Don't ask me what I felt when I saw you standing by the terrace and looking at me falling down. I kept praying it was a nightmare, and that my Neel would soon follow, and together we shall die, but my prayer wasn't answered. It was indeed a nightmare but a real one. You backed off Neel. Right when it mattered, you bloody backed off.

When your mother was in my clinic, I asked her what your past story was. She said you saw one of your classmates commit suicide. It affected your mind so deeply that you underwent manic depression, sleep and eating disorders, developed psychotic and bipolar symptoms, and also attempted suicide thrice. What they didn't know, but I knew well enough, was that you were a fucking coward. And whatever you went through, you deserved every spool of it. Cowards don't fall in love, Neel.

Your parents understood you needed serious treatment when one day they found out you'd killed your Doberman in rage and depression. Your mental illness made you forgo school for four years. You were kept locked at home most of the time, with your parents chasing every psychiatrist down for your treatment. It was only when you somewhat recovered that they thought of helping you finish your school education. The key was to keep an image in front of you that everything was normal in your life, else they feared they would lose their only child forever because of his hyper suicidal tendencies. Whenever you asked them why you were in a room, they coaxed you by saying you had some dust ailment.

Tell you what Neel, nothing is absolute in this world. Not God, not love. Everything has two sides. It's our myopic cognizance that makes us generalize the other side of things on the basis of our experience of one side. You eventually passed your twelfth board exams at the age of twenty-three, that too with grace marks. No college would have taken you because you were not fit for any.'

'But I...' Neel sounds benign. 'I qualified AIEEE exams and got into Neelkanth...' Neel's voice trails off.

'Yes, you got into a college that never existed. Your AIEEE mark sheet was a fake one. Your parents always were snobbish about the financial class they belonged to. And why wouldn't they be. All the laws of the world are bent in front of money. It was your parents' blind faith on money on the basis of which they thought they could still give their son a normal life, no matter what destiny did to him. What you were never told was once your father's sari business prospered, he got in television production. Remember the television serial where you spotted Arindam—your supposed colleague? It's produced by your father along with few a more. In the same building where they shot their other serials, they allotted a time where the set for your college was constituted. Small time actors were picked to essay the role of students, professors, and guards for a monthly payroll for four years. Unbelievable right? I too thought so but that's the difference between truth and fiction. Fiction needs to be believable whereas truth doesn't have such prerequisites. Whenever any city authority or education board staff came, they were told a television serial was being shot inside. Nobody had any issue. Tell me did you ever notice more than fifty people in your college at a tmie?'

Neel thinks hard. And nods. He didn't. In fact he did wonder at times why he kept seeing the same people again and again; every year. What Titiksha just told him now could be one reason why he was dropped by his father's car just when his college started, and was picked up immediately after it was over. Also, his friends vanished after college because they were never his friends. It was all fake. And hence it's not there anymore, Neel wonders. This is why there wasn't any ragging in his college, nobody talked to him, and he was always the one who topped; Neel surmises. As she said it's unbelievable. But, maybe, it's true.

'Your parents thought your life was almost in their control till you met Titiksha in college one day. It made things difficult because firstly your parents were not at all ready for this. Your father thought right after your fake college education, he would make you sit in his shop and relax for the rest of his life. Secondly, Titiksha was only a figment of your imagination. It was alright when you were in college with her, but when you told them you wanted to work in a bank, and then live-in with her, it perplexed them because they couldn't say no to you whereas a yes would have been tricky. Though they agreed, they had you under supervision in your rented flat. When your parents took your case to one of my colleagues, he confirmed that you had developed Dissociate Identity disorder, and there may be another personality hidden in you along with Titiksha.'

'It can't be. I was in love with Titiksha. I stayed with her. I introduced her to my parents even. We used to have sex too. How can...,' Neel exclaims. He sounds weak, as if he is trying to convince himself against what is slowly sinking in him—the truth.

'Every time you thought Titiksha and you were having sex, it was you who were masturbating with your mind playing tricks on your senses. Yes, you did introduce Titiksha to your parents but there was no Titiksha. The physical traits of Titiksha like her looks, her smile, etc was only a concoction of what your subconscious had observed in others.'

Neel now remembers how his father was composed even when he told him Titiksha was missing. How they never let him see the photographs he clicked when he brought Titiksha to meet them. It was because they were only acting as if there was some Titiksha but actually there wasn't any. They played on so that it didn't excite him unnecessarily, worsening his condition. And the camera wouldn't have lied. So Nivrita—or the real Titiksha—must have acted when she came to his rented flat while he was in the bathroom assuming she was meeting his girlfriend when in reality there was no one.

'It was when your mother told me that you used to interact with an imaginary Titiksha that I intentionally inquired why the name Titiksha and no one else. Your mother told me that Titiksha was the same classmate who had committed suicide in front of you. They said she was the root cause of all the problems in their and their son's life. Your parents still believe the real Titiksha died that night. But sorry, I didn't die Neel.'

Neel is only staring at the terrace floor. It's a dead stare.

'After the fall that night, I suffered multiple head injuries, a twisted ankle, and a fractured shoulder bone. The security guard of Sharada Heights raised an alarm seeing my body, but I was taken to the hospital much later. I had almost bled to death by then. Your friend who lived in Sharada Heights contacted your parents who came and took you home without even caring to look at me. Why are people so cruel, Neel? Why don't we understand other's pain? Why don't we get it, a simple act of yours sometimes is potent enough to destroy a life. A whole fucking life! And we still call ourselves God's best creation. Humour me.'

'There wasn't anybody to take me to a hospital that night. People of the apartment were scared because it seemed like a police case. Finally the police was summoned, and I was taken to a nearby hospital where I was in coma for 72 hours. Those 72 hours took Yo-didun's life. She died from a heart attack the next day after being in the hospital for more than 50 hours, waiting for me to regain consciousness. I lost two of my most prized possessions when I wasn't in my senses—you and Yo-didun. I never saw her again after I moved out of the house in the dead of the night to meet you.' I should have at least been given a chance to bid her goodbye.'

'I survived and came out of the coma. It took me two years to recover fully. By then even my parents had decided to disown me. I was anyway an accident for them. My mother gave me up to an NGO who took care of my medical expenses. I don't know what happened to Ashok mama and Bijoya mami much except that they left Yo-didun's place and shifted elsewhere. Right now, as I speak, a court case is going on between my mother and mama as to who should take Yo-didun's house.'

In the two years that I was recuperating, I remembered myself as yours and that's where the problem was. I was going through life but I wasn't living it. And the more difficult it was to live, the more I wanted to live. I wanted to live because I wanted to tell myself that Neel Chatterjee tried but couldn't kill me totally. That way I wanted to win. Also, I wanted to live for my love for you was real and true and genuine and I wanted to keep it alive within me. So it didn't matter how much your memory kept diluting it. I wasn't ready to pay for loving someone truly, even if I fell for a total coward who gave in to his fear at the last moment, than stand by his love for me. And the first thing I did after I recovered fully was change my name from Titiksha to Nivrita. I thought I could become a new person with such a change for the name Titiksha had a lot of story which I wanted to sever myself from.

I completed my schooling from a low-grade government school which the NGO helped me get into, passed the Pre Medical exam, and did few odd jobs to help myself pay for my medical studies in a government medical college. The only thing going for me was I was good in studies. My zeal to live made me push myself harder to become even better. I completed my MBBS at the age of twenty-six and then did my PG in Psychiatry. I was doing well in my career when your parents came to me. I took six months to follow you, research about your likes and dislikes, and present mental status. The bank you were working for was a fake one too. Ever wondered how come there were only eight employees working in that dingy two-room bank you worked in? The first thing I did was ask your father to make the job so boring that you resign yourself. And you did.'

Neel would wonder why he never got promoted even when he did his work on time. Why there was the same work again and again. And why everyone was relaxed most of the time. Just like it happened in his college days, he was dropped in his bank and picked up right when it got over without letting him spend time elsewhere. Now he knows. The work wasn't real. The bank wasn't real. His life wasn't real. How could he be so stupid? After a momentary silence, he answered by reminding himself that he isn't normal. His grasping power is below standard, his mind is inferior. He is a fucked-up case.

'Though your father wanted you to sit in his shop to avoid complications, he did agree when you said you wanted to work. At least you were by his side. The salary was given to you, and every other actor in the so called private bank by your father. If you remember Arindam didn't recognize you on the street the day we came from Jaipur, it was because he had been adequately paid not to recognize you outside the office. In fact, nobody was allowed to remain in touch with you outside office. The same was for your college buddies. They disappeared because they had been paid to disappear.'

'What about Cintus Finance and the man who picked up the phone there when I called?'

'Cintus Finance did exist when you went with your imaginary girlfriend but it was soon gone. That was the only time, your father told me, that you have ventured outside alone. Also, it wasn't Cintus Finance's number that you had with you. It was the number to your father's production office. The man had been asked to tell the same thing hence he must have sounded like a robot to you.'

Silence persists for some time.

'Your parents have doled out a fortune Neel,' Titiksha said, 'to give you a normal life... You are lucky that way Neel else you would have rotten in some locked up room forever. Do ask yourself Neel if you have done anything to deserve the goodness your parents have showered upon you?'

Neel is sitting silently on the stairs to make sense of all that he has been told so far. He wishes he had never met Nivrita—or Titiksha as he now knows her—ever. Ignorance is good. But now he knows Titiksha and his story. He has lived it in his mind. Did he really love Titiksha the way she loved him? Writing the story he felt the character Neel did love the character of Titiksha. It means he too must have loved her truly, now that he knows it was his story too. Then why didn't he jump that night if it was his plan to begin with? Why couldn't he keep his promise? Was he that shallow a person from within that he couldn't carry out something he promised his love? Is his fear more powerful than his love for Titiksha?

'Destiny is a musical instrument Neel,' he hears Titiksha say, 'And it has its limitations. It doesn't matter how big a musician you are, you can't produce percussions out of a string instrument. I did wake up after the 72 hours of coma but the day your father showed me your photograph in my clinic, I realized something in me had been in a coma from long, very long time. I know you noticed the tears in my eyes when we were in the Jaipur hotel room together. It was because I never had imagined I would lose my virginity to you. Yes, that night I lost my virginity to the one I had always loved. That possibility was beyond a dream for me. But it happened. I'm lucky. But as I told you, nothing is absolute. This good luck of mine has a pretty bad side too which you now know. Probably, it was all destined. When I learnt you had a sudden urge to become an author, I got my excuse of butting into your life. Most depression patients show signs of creative escape. I feigned being the commissioning editor of a leading publishing house. It was a trap. I booked the hotel room for you in Jaipur, I booked Lappan for you. They knew me by my name—Titiksha—and you thought it was your imaginary girlfriend. I was happy you remembered my name, but then what's in a name really? You didn't remember me; the person bearing the name. I could have told you all this on day one itself, but I wanted you to relive our story which you had forgotten. I wanted you to feel guilty, I wanted you to feel the pain that I have been hiding within me for all these years. I wanted you to hate yourself for forgetting me, like I hated myself, at times for loving you so incorrigibly. You have kept me pregnant with an inscrutable pain since a long time now. Neel—a pregnancy which I thought I'll never come out of. A pain I knew I would take to my grave.'

Neel was quiet as Titiksha clarified further.

'The earlier psychiatrists were right. There is indeed another dormant personality in you other than the imaginary Titiksha's. I probed it by enticing you to doubt the imaginary Titiksha and later by telling you I saw someone with your girlfriend in a mall. Though an out-of-the-body experience is pretty common in patients suffering from Dissociate Identity Disorder, if instigated, but I didn't want to take a chance. So I staged the power-cut in the mall as well as kept a real boy and girl with a green-grass top. I also kept the dismantled phone in the washroom which you thought belonged to your imaginary Titiksha. After you were convinced about the presence of another man in her life, I brought Parimal into the picture. I wanted you to suspect me after I threw the cigarette packet inside your flat with the note so that at least you knew something was indeed wrong, and later I stuffed your washing machine, taking the key from your parents, with chopped beyond recognition flesh pieces which were nothing but slaughtered animals I bought from a butcher shop. But you started doubting Parimal instead, as the supposed murderer of the imaginary Titiksha. Hence I had to keep him for a little more time than I thought he would be needed. The police uniform was deliberately kept in my flat because I wanted to re-direct you to me via Parimal. When you called your father about Titiksha's disappearance, he had called me for help. I'd sent the actor Parimal as a policeman to him while we were investigating the presence of a non-existent Cintus Finance in Sector V. The funniest thing, however, is that your parents still don't know who I really am. They think whatever I'm doing is part of some medical process to help you get better. And they co-operated.'

Silence persists. There's nothing more Neel needs to know. He lowers his head. What else can a coward do? Titiksha ambles towards him. She caresses his hair and suddenly grabs them tightly, pulling his head up. His shamed eyes meet her arrogant ones.

'And now I want you to suffer, Neel Chatterjee, because now you know the second half of Neel and Titiksha's twisted love story. I'll sleep well tonight and for the rest of the nights you shall remain awake, hoping and praying for death to come to you because you know you are a fucking coward, and are responsible for killing what I basically was. Your parents may still think it was suicide, but I and you now know it was homicide. My jumping off the terrace was a culpable-fucking-homicide—if you know what I mean!'

Titiksha let go of his hair and walked out of the terrace. Neel sits in agony. He can now understand what Titiksha must have undergone because of his momentary cowardice. An impulsive thinking, a simple lack of judgement, and two lives have been destroyed beyond repair. If he had not gone to Titiksha that rainy night, they would have lived, even if it was with a little bit of pain. But that pain would have been different from the one Titiksha had just told him about. It would have been a different pain from the one that he will live with from now on. Should he live on? Titiksha had asked him to question himself if he deserved the life he got in return of what he compelled Titiksha to undergo.

Neel asks himself: what do I deserve? He has to make a choice again, like that rainy night when Titiksha jumped off the terrace. Is he ready to live with whatever Titiksha told him? Will he be able to look at himself in the mirror knowing what he did that rainy night? Backed off from the promise he made to the one he loved with his heart and soul. If fear made him a coward once, can love make him atone for the cowardice now? For how long will he let his fear control him? It has already pushed him to make a miserable choice in life once before. Is he brave enough to punish himself tonight for the love he once had for Titiksha, but didn't let it attain fruition?

Neel gets up. In a trance-like state, he walks to the cemented barricade, gets on top it, and takes a deep breath.

This time he jumps off.

SHARADA HEIGHTS APARTMENT CAMPUS

Minutes later

There's a lot of light. And there are lots of people around—all of them strangers. *Is this how souls are welcomed in hell?* Neel wonders looking at them. His leg hurt a bit.

Looking down he realizes he did jump, but he hasn't touched ground yet. Neel is astonished to see a huge air mattress below him which has saved him from landing straight on the ground. *Did they know I was about to jump*?

Titiksha appears amid the crowd.

'This was the only thing that was left for me to see, my only consolation,' she says. 'Whether you still gave your cowardice an edge over love or whether, after knowing everything, you choose to dare life for love. I was waiting with bated breath, hoping you make the jump. It only means you finally respected my love for you, even if it took time. Thanks for not disappointing me this time, Neel.'

Neel is too blank to talk.

'Take my hand. It's time to treat you to normalcy.' Titiksha says.

He takes her hand and gets up. The hired men who have gathered around him help him step out of the air-mattress. 'I'm sorry Titiksha for that night and for everything that followed. I know a mere sorry won't take away what those 15 years gave you, but I don't know what else to say,' he says. Titiksha looks at him with longing.

'Don't say sorry, Neel. Say you *love* me. Please say you love me. It's more powerful than any apology. It's more healing than any medicine. It's more forgiving than any life. And it's much better a solution than any death.'

'I love you Titiksha,' Neel says and hugs her tightly. 'I really do.' Neel's voice seems choked. Titiksha hugs him back with equal fervour. Her within feels rinsed.

'There are two kinds of love: one that exists because it has never been tested and one that lives on because it has passed all its tests,' Titiksha whispers in his ear.

Acknowledgements

Much love, humble thanks, and gratitude to my parents for inspiring me and shaping my outlook towards life and for giving me enough reasons, through your actions, on why simplicity and humaneness still counts.

Gratitude to the Chowdhury family, the Rastogi family, and the Pimple family for their love, care, and blessings.

To Arindam Dey, Reetika Mishra, Rachit Varma, Pravesh Agarwal, and Rahul Saini—thank you buddies for all the emotional support, meaningful suggestions, and honest feedback I ever needed.

To Mr Prakash Mishra—it has been a privilege to be associated with you. Looking forward to learning a lot more from you. Thanks!

Extended thanks to Naman Kapur for unconditionally appreciating my work for such a long time now. I hope you like this one too.

Special thanks to Anuradha Chakraborty for setting up this story. You know what I mean.

To Kaushani Ganguly—thanks for all your amazing questions. And for helping me get an insight into today's school kids.

Anushikha Pathak—for being my youngest friend and helping me understand the psyche of today's teenagers.

Thanks to my editor, Gurveen Chadha, for sprinkling just the right spices to make this story even tastier.

Thank you Milee Ashwarya and the entire team at Random House India who are instrumental at turning this book into reality.

To my readers—love and thanks to each one of you who have reached out to me in the virtual world after reading my books and also those whom I don't know yet but I'm sure have kept me in their silent prayers. This story, the ones before, and hopefully the ones coming up are a result of those prayers.

Lastly...

To R—you are that sun, I know, which is and which will be there, even if every other light source fails me. For you—anytime, all the time.